# FIRE IN THE MOONLIGHT

*a story of persecution*

# JOHN MATTHEW WALKER

ISBN-13: 978-1-7355975-4-6 (eBook)

ISBN: 978-1-7355975-5-3 (Paperback)

Cover design by: John Matthew Walker

Cover photo by: Pissarova Marina and Kostuyrin Alexandr (pikoso.kz)

Library of Congress Control Number: 2020924127

Published in the United States of America

to the voices silenced by persecution

*And I saw the souls of those who had been beheaded because of their*

*testimony about Jesus and because of the word of God.*

Revelation 20:4

# CHAPTER 1

Taylor University, Zondervan Library
Monday, August 25, 2008

Andrea's latte failed. She drifted to sleep and found herself beneath a coal black sky.

*Strange. Where are the stars?*

A sudden crackle startled her. She whirled around and faced a rising wall of flames and a shower of sparks.

A voice beyond the flames whispered. "*Walk through the fire.*"

"Who said that?" Not a soul in sight. Only flames.

"*Come closer.*"

Inexplicable calm surrounded her—the kind one would only expect in a dream. With one step, the flames engulfed her. Like strong arms, they carried her into a small empty building with white block walls and a metal roof. No chairs, no carpet, and no lights. Burning rafters collapsed around her. The walls on either side hissed and cracked, but the wall straight ahead remained intact. A simple stage. No pulpit. No instruments. On the left, she noted a closed door. But the dead center of the wall held a wooden cross.

Flames destroyed everything in the tiny church except the cross.

*Why isn't it burning? Why am I not scared? Why am I not burning?*

Despite the fire's roar, the soft voice spoke to her heart as though the flames were silent. *"Come closer."* The voice seemed to come from the cross or somewhere beyond the cross.

Another step. The flames raged. Her pulse soared and pain blistered her skin. The door to her left creaked open. Smoke and darkness filled the room. She opened her mouth and drew a deep breath to scream, but everything fell silent.

She strained to hear. *Where is that voice?*

Sudden warmth rushed over her. *God, help me.*

Then a child's sniffling broke the silence. The sound came from outside. Andrea rushed out the open door. The church vanished.

She awakened to steaming coffee in her lap and an empty cup in her hand.

# CHAPTER 2

Before Dawn in Orissa
Monday, September 8, 2008

Indu was a princess riding a white stallion through a valley of flowers. Her father was a kindly king, and her mother a beautiful queen. In her dream, there was no dusty village with tiny houses. She did not share a bed with her sister. No violence entered her kingdom.

Indu jolted from sleep as men exploded into her home. A fierce grip tore her from her bed and dragged her into the street. The deafening chaos voided her scream.

Her attacker clamped his hand over her mouth and slammed her to the ground. She glanced at his scowling face. *He is so young! How could he do this?* She wrestled free from his trembling, sweaty hands but froze as he pulled out a knife.

Time stopped as she stared into his eyes. *He is no monster. He is scared.* Her father's words rang in her mind. *"Bless those who persecute you. Bless and do not curse."*

*Dear Jesus, forgive him.*

A chill shot up her spine as flames danced in the young man's eyes. Hatred melted into shock as his face softened and his grasp fell limp. Tears swelled as he dropped the knife.

Indu pushed with her heels and slipped away unnoticed. She slid behind the tree near her bedroom window. She clung to the sturdy trunk, shaking as she held it tightly. She watched in disbelief while the men who destroyed her home dragged her mother into the street. She buried her head and prayed as they ravaged her. She cried at her father's wailing as the evil men forced him to watch. Indu squeezed her eyes shut at her mother's screams. Tears soaked her nightgown as her mother's shrieks faded and her father's grief echoed.

As the moaning waned, she slowly lifted her head to peek at her father. So much blood! Her heart leapt as his pummeled form moved, but she recoiled as the wave of angry men lifted him and tossed him recklessly toward his church.

As the crowd moved down the street, Indu's heart stopped at the sight of her mother as she lay still in blood-spattered dust. "No! Dear Jesus!" Indu rushed to the crumpled mess of torn clothes and gaping flesh. *Mother!*

Shaking and sobbing, Indu removed her sari and draped it over her mother. She pressed her tiny naked body against her mother and closed her eyes. *I want it to be a bad dream. Make it go away, and let me wake up in my bed.*

Indu startled at footsteps shuffling behind her and the crackling voice that followed.

"Your mother was always so beautiful."

Indu peeked at the aged eyes peering over her.

The woman bent low and touched her cheek. "Child, you cannot stay here in the road. You are not safe."

Indu clung to her mother's body.
"Your mother wants you to be safe. Come."

Spindly fingers pried Indu from her mother. Her heart lay broken in the dust. Smoke obscured the street, but Indu blindly followed. Nearing the old woman's home, Indu paused for one more look. *I love you, Mother.* Tears, dust, and smoke clouded her eyes. *I can't look anymore.*

As the old woman scurried into her house, Indu slumped

against the wall. Her life whirled through her mind. She clung to every memory, aching at the thought of life without new memories. *How can I go on? Dear God, I don't know what to do. Please help me.*

The old woman hobbled out the door holding a new sari. She wrapped it around Indu. "Child, what will you do? You can't go back and you can't stay here. You must hide or these men will find you." As villagers clamored into the dusty street, the old woman retreated into her house.

Indu slid behind the house and listened. *No more shouting. Maybe those men are gone.* She peeked around the corner and spied the idle crowd gawking at the dead. *None of them are holding sticks or wearing bandanas.* She drew a deep breath and ducked behind a tree. Her pulse slowed as she caught her breath.

*If they are gone, where is my father?* She imagined his gracious eyes and the touch of his gentle hands. She imagined him tucking her into bed and whispering a prayer. She warmed at his smile. His grasp on her shoulders strengthened her resolve. Then she heard his voice. *"It's not a dream, my child. Indu, I want you to live. Go. Run. Hide. God is always with you."*

She opened her eyes and turned toward the woods. She ran for her life. Her world had been destroyed. There would be no turning back.

\* \* \*

Indu's father, Jeevan, saw no faces, only hate-filled eyes. Soaked with tears and sweat, he felt a harsh rip through his scalp as the grip of hatred forced him to gaze at his burning home.

Jeevan silently cried. *God, please don't let them burn our church.* He fell limp as the mob dragged him down the street. He offered no resistance as they stood him up facing the humble church. The smell of kerosene melted his remaining resolve. As he stared at the tiny spire, he felt the cold fluid and warm sting pouring down his face into his eyes and every inch of torn and beaten flesh. Squinting through the pain, he wept as his church erupted in flames.

He felt his heart break at the glowing smiles flickering from the flames. "Father, forgive them," he whispered. His gut wrenched as he trained his eyes on the one pouring the kerosene. He sensed the young man's awkward ambivalence. *He is so young. God, open his eyes. Forgive him.*

Staring at those bewildered eyes, Jeevan remembered the day he turned his back on his old life. He could still hear the song calling him to the front of that meeting. *I have decided to follow Jesus... Though none go with me, still I will follow. No turning back. No turning back.*

Choosing Christ meant death to who he was. He still felt his father's crushing words. "*You are no longer, Gurdeep, my son. You are dead to me.*" His father remembered him with a funeral, and Jeevan never saw him again.

Jeevan cried loudly, one last time, "God, send your mercies to my father."

His world grew dark. His pain faded as he blinked at the sudden darkness. Glimmers of light danced around the silhouettes above him. As the light grew so did his pain. He felt the repulsion of those gawking at him. His appearance was disfigured, marred beyond human likeness.

Jeevan felt his life slipping as the mob lifted him up and discarded him into the flames of his crumbling church. He landed on his back. He felt no pain. He could see the clouds and the welcoming blue above the smoke. His flesh melted away as he felt himself slowly rising through the glow where he saw the two most beautiful faces. Although they said nothing, he could hear their chorus of welcomes harmonized with hope, courage and comfort. He felt their words as if they said, "We will carry His mercy to your father." Their gentle faces seemed to fall behind him and disappear. He looked down on his church and the mob below as the world grew smaller and less significant. He felt the warm touch of his wife and saw his children and many whom he loved and knew from days and years past.

Light and music surrounded him and many others, whom he had never met but somehow knew. Sorrow was not even a memory. Although Indu was not with him, Jeevan had no fear for her. He knew the hands that guided him home would guide her, too.

# CHAPTER 3

Amsterdam Airport Schiphol
Sunday afternoon, September 7, 2008

Mitch Hawkins browsed the bookstore as he waited for his flight to Delhi. Amsterdam was one of his favorite stops. He glanced at his boarding pass and checked his watch. *No time for ecstasy.*

With glossy fantasies in hand, he dusted by the postcards and bumped into two charming innocents. *Americans.* He eyed up and down over each young woman. He brushed past them, dropped off his Euros and plodded toward his gate.

He clomped through the airport in his shorts, flip-flops, and untucked shirt. His bifocals dangled precariously as he scratched his tousled hair. After checking his ticket, he wheeled around for one more peek at the two naïve Americans.

\* \* \*

*Andrea Widener, look at you!* She spun like a preschool ballerina almost falling down. "Can you believe it, Marci? Here we are in Amsterdam! Next stop, India." She breathed deeply, trying to soak in the moment. *I know this seems crazy to everyone else, God, but thanks for making it all work. And thanks, Mom, for sharing your dream.*

"I don't know how I let you talk me into this. You know this is nuts."

"Hold it." Andrea saved her friend from backing into a stranger. She ducked her head to avoid eye-contact as the man thumbed through the openly displayed porn.

Andrea cringed as he pressed against Marci on his way toward the cashier. A sudden chill swept over her as his eyes studied her. She sputtered at his overpowering cologne.

Marci scowled. "Can you believe that guy?"

Andrea followed him with her eyes. *Camera bag. Sturdy carry-on. Tilly hat.* "Do you think he's a journalist?"

Marci nudged her. "No idea, but I'm sure he's a pervert. Didn't you see him poring over that trash? He wasn't trying to hide. He didn't look excited or even interested. He was unfazed. He might as well have been reading legal notices."

Andrea sighed and pretended she hadn't been listening. Stuffing postcards into her bag, she prodded Marci toward their gate.

"Marci, which seat are you in?"

"I've got the aisle. You'll probably be sitting by Captain Schmuck."

Andrea was hardly amused. "Very funny. There are a thousand flights. What are the chances?"

"But how many guys look like that?" She was smiling ear-to-ear and laughing, imaging Andrea crunched next to their new friend from the bookstore.

Andrea took Marci's hand and they joined the mob and waited their turn to enter 11 hours of mind-numbing nothing. They climbed aboard and wiggled and twisted through the maze of people: a Chinese businessman, women in saris, diplomats from the Congo, and European travelers.

Andrea looked straight ahead. *God, I know that you want us to go on this trip. It's such a big world, and I feel so small with all these people. I imagine their hurts and wish I could help them all. Please use me to help the hurting souls of Orissa.*

She felt Marci's breath on her neck as she inched her way down the aisle.

"What is that smell? This plane is so cramped. It has to be overbooked."

Andrea sighed at her grumbling. *Marci, please give it up.* Distracted, she walked past her row.

Marci grabbed her sweater and motioned her toward the correct row. A sudden swell of nausea rose as Marci looked down on Captain Schmuck and his airbrushed magazine. "You're in my seat!" she said.

The man widened his eyes as if startled, but Marci said, "No, it's ok. I'll take the window."

Andrea squeezed past, sandwiched between Mr. Smutfest and Marci.

Less than an hour into the flight, her new friend had lost interest in Miss Amsterdam. He rolled up the magazine and stuffed it in the seat. Andrea felt his eyes dance across her chest. He sniffed and reclined.

*Thank you, God. He finally closed his eyes.* She felt exposed sitting next to this stranger. She withheld judgment, but she could not help feeling repulsed. She buried her thoughts in her Bible.

* * *

Marci eyed the stranger. Hat hair. Untucked shirt. Frayed shorts. *What a self-absorbed lust-glutton. Five minutes with this urchin would be too much. How am I going to endure an entire flight? There isn't one decent movie.* She tried to start a few, but none could capture her attention without filling her with disgust. *I hope I can sleep.*

With the cabin lights dimmed, she sat in silence staring out the window. At thirty thousand feet above the Afghan mountains Marci spotted tiny specks of firelight and little else. *The world seems so dark and cold. God, I hope we're doing the right thing. I'm not sure we know what we're walking into.*

Marci welcomed sleep when it finally came.

\* \* \*

Mitch awakened to the familiar rustling of the attendant's cart. "I'll take a lite beer, and I saw the ladies drinking diet Coke earlier, so two for them. Thanks." He eyed the slender attendant. *I'll bet you'd be a lot of fun.* He checked his watch. *Over halfway there.*

As he sipped his beer, he noticed the young woman shaking beside him. He reached overhead and milled around for a blanket. As he covered her, he caught the wary eye of her friend.

"She seemed a little cold." He mused as she ignored him and turned to the window. "Not much to see down there," he said. *Nothing. This girl is tough.* His eyes traced her profile, slowly working their way down. She adjusted, turning away from him as though she felt his stare. A switch flipped in his mind as he spied the Bible in her lap. "I see you have a Bible."

She nodded, still staring into the cold black world.

"Who is my neighbor?" he asked.

"Huh?"

Her transparent look revealed her amazement at the question. He felt like a fisherman casting his favorite lure. "Who is my neighbor? The Bible says love your neighbor as yourself, but whom should I love?"

Marci said, "I'm no scholar, but surely you've heard the story of the Good Samaritan."

"Yes, I have. Who would you say is the Good Samaritan tonight? Your friend is crowded next to a man she doesn't know yet loathes, but when she is shifting and trying to find warmth, her friend, who chose the window seat, fails to notice, but the loathsome stranger silently covers her with a blanket."

"Well, I guess, you…"

"You needn't explain," Mitch continued. "You judge me without even knowing my name or anything about me. I knew you were a Christian before I saw your Bible. Your faith is evident in your vacuous eyes, your upturned nose, and your pointing finger. Isn't that what your Savior said, 'By this all men will know that you are my disciples, if you love one another and snub everyone else?'"

"I'm sorry if I came across that way. It's a long trip and I'm tired and anxious," Marci said.

*Gotcha! I can taste the juicy Christian flesh.* "Oh, you came across 'that way,' but aren't you 'that way' and why are you anxious? 'Do not be anxious about anything.' Isn't that what the good book says, kind of like 'be carefree and go with the flow or something like that?"

"I don't care for your sarcasm."

Marci's shrill tone awakened Andrea. "What's going on?" She embraced the warm blanket. *Where did this come from?* She smiled at Marci. "Thanks for my blanket."

She hugged herself and smiled, but Marci's eyes told her it was Captain Schmuck of the Mr. Smutfest Schmucks that gave her the blanket. "Oh. Thank you, Mr.?"

"Hawkins, Mitch Hawkins." Offering his hand, he said, "How do you do?" He smugly glared at Marci as he stretched his hand toward Andrea.

"Mr. Hawkins, thank you. I was cold, but I was afraid to ask."

"You're quite welcome, but to whom have I given this blanket?"

"I'm sorry. My name is Andrea Widener, and this is my friend Marci Beaufort."

"Byoo-furt, did you say? Is that spelled Bo-for?"

Marci replied, "I'm grew up in Goose Creek, South Carolina. In the lowcountry we pronounce it Byoo-furt, but I'll answer to anything as long as it's Marci Byoo-furt."

"Goose Creek," Mitch snorted. "You have more charm that I realized."

Marci feigned a curtsy. "Perhaps I wasn't the only one quick to judge."

The tone and lights signaled them to fasten their seatbelts for their descent. Mitch clicked his seatbelt. "So what are you lovely ladies planning to do in Delhi?"

Andrea smiled. "Oh we're not staying in Delhi. Tomorrow morning we're taking a train for Orissa."

"Orissa?" *What are they thinking?* "Orissa could be dangerous—*is dangerous.* Are you sure that's a good idea?"

"Mr. Hawkins, I heard you quoting scripture. Perhaps you know this one. 'If anyone would come after me, he must deny himself and take up his cross and follow me. For whoever wants to save his life will lose it, but whoever loses his life for me will find it.'"

Mitch folded his arms and shook his head. *You have no idea what you're doing.* He looked Andrea square-in-the-eye. "I see two toddlers stumbling into a fire."

Andrea and Marci stared, unfazed.

"You must be meeting someone."

*Oh no. Blank stares.* "You're not going to Orissa by yourselves?"

Andrea's sappy smile and knowing look revealed the truth. *That look is always followed by a cheesy sermonette.* He suppressed a brief wave of nausea and interrupted before Andrea could speak. "Please don't give me that stuff about the *spirit* going with you."

Marci clenched her teeth.

Andrea swallowed her tears.

Mitch sensed their frustration but did not realize Andrea's tears spilled for him. His self-piety erupted as he continued to blast Marci and Andrea and their god. "You need flesh and bone, muscle, a real person to guide you. You need someone with some sense. Personally, I am utterly disgusted at your self-righteous naivety, but it is my job to look at life somewhat dispassionately. I am a journalist. I see a story in Orissa." *There will certainly be a story if you're killed—for your ignorance.*

Marci leaned in front of Andrea. "You can scoff all you want, but..."

Andrea covered Marci's mouth. "We welcome your company, Mr. Hawkins."

"Friends call me Mitch."

Andrea swallowed hard, still holding her hand over Marci's mouth. *Dear God, give me the words, and help me speak with compassion. Speak to Mitch through me.* "Mitch, many scoff at the power of the Holy Spirit. If He were a fantasy or a man-made notion, then we would truly be lost and alone, but He is real. I know that He is - more surely than I know where I am or what I am doing. On my own, I would never dream of coming to India, but Christ, through His Spirit within me, is calling me to reach out to my brothers and sisters in India. I made the choice to lay down the comforts and ease of my life." She paused and looked into his eyes. "...to give them a warm blanket on a cold flight."

Mitch was silent. He had never had a conversation with a Christian without feeling like he was under siege. There he sat, completely disarmed by a girl following her deepest emotions to care for people she did not know and had never seen. He shook his head and felt the beginnings of a real story. He savored the headline.

# CHAPTER 4

The Hotel Grand International
New Delhi
Monday, September 8, 2008
Breakfast

As Mitch strolled the hotel grounds, he spied a picture of Southern beauty. *Marci Beaufort.* He drew a deep breath and sneaked behind her. *Keep walking gorgeous.*

Marci stopped at the breakfast buffet and lifted a pineapple wedge to her lips.

*How I would love to taste her forbidden fruit.* Mitch slid beside her and grabbed her wrist. "Don't eat the fresh fruit."

Marci recoiled and he released her hand.

"Miss Beaufort, normally in a five-star hotel, you should feel free to do as you choose, but trust me, eat no fruit unless you peel it yourself; no salad, no ice, no dairy. Only eat what's cooked or packaged, and only drink bottled drinks or for you, vodka."

Andrea approached with a loaded plate.

"Don't eat the fresh fruit."

"Too late." Andrea muttered as pineapple juice escaped her lips.

"Do you ladies mind if we eat outside?"

Mitch collapsed on the lawn. He stared at the blank sky. He sighed at the overpowering noise of the street. *How many more of these long flights am I going to take?* He followed a jet across the sky and wondered, *how many hours of my life have I wasted on one of those?*

\* \* \*

Andrea sat beside Mitch. *God, I don't know what you have in store, but here we are. Thank you for our safe trip and thanks for breakfast. I'm not sure where we fit with Mitch, but please speak to him through Marci and me.*

"Tired from the flight?"

Mitch nodded, still watching the sky.

Andrea counted the years in his face. Although his eyes were deep and thoughtful, she could feel a hollow soul behind them. *I can only imagine what his eyes have seen.* She studied his sturdy jaw, his wrinkles, and his streaks of gray. She could almost read the stories etched in those lines. She sensed his continuous longing to find that one great story, a career capstone. Her heart begged, *God, help him see the bigger story.*

Andrea patted Mitch's shoulder. "Marci and I like to start our day, talking with God. You don't have to participate, but please stay with us."

Mitch sat up.

Andrea opened her Bible and read aloud, "Do nothing out of selfish ambition or vain conceit, but in humility consider others better than yourselves. Each of you should look not only to your own interests, but also to the interests of others. Your attitude should be the same as that of Christ Jesus: Who, being in very nature God, did not consider equality with God something to be grasped, but made himself nothing, taking the very nature of a servant, being made in human likeness. And being

21

found in appearance as a man, he humbled himself and became obedient to death, even death on a cross!"

Mitch couldn't restrain himself. "Do you girls have a death wish? It seems like you're discarding reason to intentionally risk your lives."

Marci tried to speak, but Andrea covered her mouth and glared at her. *Don't you dare!* Andrea turned to Mitch and peered into his soul. "Mitch, you see the world very differently from the way we see it. I have chosen to live for Christ. My life is otherwise meaningless. What would I do if I were not here? I would finish school, get a job, marry, have kids, send them to college, pay my debts, retire, grow old, dwindle and... die, all the while living for myself. I want my life to be something more."

Mitch interrupted. "Andrea, everyone wants to find meaning in life, but there is none. Life is what it is. It's what you put into it, and it's what you can get out of it. Nothing more. Life is the experience, so make it good. Enjoy it.

My life is my life. I make my own choices. I live as I work, freelance. I answer to me. No rules. I follow my own path."

"Mitch, do you remember the verse I quoted last night?"

"You mean the one about losing your life? Yes, I remember quite well." Mitch was in disbelief at her disarming naivety.

Andrea stood. "The last part of that scripture says, 'whoever loses his life for me will find it.' I have found life."

Mitch was stunned once again by this child. *Who are you, Andrea Widener?*

# CHAPTER 5

On the Train
Monday, September 8, 2008

Marci braced herself as she sat up and looked at Mitch and Andrea sleeping. *How can they sleep on this thing?* A cloud of dust covered her as she opened the curtain. The countryside seemed a blur through the greasy window. As the train lurched she felt immense gurgling. She choked on the lingering odor of urine. *It's everywhere.*

Clutching her stomach, she wondered, *what did I eat?* One more rumble and she jumped up and scurried through the car. She stepped over a couple of sleeping children, she bounded toward the next car.

The noise and shaking intensified as she stepped through the door. She smiled at a couple of stowaways hitching a ride between the cars. She stretched to cross over to the next car when the train lurched. The blurred ground vibrated beneath her.

"Oh no!" *Why did I look down?* Marci leaned over the side and heaved. Her hands clutched the railing as she paused to breathe. *I've got to get to that bathroom.* She straightened, nodded at her two spectators and climbed through the rusted door.

*I've heard the stories, but there it is, a hole staring at the ground rushing by.* There was nothing to grab, no seat, no bar. One more lurch pulled the invisible rug from beneath her. She slipped on the urine-waxed floor and landed face down over the hole. Her stomach erupted onto the beams and gravel racing past.

*Oh! Dear God! My hands. My face. I'm covered.* She turned away from the hole overcome by her own stench and the train's exhaust.

Struggling to find footing, Marci scanned the room for a towel or something to wipe off the disgust. *There's no shower, not even a room to change.* She held up her hands as if to wait for some magic to whirl around her and make her fresh and new. She caught her reflection and chuckled at her matted hair and sticky face. *I look like a dirty little kid.* A splash here and there was all she could stand from the germ-infested sink. *I have to get out of here!*

\* \* \*

Mitch heard the creaking of the door and watched the disheveled angel walking toward him. One whiff of Marci amplified the stench that Mitch thought could not get any worse. "My God, what happened to you?" he said half laughing and half choking.

Marci's glaring eyes ripped him. Smiling boldly, she stepped toward him with her arms wide-open and forced a giant hug on him.

Mitch coughed and sputtered. *I was wrong. The smell could get worse.* Despite her stench, he hung on to her embrace and looked into her eyes. He could not see the judge he met on the plane, just another vulnerable human, much like himself.

His thoughts evaporated as Marci puckered, closed her eyes and softly belched in his face. Mitch plucked a handkerchief from his pocket and handed it to Marci. "My gift to you."

He turned and looked up at Andrea dozing in her bunk. "How can she sleep?"

# CHAPTER 6

Early Morning in an Orissa Village
Monday, September 8, 2008

Satyajit struggled to find rest. His heart leapt at the blood-covered face of a stranger in his dream. Deep midnight eyes peered into his soul. Flames danced around them. Despite the heat and glare, he saw the man's tears. *His tears are for me.*

Brightness grew as Satyajit noticed two goddesses flanking the man. Radiant and smiling, the goddesses stepped through the fire toward him. Fire engulfed the man. He closed his eyes. Satyajit heard his voice, though his lips failed to move. "Go to Sambalpur." The man opened his eyes once more. He smiled, lifted his arms, and disappeared.

Satyajit felt a hand on his shoulder.

"Wake up. It's time to go."

He opened his eyes to his friend, Natraj.

The two young men left the house quietly. Faint moonlight guided their steps through the village. They climbed aboard an over-loaded bus.

Their village grew smaller and disappeared as the bus drove on for two hours, stopping twice to pick up more young men, ultimately piling a few atop the bus.

As the bus rumbled through the dark countryside, Satyajit could feel the rush of night air whirring past. Dust covered him as the bus reeled to a stop.

A mob of young men swelled from the bus. The cloud of dust drifted over them toward their target, the sleepy village of Pahireju. A pronounced silhouette interrupted the dusky blue as their angry leader jumped on an over-turned crate and shouted a torrent of Hindi and Oriya.

"You know why we are here! These Christians are murderers. They must pay with blood. We will earn $250.00 for every priest or preacher killed. We must kill them all."

*$250.00 is more than two men in my village earn in a year.* But money was not why Satyajit was carrying a club and marching with a mob. He simply wanted to belong.

Satyajit wanted respect. His grandfather was a sadhu. This holy man and all his family before him were Hindu. Like their leader, Uttar Basu, his grandfather would say, "India always has always been, is, and forever will be a Hindu nation. Whoever stands against the rights of the Hindus, we will finish him." Although he was a tender youth and the pride of his mother's heart, Satyajit was nursed on the elixir of hate. He detested anything Christian.

Sunlight hid beyond the forest. Deep purple slowly awakened to a softer blue. Quiet footsteps crept through the unsuspecting village. The homes of Christians had been marked, particularly that of Pastor Jeevan Joseph. Satyajit and his friend, Natraj followed the shadowed mob to the pastor's house. A flashlight and screaming disrupted the darkness.

Satyajit felt a warm surge at the horrified faces of the pastor and his family. His stomach churned as the men tore the pastor out of his bed and dragged him into the street. He shook, unable to move as his friends battered the pastor with sticks, clubs, and stones. Satyajit froze as the pastor's wife clawed her way through the mob toward her husband. His blood chilled as one brutal stone silenced her shrieking.

A shove in the back encouraged Satyajit to fill his role. Hatred did not satisfy his doubt as he pounded the bleeding face of the unconscious stranger. The screaming children were forced back into the home just as it ignited. Satyajit followed the mob to the next home as he imagined himself a small, terrified child, orphaned in a burning home. *They are Christians and they deserve to die.* He clutched his club as he tried to console himself, but the warm trickle of the woman's blood was impossible to ignore. He shook uncontrollably and would have let go of the club except for the flood of hatred pouring around him. The mob engulfed him as they pressed toward Pastor Joseph's house.

Satyajit stood frozen and numb as his friends took turns using the pastor's wife. He spied the pastor, held and forced to watch. Satyajit could not see his face, but he could hear his agony.

The unconscious, unclad remains of the once beautiful bride were raucously exalted and carried toward her husband. The vicious parade complete, her limp corpse was cast down at her husband's feet.

The powerless pastor crumpled to his knees. His tears showered his wife as his wailing faded into raspy moans. Her abusers spattered urine across her body and in his face. The pastor convulsed silently as his tears ran dry. He tried to cover her with his robe, but restless hands wrenched him away, leaving her limp body in the street. His desperate eyes fixed on her battered face.

\* \* \*

The subtle warmth of the rising sun brought no consolation. The flood of brutality pushed Pastor Joseph through the village toward his church. Through the fog of smoke and tears, his world disappeared. He captured the glare of neighbors hiding in the shadows, some scowling, others smiling on his ruin.

He prayed for those he hoped were fleeing through the forest.

His heart melted at the unashamed laughter of those looting his church. He suppressed his anger as he prayed for the young hands tearing and igniting Bibles.

Jeevan felt an unseen comfort. The hands that gripped him fell limp. Disregarding all hatred and scorn, he lifted his head and raised his hands. *God forgive them.*

\* \* \*

Satyajit stumbled as Natraj shoved a can of kerosene into his chest and nudged him toward Pastor Joseph. One of the men grabbed him by the arm and patted his back. "We are making history, my young friend. This night is the beginning of our quest to rid our land of all false religion, especially Islam and Christianity." He placed his hand on Satyajit's and lifted the can over the praying pastor.

Kerosene and tears streamed down the pastor's face. His eyes followed a torch arching through the air. As it fell, his church burst into flame.

His attackers released him as though they were pulled away. Jeevan stood still. He did not scream. He did not curse. He did not run. He lowered his praying hands and turned around. He opened his blood-covered eyes and looked directly into the soul of Satyajit without saying a word.

*The man from my dream.*

The pastor's face was marred beyond recognition, but his unwavering eyes held Satyajit captive. Satyajit felt draw to those black holes circled by blood. Time stopped until he heard that unmistakable voice within.

"Go find them for me. Bring them here."

No one else heard the voice.

All eyes fixed on the blazing church. Glowing faces and smiles turned to scowls as Pastor Joseph unleashed his final prayer. "God, send your mercies to my father!"

Satyajit stood numb and detached as the mob cast Pastor Joseph into the fiery church. Tongues of fire licked up the kerosene. Pastor Joseph disappeared in the flames.

Satyajit shook his head as if to rattle something loose when he fell into his dream again. He heard that same voice saying, "Go to Sambalpur."

With blood on their hands, the band of young men and their leaders ran from the village. Dirt-covered faces smiled, victorious. The village behind them smoldered in the early morning light.

Dust whirled around the bewildered survivors. Many had fled to the jungle.

One girl quivered beneath her blanket of tears as she remained hidden at the edge of the village.

# CHAPTER 7

The Train Stops
Tuesday, September 9, 2008

Andrea smiled and stretched, opening her eyes to greet the morning. "What could go wrong on a day like this?" she wondered as she drew the tired, dust-drenched curtain to welcome the daylight.

"Well, that was certainly a mistake," Mitch chimed as they all inhaled thousand year old filth from the seldom, as in never, cleaned drapes. Still coughing from the dust, Mitch said, "Just how far are you planning on taking this train?"

Andrea answered, "Bhubaneshwar."

Mitch moaned and leaned against her bunk. He stared through the hazy window at the world passing by. "I'm not sure I can last that long. I think I have had enough of this train for a few lifetimes. Wouldn't you agree Marci?" Mitch almost laughed as he pointed at the streaks of yesterday's lunch on her skirt.

Andrea squinted, peering through the window. "Where are we anyway?"

Mitch yawned. "That little nowhere we just passed was Brajrajnagar. Try saying that fast three times. The next town of insignificance is Jharsuguda. If we stop there, I'm sure we can find a car or some less nauseating transportation to take us the rest of the way to Bhubaneshwar."

"Sounds good to me," said Marci.

"As long as we get there in one piece," said Andrea as she grabbed her toothbrush and headed toward the bathroom.

Mitch plopped down on his lower bunk. As the man above him parachuted to the floor in his kurta and flip-flops, Mitch buried his head in his hands wishing for a Starbucks.

* * *

Mitch wondered how Andrea could live such a naïve, contented life as she waltzed from the restroom, smiling and unaffected by her dismal surroundings. Unlike his upstairs neighbor, Andrea clasped her skirt as she climbed back up to her bunk. Mitch pursed his lips in silent disappointment and attempted to distract himself with writing. He was somewhat lost without his wireless connection, and his satellite phone needed a charge.

Mitch nestled into the corner of his bunk with pen and paper ready. He could not escape Marci's stench. He hoped she would climb up beside Andrea to share morning devotions, taking her eau de toilette with her. Instead she stood at Andrea's bedside and began changing her clothes. Mitch caught Marci's brief stare and he quickly hid his face in his work. Despite her odor, the glimpse of her firm unfettered body tested his resolve.

He pressed his eyes into his notebook and attempted to write, but he was thwarted by Andrea's voice. He could not make out her whispers, but he felt the passion and energy in her prayer. Although he could not see her point of view, he recognized and respected her sincerity.

Mitch covered his ears as the rusty horse whined to a stop. *I can scarcely wait to rid myself of this vile contraption.*

Mitch gathered his things and climbed down from the train. He exchanged the smell of dried urine for smoke and dust. As he helped Marci from the train, he asked, "So, have you ever been to Jharsuguda?"

Marci gave him a shove.

The two of them stood waiting as Andrea waved her goodbyes to everyone and thanked the attendant.

Stepping out of the railway station, they met a slender young man holding a sign, "The Aryan Hotel."

Mitch asked, "Hot shower and internet?"

"No problem." The man smiled and nodded as he led them toward an oversized matchbox car. The passenger's seat was already occupied with a woman and her child. The driver removed the woman's older child from the back seat, cramming the mother and both of her children into the front seat. He squeezed Marci, Andrea and Mitch into the back of his tiny box.

Mitch groaned. "I feel like a used air mattress." He smiled at Marci. "Perhaps, we would make a better fit if you sat on my lap."

Marci stuck out her tongue and pretended to gag herself.

Andrea chuckled.

Their driver looked over his shoulder. "Everyone, ok?" Then he steered the cramped vessel into the flood of people wading through Jharsuguda.

The tiny car lurched and the horn squeaked, joining the discord of cows, chickens, children and people of all sorts, bicycles, rickshaws, motorcycles, buses, huge trucks, goats, and more. It seemed the entire world was finding its way through the stream of confusion.

The endless barrage of toots and beeps was a language unto itself. The driver thumped the brakes like a kick drum and tapped the horn in rhythm, wiggling through the maze toward

The Aryan Hotel.

Wedged between two twenty-year-olds, Mitch leaned toward Marci, but she smelled like vomit. He turned to breathe in Andrea. All he could smell was after 36 hours without a shower. "How much further to the hotel?"

When the car finally stopped at their hotel, Andrea bounded out, smiling and soaking it all in. Her smile disappeared as smoke flooded the street like a heavy fog. "Where is that smoke coming from?"

The driver nodded toward the smoke as he carried her bags. "The steel mill. It depends on the wind."

Mitch wriggled his way out of the car and up the steps. He left the dust and smoke on the outside to discover marble floors and fine lighting on the inside, a welcome reprieve. He followed Andrea to the front desk.

Mitch said, "Rather fancy for the middle of nowhere."

"Should we be doing this?" Marci protested. "We need to watch our money."

Andrea smiled. "That's why we're only getting one room."

Marci and Mitch raised their eyebrows.

Andrea continued, "We're not going to spend the night. We can all take a shower." Rolling her eyes at the smiling journalist, she corrected herself. "We can EACH take a shower. We have two queen beds, so you and Mitch can catch a nap. We'll get something to eat and find a car."

# CHAPTER 8

Road to Sambalpur
Tuesday Morning, September 9, 2008

Satyajit lay awake, watching a lizard scurry up the wall. Its tiny feet clung to the ceiling. He imagined himself holding tightly, but, unlike the lizard,

*"How do you not fall?"* Jeevan Joseph's voice echoed through his mind. *"Send your mercies to my father."* Blood-drenched eyes dripped a mix of kerosene and sweat. Flames danced around him, mocking the children's cries.

Satyajit jolted out of bed. Drenched with sweat, pulse racing, he buried his thoughts and slipped on his shoes in the dark. He tip-toed in silence, clenched his stomach and stumbled out the door. *I can't see anything.*

He followed the path from memory, counting his footsteps on the packed earth. He followed the darkness to the edge of the village. He stopped as he felt the crunch of the road under his feet.

He hid in a cluster of teak trees as a herd of cows meandered across the road. A large truck slowed to a stop, waiting for the sacred beasts to pass. Satyajit slid from his perch and climbed the back of the truck. The truck lurched, tossing Satyajit onto a mountain of rice bags. One of the bags spilled onto the road. The driver failed to notice as he maneuvered around the cows.

Satyajit collapsed on the mountain of rice and propped his feet against the back of the truck. His eyes burning from lack of sleep, his throat parched, he stared at the sky as the truck rumbled over the broken asphalt.

On his left, the deep blue grew softer. Above him the stars began to fade. Faint wisps of clouds only teased, for the rains had died earlier in the season. Despite the precarious nature of his rice bed, Satyajit somehow managed to fall asleep.

\* \* \*

Screaming woke Satyajit in time to feel a sharp sting across face and an angry fist in his gut. Instinctively he kicked his attacker knocking him from the truck. Onlookers broke the driver's fall and hurled insults at Satyajit. Still wearing his crumpled bandana, he was obviously a bandit.

Staring down at the small crowd, Satyajit understood the inevitable. *If they catch me, they will kill me.* He looked for his quickest escape, but the crowd was surrounding the trunk and some were starting to climb the sides. The crowd was like a hungry tiger, circling and waiting to pounce. *Think, Satyajit. Think!* He crouched on the mound of rice and began tossing out bags. The tone transformed from anger to delight. Everyone scrambled for a free bag of rice. Satyajit climbed toward the front of the truck. He tossed one more bag, slid down the side of the truck, and ran as fast as he could.

The fist-shaking, screaming driver dared not leave his truck. He hustled to get behind the wheel and make the town of Dhama a memory. "Why did I stop in this ant hole?" he cursed.

Satyajit stopped running and caught his breath. He shielded his eyes from the glaring sun and watched the truck lumber around another cluster of cows. Glad to be alive, he removed his bandana, tucked it in his pocket, and headed north toward Sambalpur.

# CHAPTER 9

On to Bhubaneshwar
Tuesday afternoon, September 9, 2008

Andrea prodded. "Are you sure it's a good idea to let Marci drive? She's not accustomed to driving on the left side of the... Whoa! ...or swerving to miss cows."

Without looking up, Mitch said, "Speed is limited by the miserable quality of these roads. She is driving remarkably well, all things considered. A normal speed, would break this car into pieces." He blithely folded his newspaper. "That said, I'm quite sure you have much bigger worries than Marci's driving."

"What do you mean?"

Mitch shrugged. "Coming to Orissa... and at this time." "I'm not sure it was a good idea. Well, actually I feel certain it was a mistake since Lakshmana Datta was killed two weeks ago Saturday."

"Laxma-who?" Marci asked.

"Lakshmana Datta was the leader of the Vishwa Hindu Parishad, the VHP."

Andrea crinkled her brow. "The VHP?"

"Essentially the World Hindu Council. They are quite open with their hatred of Christians, Jews, and Muslims. Orissa is one of many less developed areas where the VHP is strong. It's a troublesome area anytime, but at present, it is particularly worrisome. The VHP has blamed their leader's murder on

Christians, and they have vowed to kill *all* Christians in the Kandhamal district."

Andrea took a deep breath. "That's where we're headed, right into its capital." *God help us!*

Marci drove with one hand, and gestured with the other. "I can see the headlines. Two Americans Killed, and I can hear the snide little voices, 'What were they doing going to that part of the world anyway?' Mitch if you knew it was so dangerous, why did you come with us?"

Mitch felt a sour taste as he stared at the floor. He gulped as he tried to answer. "Well, first of all, I'm not a Christian." *Thank god!* "Second, I'm a journalist. Part of my job is to edge as close to the fire as possible." *I thought this trip would be one of mutual contempt, but I feel closer to these girls by the hour.*

"So, you're going to walk us into the flames and watch us burn?"

Andrea interrupted. "If we are thrown into the fire, God is able to save us from it, and he will rescue us."

Mitch caught her elusion to Shadrach, Meshach, and Abednego and the story of the fiery furnace. *What a fairy tale! Who are these two Sunday school girls? They have barely tasted life, but they want to turn the world upside down.*

Andrea studied his eyes. "Mitch I cannot read your thoughts, but I feel your heart. I don't expect you to believe the way Marci and I do, and please don't feel compelled to go with us. You don't have to understand the way we think or why we believe what we believe, but please be understanding. We all know we are going to die some time, but, in the meantime, what are we living for?"

Mitch chewed her words. *Normally I would charge with an argument or a personal attack, but these girls are different.* After a long silence, he sighed deeply. "There is more to me than finding a story. I don't want any harm to come to either of you. I will stay with you until I am sure you are safe."

Andrea smiled. "Mitch, thank you for your concern, but we are already safe. God is with us, and He has gone before us to guide our steps."

Mitch rolled his eyes and muttered, "Dear God!"

* * *

As they ambled over the broken road, Andrea inhaled the coarse beauty of the scattered hills. *This place is so dry, like a heart void of emotion. God, what's in store for us?* She swallowed hard and braced herself against fear. *Only you know the trouble ahead. Help me trust you. Please calm my fear.*

Andrea stared at the world passing by as Marci slowed the car for another cow. *What have I gotten her into? Lord, help us.*

As they ambled around the cow, Andrea felt a sense of calm. No obstacle is too big for God.

She placed her hand on Mitch's shoulder. "I think you may find a bigger story than you thought possible. I know you think we are adolescent. You're probably right, but I have to trust God no matter what, and He is calling us to Orissa. Only He knows why."

* * *

Mitch did not say a word. He knew Andrea was sincere, but his face could not disguise his frustration. He wanted to mock these two Bible school girls. He wanted to argue all the way to Bhubaneshwar. He wanted to despise them, use them, and then watch them fall on their faces.

He wanted to hear them beg for his help. He could see himself wiping their tears as they give up on their pathetic nursery rhyme beliefs, but, at the same time, a tiny part of him wished it were true. So much of life had let him down, leaving him reluctant to trust, but these two young women captured his heart. They held tightly to a surety and love for life he could not accept, but he was falling into their trance.

Mitch melted with the soothing voice and gentle heart of Andrea, and he loved the brass and spunk of Marci. Marci and he were like boxers, toe-to-toe and nose-to-nose, insulting and jibing, sweating and salivating, anxious for the next round to begin. Marci packed a wicked punch, but he recognized her outward contempt as genuine inner respect.

His off-road thoughts were bouncing about when he realized they were headed south instead of southeast. "Marci, do we know where we are?"

"Hey, you said this was the way to Bhubaneshwar."

"Some time ago, yes, but I think we missed a turn. We should be heading southeast, not south." Mitch didn't hate being lost half as much as he loved being right.

"It's all right, Marci," Andrea answered.

Mitch rolled his eyes again, bracing for a "we're following the Spirit speech."

Andrea sighed. "There is more than one road to Bhubaneshwar, but there is only one capital of Orissa, and that's where we're going."

Marci chirped the horn at a couple of scampering goats and two boys laughing and chasing each other. Small mounds of garbage smoldered at the road's edge as they passed through the town of Regali. Women, colorfully adorned, carried bundles, corralled children, and sold produce. A cluster of aimless men warily stared as they passed through the village.

Andrea gazed through the rear window. Regali grew smaller as she fixed on one child, not much more than a toddler. Wide eyes and a bright smile overshadowed her surroundings. Andrea waved at the little girl. As the child waved, Andrea beamed. She watched the girl as long as she could, wondering what life would take from her. She prayed silently, not wanting Mitch to know her thoughts. She knew that God would understand.

Marci broke the silence. "Did you see the way the men in that town looked at us?"

Mitch nodded. "I don't think we would want to find ourselves in Regali after dark."

The sun was well overhead and beating down. "Is the air-conditioner working?" asked Andrea. "I can hardly breathe. There is no air back here."

Marci noted the temperature gauge leaning on red.

Mitch said, "It's well over 100. I don't think this little maggot will make it any further."

The car began to hiss. Marci pulled off the road as steam escaped from the hood.

Mitch swore under his breath and looked at the girls apologetically.

The steam disappeared in the dry heat. India suddenly became more real, in-your-face and frightening. The broken-down road looked longer. The air felt thick. Time would not wait for them as the sun seemed to sink faster. Three became a smaller number.

Marci grasped Andrea's hand while Mitch scratched his head and stared at the engine.

# CHAPTER 10

Sambalpur
Tuesday, September 9, 2008

The day was slipping away. Thirst, hunger, and heat were stealing life and passion from young Satyajit. His tongue languished like a fish in a dry pond. He choked while trying to swallow, his mouth glued shut. His eyes drifted ahead, spying a well a few hundred yards away. He could taste the invigorating coolness. The need for water motivated every step.

As he neared the well, he stumbled and fell onto the hand pump.

"What are you doing?" A stern and gruff voice dismissed his thirst. "This well is not for you."

"But I am so faint from thirst."

"You are a fool to walk so far without water. What can you give me for a drink?"

Satyajit reached into his pocket. Before he could count his money, the man tore it from his hand with a "hmpff, 50 rupees will buy you three seconds." Satyajit thrust himself beneath the spigot as the well pumped life. He lay beneath the fountain until an abrupt kick awakened him to reality. Scooting away from the well, he offered his thanks and scurried on through the town.

His long shadow followed him. The rocky hills were slowly shrinking over his right shoulder. With the Mahanandi River weaving along on his left, Sambalpur grew closer.

Shadows grew and night's mantle stretched over the sleeping town as Satyajit reached its edge. Almost no street lights, a scattered lamp here and there along the main street, the city was dark. A rare home was dimly lit. Yet the darkness did not stir fear.

Satyajit knew how to find his way in the dark. The only light in his village was moonlight and a rare lamp. Stumbling along, he almost stepped on a startled chicken. As the hen squawked, his stomach lurched. If he was at home, he would have chased the chicken and tried to catch it. He thought of his mother's chicken-and-rice. But the night was too dark, and his startled meal was too fast.

He sighed as he gave up hope of scrounging anything for supper. As he plodded along, he remembered the days when he roamed everywhere barefoot. *My feet are so hot. I think my toes are melting together.*

He followed Ring Road toward the river. Tumbling down the bank, he cast off his shoes and soaked his feet in the muddy water. A man nearby was bathing himself with one hand, the other resting on a cow. Neither said a word. Satyajit stood watching thin streams of light dancing across the river. A soft orange glow faded against the distant hills.

Satyajit ambled along the edge of the river to where the ground was firm. He carried his socks and shoes, remembering simpler days. A distant fire reminded him of the funeral pyres he once saw on the Ganges. The tiny blazes grew closer with every step. As the flames grew, his pulse quickened. His mind could not escape the image of the man in his dreams.

*Why am I here? I should run as far and as fast as I can.* His thoughts drifted to the inescapable memory of his dream and the unmistakable voice that said, "Go to Sambalpur."

Satyajit flopped down, exhausted, and hungry. His stomach ached as if he had not eaten for days. He was too tired to climb the bank. He stretched out on his side. He wanted desperately to lose himself in the endless sea of stars. Darkness was his blanket. Tears were his pillow. A fresh new day was his dream. Again, he wondered, *why am I here? There are no goddesses. I hear no voice. I know no direction.* He saw himself like a stick drifting aimlessly, pushed along with the current, floating without reason or direction.

# CHAPTER 11

On the Road
Tuesday Afternoon, September 9, 2008

With his satellite phone glued to his ear, Mitch paced furiously. "What do you mean, we need to bring the car to Sambalpur! Steam is spewing from the engine! You need to come get it and bring us a new one. Of course, that's what I expect! No! You listen to me. We are done with this car."

Marci smirked. "Well, it sounded like that went well."

Mitch glared. "We are on our own. They can't help us until tomorrow."

"That's just great. So, you're going to carry our bags, right?"

"Hardly!" replied Mitch. "I believe in you, Marci. You are a strong and capable woman."

Andrea ignored them, popped the trunk, and removed her bags. Backpack on her shoulder, suitcase on rollers, she headed south. She stopped and turned abruptly. "It's going to be dark in less than two hours. I would prefer to be safely indoors."

* * *

The unlikely trio continued their journey in silence until a farmer came by on his tractor. He stopped beside them, leaned over and lifted his voice above the clanking engine. "Sambalpur?"

"Yes! Can you take us?" Mitch shrugged his shoulders to

suggest putting his bags on the wagon."

The farmer nodded. "Come. Come. I take you."

\* \* \*

It was a jarring ride, yet quite comfortable compared to walking for hours. As the sun began to fade, the tractor slowed. The bouncing and rumbling lessened. As they drew nearer to the town, the road grew congested with life: cars and busses slowing for cows, motorcycles weaving in and out like a bizarre parade.

Andrea desperately wanted to sleep, but her nerves were on edge. Reality struck. *I'm 10,000 miles from home, headed to a strange town at dusk with no plan, no reservations, and no idea of what I am doing.*

The road was perilous as only every fifth car donned their headlights. Their tractor, of course, had no lights. Exhaustion had gotten the best of them. Despite the chaos, eyelids were sagging. Heads were bobbing. Sleep eventually won, and Marci, Mitch, and Andrea nestled against their luggage in the bed of the wagon.

\* \* \*

They jolted to a stop. The farmer jumped onto the wagon, shouting, "No move. Hide!" He covered them with a large canvas and weighted the corners with stones.

Mitch tried to peek, but he could not see anything. "What is it?"

The driver waved his hand furiously as if to say, "Be quiet and lay still."

Marci elbowed Mitch. "I think you should keep it shut like he said." She could not see Mitch's eyes, but Andrea's sharp pinch was unmistakable.

As the tractor resumed its course, the noise of the engine was muffled by shouts and gunfire. Marci, Andrea, and Mitch huddled close and remained perfectly still. Fear had surpassed exhaustion. Their driver tried to speed up.

The floor of the wagon dimly reflected the glow of raging fire as they drew close enough to feel the heat. The tractor's engine was silent compared to the noise of the mob.

Mitch heard pressured whispers as Andrea splayed her heart open before God. Mitch wished that he had not come along, or that he had, at least, brought a gun. His fears opened wide as the tractor stopped. Mitch held his breath as voices grew louder and nearer and the fire's glow dimmed behind darting shadows.

The wagon shook as men clamored up the sides. Not wishing to lose his tractor, the farmer waved his arm, inviting any who would to climb aboard. Dozens of men fled the conflagration to enjoy a free ride into Sambalpur.

Mitch turned off his sat-phone and wished he could pray. Being a journalist would not protect him with this crowd. He slid his hand across Marci who cringed until she felt his hand squeeze Andrea's. He put his microbe of faith in her hand and her prayers.

Andrea prayed in silence. *Dear God, let us be stones to these men. Protect us from harm, Oh Lord.* Her prayer continued with fervor and without pause.

Originally the three had hoped for a half hour ride to the city. Three hours later, they finally stopped. A flurry of footsteps and jumping signaled the departure of the men from the wagon.

When the thumps and voices faded into silence, the farmer leapt from the tractor onto the wagon. He was screaming inconsolably, hands to his head and spitting words rapid-fire between cries and moans.

"What is he saying?" Marci asked.

Mitch pulled off the canvas. Blinking and choking from the dust, he held out his hand to calm the man, and answered Marci. "I don't know. I can understand a scattered word here and there, but he must be speaking Oriya."

Andrea flinched as she captured a set of dark eyes drenched with blood and soot. The mob had left a dead man in the wagon. Andrea cringed and gripped her stomach.

Mitch crawled toward the man as Marci offered her flashlight. "He has a pulse." Mitch glared at the driver. "Where the hell are we?"

Andrea tried to forget herself. She cast her attention toward the farmer. He was visibly shaken, too delirious to speak. Looking past him, Andrea noticed one of the rare lights in town, a sign pointing to a hospital. "Do you know anything about this hospital? Can you take us there?"

Andrea repeated the question slowly and louder.

The farmer looked puzzled until Mitch repeated the question in Hindi. He understood enough, and he jumped back onto the tractor and shouted at them to sit down.

# CHAPTER 12

All Saints Hospital
Tuesday Night, September 9, 2008

The lights flickered as Chandrika observed her patients. Footsteps behind her meant that Naomi was coming to relieve her. Chandrika turned and said, "The power went out seven times today. Once while Dr. David was in surgery."

Naomi crinkled her brow and smiled. "Be thankful we have a generator that works, Chandrika. How is our patient?"

Chandrika motioned Naomi toward the door. She tiptoed and whispered. "He is sleeping. The surgery went well. He had a large tumor, but Dr. David removed all of it."

Thunderous pounding at the door startled them. Naomi tensed her lips. "Go see what it is, please."

\* \* \*

What would have been a two-minute drive in daylight had taken 15 minutes. The farmer measured every movement of his tractor and wagon in the darkness, winding along the dirt road to obscurity. At the outskirts of nowhere, they reached a dead end with only one building that could be a hospital.

As the light fluttered across the sign, Marci announced, "All Saints Hospital."

Mitch dashed to the door and began pounding. Soon after, the door swung open. A slender, youthful nurse greeted him. Mitch clutched her arm. "Please help us. This man is dying."

Mitch and the farmer lifted the man from the wagon to an ancient litter and wheeled him into the hospital.

Chandrika led them through the dark corridors to a modest procedure room. She flipped on the lights. "We have no doctor until morning, but you are welcome to stay with him, and I will do what I can to help."

Mitch thought to offer the farmer money for his trouble, but the farmer's feet were faster. "Well, there goes our ride."

Marci's eyes widened. "Our bags!" She grabbed Mitch by the arm and tore out of the hospital, leaving Andrea with the dying man.

Andrea gave no thought to her things or time or place. She stood over the unknown soul. She stared at his weary face, gently wiping his forehead with a damp cloth.

Chandrika prepped his arm and established an IV. "I will give him fluids. He does not appear to be bleeding, but his pulse is fast and weak. How did he get covered with such filth?"

"We don't know what happened to him. We were hiding on the farmer's wagon. There was a fire and a mob. I think it was a car burning. All these men climbed on board the wagon while we hid beneath a tarp. When the tractor finally stopped, the men jumped off the wagon. When they were all gone, we discovered this man and realized that they had left him for dead."

As Chandrika worked in silence, Andrea could see tears dribbling down her cheek. The young nurse bit her lip and sniffled. Andrea felt an unexplained rush. For a split second, she envisioned a frightened Chandrika, crying and running. Watching this humble nurse tearfully caring for her patient, she wondered if Chandrika had suffered some great loss at the hands of someone like this stranger. A chill prompted Andrea to say *you can feel safe with me*, but fear overpowered boldness, and she kept her thoughts to herself.

The IV was running smoothly. Chandrika breathed a sigh as his blood pressure rose even slightly. She turned to Andrea. "Why are you here?"

Andrea stared in silence, wondering the same question.

Chandrika draped her arm around Andrea. "We are not here by our own design, but by the will of Him who knows our hearts."

The same warm rush swelled in Andrea's heart. *God bless this angel's hands and save this man.*

* * *

Chandrika smiled as she labored over the unconscious man. She focused on his eminent needs. When she had done everything to stabilize him, she paused to look at him. Sweat and dirt mired his face. Chandrika blotted his forehead with a clean towel. *His face is gentle, but he has seen so much. The years had etched their marks.*

As she wiped the last remnant of soot from his face, she whispered, "You remind me of my grandfather. I miss him. I see him in your eyebrows and wrinkles."

The man gasped but remained asleep. The quickening heart monitor brought Chandrika back to reality. She watched him closely until his pulse returned to normal. Breathing a heavy sigh, she sat down to capture a moment's rest.

"Is he one of the extremists, or was he with you?"

Andrea shrugged. "He was not with us, but I am not sure if he was with them. We could not see what was happening. All I know is they left him for dead."

*She has such kind eyes. Why is she here? God, why did you*

*bring her to this place of pain? She is a perfect lotus in a dry land. Do I trust her? Can I share my soul with her?*

Andrea broke the silence. "I don't know this man, but I can see he has awakened painful memories."

Chandrika stared at the life dangling before her. *Who is this man that opens the wounds of my soul and this woman who sees my pain?* She watched him breathing and checked his pulse once more.

Tears welled and dribbled down her cheek. "When I was 10, my father and mother accepted Christ. My mother's parents cursed my father. They said, 'You have corrupted our daughter. She is dead to us.' This man reminds me of my grandfather. I never saw him again after that day. When I was 12, extremists killed my parents. I ran away, but I have never been able to fully escape. Even now, I am faced with hatred. I struggle when I take care of someone like this man. Anger and bitterness would have me fail in my duty. Look at him. He hangs on the edge of life." *I could be slow in giving him fluids. I could withhold pain medication. I could say he died shortly after he arrived, but I do not hate or fear this man.* "Even though he has done a great evil, he is not my enemy. He believes in a lie, and does not know what he is doing. He has become an instrument of hate."

Chandrika grasped Andrea's hand. "I fear they have killed one of our pastors tonight. It is by God's mercy that you are safe and have brought this man to us."

The man moaned and gasped. Chandrika gently patted his cheek and spoke to him in Oriya. "Wake up. Wake up, sir. You are in a hospital."

He grimaced and mumbled. The heart monitor raced. He briefly opened his eyes but could not stay awake.

"What was he saying?" asked Andrea.

"I could not understand. It sounded like English or a name."

*  *  *

Mitch plopped the last of their bags in the hall and entered the ward. "Well, is he waking up? Has he said anything?"

"He tried to say something, but I think his pain was too much. Chandrika gave him some morphine, and he is sleeping."

"His pulse and breathing are stable. Dr. David will be here at 7 o'clock."

*  *  *

There was no comfortable lounge, no family waiting area, no adjacent hotel.

Marci slept on a gurney in the hall.

Mitch sank into the sofa in Dr. David's office.

Andrea unrolled a mat on the floor near the wounded stranger. She emptied her heart to God, praying until her eyelids fell.

# CHAPTER 13

The Temple
Tuesday Night, September 9, 2008

The world vanished in shadow. The ghostly river rushed by with a low rumble. The midnight sky fought the darkness with tiny gleams of hope. Satyajit lay still, longing for daylight.

He closed his eyes only to be gripped by Pastor Joseph's blood-covered face. He could still see the skin peeling and rolling off his body like melting chocolate. He could not quiet the voice, *"Go! Find them for me. Bring them here."*

The words played over and over. Satyajit wondered who he was supposed to find. He pictured the two goddesses that flanked the dying preacher. *Surely not them.* They appeared as flames, shimmering light, wrapped around dissolving flesh. They drew together, stretching high above the empty, discarded shell.

Satyajit felt a strange sense of destiny as though somehow chosen by the gods. He had always been a follower his whole life, chasing someone else's dreams. His only dream had been to be accepted. This new dream superseded all others.

As he sat against the Mahanandi's dusty bank, a blaze danced behind him, casting shadows toward the river. A flood of youths poured over the bank and down to the river's edge, chanting, drumming, dancing, and yelling. *Bandits.* Their bandanas gave them away.

Satyajit quickly tied his bandana around his neck and slid into the shadows. He scurried north along the bank, clawing and scratching his way up through the dirt and across the road.

He stumbled through the darkness and fell beneath a large fountain in the shape of a giant lotus blossom. *The temple of Samaleswari*. He dared not enter the temple after dark. He collapsed against the temple wall until sleep finally won.

# CHAPTER 14

At the Crime Scene
Wednesday, September 10, 2008

Early in the morning, Mitch secured a matchbox SUV. Taking his camera and a digital recorder, he drove to the northern outskirts of town and shot a series of photos of the burned-out vehicle.

As police cars approached, he stepped back and hid his camera. He watched in silence, sneaking photos as the police forced open the burnt car door revealing the charred remains.

A man shouted, "That's pastor Singh!"

Mitch turned toward the shouting and fired off several more photos. He captured a cluster of stunned souls. Weeping, screaming, some silent and some fainting, he unloaded his camera on them.

The car, the bodies, the ground around the vehicle, were scorched and black. Two young, disinterested policemen talked to onlookers and took notes. The swell of charred earth around the vehicle made it clear an accelerant had been used. Scattered clubs and sticks implied a violent mob.

His lens was an open window to the world. With each click he captured life at its worst: the blank faces of police, streams of tears, confused children, and the discarded remains of lives both loved and despised.

\* \* \*

"It appears to have been an accident," one of the officers said.

The searing lie burned into Mitch Hawkins. He stormed toward the two officers. Waving his sat-phone, he displayed a photo of the two of them and the torched car. "I transmitted this and other photos of this crime to my editors in London. You know exactly what happened here. A gang of extremists surrounded and stopped the car. They trapped the pastor and his family inside while they doused it, set it ablaze and watched it burn." *If they realize I was here during the attack, they will hold me for questioning for who knows how long.*

A down-turned lip and hostile eyes did not welcome his words. Stepping toward him, the officer flipped open his notepad and reluctantly began to write.

One witness reported a gang of bandits on a tractor. Another saw them unload and disperse along the bank of the Mahanandi.

"That is where we must begin our search."

Mitch captured a few more stills after the police left. He felt the curious eyes of onlookers and spied a few children giggling behind him as they watched the images popping up on his view screen. He smiled at their coy innocence as he packed up his gear and left for the hospital.

# CHAPTER 15

All Saints Hospital
Wednesday Morning, September 10, 2008

Andrea opened her eyes and groaned. *Nothing like a short night on a marble floor to stiffen every joint.* She rubbed sleep from her eyes and climbed into the chair beside the injured man. *He's awake.*

He stared at the ceiling. His sullen eyes did not move. He drew a deep breath and said, "I could not do it."

He closed his eyes and turned toward the window. "Some years ago, pastor Singh came to our town preaching his gospel. We are Hindu. We did not want him coercing our people to become Christian. We warned him more than once. This past week, we decided it was time. One of our families buried their son. When he accepted Christ, he turned his back on everything we believe in. He turned his back on his mother and father."

Andrea gasped but held her tongue.

He twisted around to see her. "You are American! Why are you here?"

"My name is Andrea. My friends and I brought you here. I did not mean to interrupt you."

He scowled but continued. "Their son was dead to them. They published a notice in the newspaper, stating he was no longer their son. They followed the notice with an obituary and a memorial service."

"Their son became a discarded memory." He looked deep into Andrea's eyes. "Sons should never be memories. We had to stop Pastor Singh. We conspired to kill him." He gritted his teeth and swallowed hard, fighting tears. "I did not know he was married. I did not know he had children. I did not care. I knew they were Christian. I had every reason to hate them.

As I leaned against his car, Pastor Singh looked into my eyes. He recognized me. His eyes begged. He screamed, kicking and pushing at the door. His children huddled behind the seat."

His tears slowed. "While Pastor Singh was kicking the door, his wife stretched out her hand to grasp his arm. Her fingers slid down to his hand. He looked at her. His feet stopped pressing the door. He looked at me again. His lips did not move, but I heard his voice. A strange silence surrounded me, and I heard his voice as though he spoke above all the noise. 'Jeevan sadaiva.'

He held his wife, and they prayed. I stood, gazing at them. I had believed we were right, that Pastor Singh deserved to die, but in his death, he was at peace. His eyes were gentle, while anger and hate boiled around him. As I watched them hold each other and pray, my hate felt so empty. Why were we outraged and violent, while this man and his wife were calm and at peace? We were safe, while they faced death. He opened his eyes one last time. He looked at me, and I realized he was not praying for deliverance. He was praying for me.

The mob pressed me toward the car and passed me a can of petrol. I turned around to see faces steaming with rage. I could not do it. I stood still.

They crushed me against the door handle. Petrol spilled everywhere and flames burst around me."

He buckled his lips, tears streaming, he shook his head. "I don't know who I am today. I feel empty. I thought killing him would free my soul, but he is the one who is free. I have never felt the calm I saw in his eyes, the calm I now see in yours."

He swallowed his tears and closed his eyes. "Why am I here? Why did I not die?"

*This young American is so out of place, so innocent. Why is she here? Why does she care? Her tears reveal her compassion.*

He stared at her, blinking through his tears, his heart bursting. *I am a murderer and a coward, a lost soul in a world I no longer recognize. Who is this young woman who shares my tears?*

Andrea couldn't speak. Sorrow blended with anger. She restrained her hand, unsure if she wanted to reach out to such a violent man, but she could not restrain her heart. "My name is Andrea."

He looked away, far beyond the ceiling. *I cannot hide from my thoughts. They will pursue me until I die.* He turned to Andrea in frustration. "Why did you not leave me to die?"

She was stunned. *How do I answer that? God speak through me.* A familiar warmth rushed over her. "God gave you life, and God has delivered you from death. You have been running from Him, but you cannot escape his reach. You have heard His voice calling you through Pastor Singh, and even now, His voice is calling you."

His face tensed. He tried to retreat into himself, but he could not escape her words. He could not escape the voice. For the first time, he listened. Although he was silent, inside he was screaming. He felt transparent, Andrea's eyes studying him as if she were reading his thoughts.

"My name is Vishal."

Andrea's eyes brightened. "I know very little Hindi, but your name means unstoppable."

He smirked. "I don't feel unstoppable."

The same warmth overwhelmed Andrea, and she spoke. "You have been a hard man, fierce and unafraid. I want to tell you a story."

He nodded. He had nowhere else to go and no one else to visit him.

Andrea folded her hands in her lap and straightened in her seat. "A powerful king heard fantastic claims about a great wizard, known for his power and wit. The king prided himself in wisdom. He called for the wizard and challenged him, saying, 'I have no doubt I can outwit you, oh greatest of wizards.' The wizard answered, 'There is no one capable of outwitting me, your highness.' The king continued, 'I challenge you only to do two things for me. The first, conjure a stone so massive, so sturdy and dense, that no one could possibly move it.' The wizard scoffed and began working to conjure the stone. Before the king, and all who were present, a tiny speck of sand began to grow. A tiny storm of dust and rocks flew through the crowd from all directions, building into a massive stone. The stone grew and pushed the crowd away."

"The king stepped backward and shouted, 'Make it stop!'"

"With a wave of the wizard's hand, the stone settled."

"The clever wizard mused to himself, *I don't think you meant to offer that command as your second request, so I will allow you a third.*"

"No one dared try to move the stone. It was larger than any house. The king had to walk around the stone to see the wizard. The king was indeed impressed, but, slapping his knees and bellowing with laughter, he said, 'I've got you now, great wizard! Now that you have conjured the immovable stone, move it.'"

"The wizard smiled and folded his arms as the stone began to crack. Its edges bulged. The stone shook the ground."

"The king asked the wizard, 'What are you doing? I told you to make a stone no one could move.'"

"The wizard shrugged his shoulders with open hands and answered, 'I am doing nothing.'"

"The crowd roared with awe. Some fled. Others backed away while watching the once tiny speck of sand grow into a stone giant. The king and his subjects braced themselves as thunderous footsteps pounded down the slope and into the sea. The giant dissolved into sand."

"No one could move the stone but the stone itself. When the wizard created it, he gave it life and a will to move."

Andrea looked into his eyes. "Vishal, the unstoppable one, the only one who can move your soul is you. God created you. He gave you life and your own will. He is the voice you heard. 'Jeevan sadaiva' means 'life forever,' but to you it means something more."

Andrea could not believe her own boldness as she spoke to this stranger. She stood as she heard Marci entering the room behind her. The doctor followed closely. As Andrea turned to make room for the doctor, Vishal stretched out his hand and grasped her arm. He had spent all his tears. His throat was dry, and he could not speak, but Andrea understood every word.

# CHAPTER 16

### The Samaleswari Temple
### Wednesday Morning, September 10, 2008

The warm caress of sunlight awakened Satyajit, who was accustomed to sleeping on dirt or stone. He stretched and almost smiled, feeling refreshed despite the emptiness in his stomach. He opened his eyes and admired the intricate temple. *Perhaps the temple is where I will find the goddesses from the fire.* Rubbing his face, he felt the bandana hanging loosely around his neck. He removed it and stuffed it in his pocket.

As he stood near a tree to relieve himself, his simple plans were abruptly thwarted.

"Stop. Do not move!" one policeman shouted. Another, running from the other side of the temple, grabbed Satyajit by the arm. The two policemen led him to the investigating officer.

The investigator plucked the smoky bandana from Satyajit's pocket. "What's this?" Waving it in the air, he almost sang. "It looks like we have found their ring leader." It was obvious that Satyajit was a villager, not from Sambalpur. He was unknown and unimportant. "These Christians want blood. This one should be enough to satisfy their thirst."

Satyajit tried to argue his case, but no one heard or cared.

# CHAPTER 17

Back at the Hospital
Wednesday, September 10, 2008

The doctor left the room with Andrea and Marci. "Minor injuries really, he should be ready to go home in the morning. Let him rest awhile."

Vishal could not rest. The voice was calling, tugging, and tormenting him. Although calm and peaceful, the voice wrestled with his very nature. It rang over and over in his mind. "Jeevan sadaiva." He remembered the first time he heard the voice, and the anger that ensued. Mulling over memories, he saw the strained face of his beautiful wife. Their children were grown. They had been married for almost 30 years.

He would never forget the day when he walked into the bedroom and caught her hiding something. He did not want to know what it was, although his heart believed it was a Bible. She hid it well for months. If he suspected she was praying, he would make some noise to alert her to his coming, but one day he had enough. He silently walked into the room. Looking over her shoulder, he saw a photograph of a young Christian family. She muttered a prayer for them. When she finished, she kissed the photo and tucked it in her Bible.

He kicked the book from her hands, ripping pages and sending the picture flying. Slapping her as hard as he could, he screamed, "What is this? This is how you dishonor me? You reject our beliefs, our family, and our tradition." Thrusting his foot into her stomach, he pressed her. "You are a Christian, aren't you? Aren't you? Say it." He screamed in her face.

She sobbed miserably, while scrambling to back away and protect herself. Hitting the wall, she used it to push herself to her feet. Then she scrambled out the door and fled with nothing.

Vishal knew where she would go. He gathered his brothers and a few close friends. He no longer considered her his wife. The woman he hated was a stranger. He could not even capture her face in his mind. His eyesight blurred with seething hatred.

He remembered all too well that night his band visited her parent's home. In respect for her parents, who knew nothing of her conversion, he snuck into the house. Two friends and he quickly subdued her. Stuffing a gag in her mouth while holding her down and binding her, they lifted and carried her out of the home unnoticed.

When they reached a quiet spot in the forest, they unbound her and removed the gag. She tried to speak, but he punched her mouth with his fist. Blood on his torn knuckles added to his fury. Before he slapped her, someone grabbed his arm.

She screamed through tears. "Vishal, I will always love you, and I forgive you for what you are about to do."

As she finished, his hand released his rage. His friends and he beat her, stripping her of her clothes and jewels. Then they abandoned her lifeless body.

Vishal gritted his teeth. "Who grabbed my arm to let her speak?"

"There was no one behind you, Vishal. No one grabbed your arm."

His tears exploded as he remembered that night. Life as he knew it was over. His family gone, empty from fruitless revenge and hate, again he wished he had died in the flames with pastor Singh.

Against the wishes of the nurse and Andrea, Vishal climbed out of his bed, put on his smoke-riddled, charred clothes and left to go home, refusing to let anyone follow.

At home, Vishal went straight to his bedroom and picked up his wife's Bible. He had no intention of reading it. His hands felt weak and guilty as they held it. He removed the picture he had neatly tucked back inside the pages. He stared at the young family for what seemed like hours.

# CHAPTER 18

At the Police Station
Wednesday, September 10, 2008

Driving away from the hospital, Mitch flipped open his phone and handed it to Marci. "Here are some photos of the car."

Marci grimaced. "Are you sick? Why would I want to see that?"

"These are your brothers and sisters, are they not? Shouldn't you be angry or frightened or showing some kind of concern? I thought you would want to see them."

"Well, I don't!"

Andrea calmed the storm. "Of course we are hurt by the killing of the pastor and his family, but our hurt runs deeper. You know the words of Scripture, Mitch. 'Our struggle is not with flesh and blood...' We are fighting against spiritual forces and ideologies. It's a battle of ideas, a battle for the mind."

Mitch did not expect her to say anything remotely intellectual, but he was genuinely impressed she understood. It was, indeed, a raging war for the mind, an unceasing war, dragging its charred, beaten and bloody remains throughout history. Mitch refused to accept the concept of an eternal soul, but he esteemed intellect. The wrestling of superstitions and traditions had no relevance to reason, and everything to do with ignorant, irrational, delusional dogmatism. For a Christian or any person of religion to, even slightly, embrace reason seemed miraculous to Mitch Hawkins.

Marci disrupted his intellectual muse. "Where are we going?"

Mitch fell from his ivory tower of reason back into the tangible world. "You have not forgotten I am a journalist? We are stopping at the police station. They caught one of the extremists, and are holding him for questioning. They will blindly deem him the leader of the mob. Whether he is or not doesn't really matter. It's doubtful they will pursue a full investigation. This government only offers tacit concern for Christians. In their minds India is Hindu. They will likely pin the entire crime on this one man."

"Sounds familiar," Marci said.

Mitch gave her a puzzled look. "We're almost there." He pointed to the Rani Lodge on the left. "I once stayed there, not too bad actually."

Marci wished they could stop as she tousled her flat, limp hair.

"Oh, I think it looks great," said Mitch.

"Well, you don't look so hot yourself."

"Oh, so if I were clean and shaven, I would look hot to you?" Mitch moaned as Marci punched his side, "Oh...we're here."

An officer in tan, shouldering an AK-47, greeted them. "You cannot come in here."

Walking toward the fully-loaded clip of a young, fervent officer, Mitch performed his best "John Wayne." With his cocky swagger, he waved some credentials and claimed, "I am a reporter for *The London Times*. After photographing the crime scene, I am following up. I need to see the prisoner."

The officer reluctantly let him pass. "But those two must

stay."

"But they are my personal escorts; my secretary, and," pointing to Marci, "my cosmetology consultant." Fortunately, the officer understood only rudimentary English, and he waved them toward the station.

Mitch felt like a Jedi, using the *force* on the weak-minded as they squeezed and nudged their way through the maze of people. Reaching the hub of activity, he turned toward his personal escorts. "Why don't you two wait outside? I might have a chance, by myself, to see the suspect."

Mitch focused on the lead investigator and left Marci and Andrea in his wake. He stiffened his jaw and maintained his gait as the officer approached him.

"Who are you and why are you here?"

"I am an investigative reporter for *The London Times*. I am researching the coercive behavior of Christians in India. I would like to speak with your suspect."

The officer's twisted smile and extended arm welcomed Mitch into the interrogation room.

Frightened childish eyes gleamed from the young suspect. His dark complexion camouflaged the lines of filth on his face and hands. His clothes bore the marks of days and days of constant wear. Beads of sweat mixed with tears trickled down his cheeks. "Why am I here? I have done nothing."

"Please, sit. I am not with the police. My name is Mitch Hawkins."

"Are you a lawyer? Are you here to help me? I am Satyajit."

"I'm not a lawyer, but I may be able to help. Tell me what you can remember about last night." Mitch sat down on Satyajit's left, a gesture of respect to place him on his right. "I will do my best to help you."

Satyajit nodded. "I am only guilty of wearing a bandana. Last night while I was trying to sleep along the river bank, a gang came running down to the river. I was afraid and so I ran. I fell asleep behind the temple, which is where they found me."

Mitch listened intently, watching the emotion in the young man's face. "You are not from Sambalpur?"

Satyajit looked up with surprise.

Mitch continued. "You have obviously come some distance, mostly on foot, traveling at least a few days. You are not here to see family, and you are not here for work, so why are you here?"

"How do you know these things?"

Mitch looked him up and down. "The condition of your clothes and your appearance tells me you have neither bathed nor changed your clothes in at least a few days. If you were here for work, you would not be in such condition. If you were here for family, you would not be hiding at the river's edge or sleeping outside. The police caught you with a bandit's bandana. It would seem apparent that crime is why you are here. What other reason would you have?"

A shrill squeak from his chair matched his emotion as Satyajit twisted swiftly. "You would not believe me."

"Convince me."

Satyajit shook his head. "I'm not sure I believe it myself, and I know that it will sound crazy to you, so leave... and leave me alone. I will pay for my crimes."

Mitch nodded knowingly. "So, you truly are not guilty of this crime, but your alibi relates to another offense. If you are honest with me, I might be able to help you. Remember, I am not with the police, and I strongly doubt that they are listening to our conversation."

Satyajit recounted the attack on Pahireju. He left out his vision and made no mention of the voice. He claimed only to be running away to find sanctuary.

Mitch frowned. *Something is still missing. That's not enough to explain why he would walk for days, or why he would come here. Most people would go to someone they know. He is here looking for something or someone. I need to dig deeper, but I don't think he is ready to budge.*

Mitch stood and gave him his card. "This has my email address and my cell phone number. I know you are here looking for someone or something. When you are ready to talk or when you need help, have someone call me or send me an email. I am staying at the Rani Lodge."

Satyajit stared at the card as Mitch stood to leave. He tossed the card on the table and plopped his head in his hands. When he closed his eyes, he saw the face of Jeevan Joseph. He could not escape the commanding voice. *"Go find them for me. Bring them here."*

*Why can't I have some peace?* Satyajit opened his eyes to shut out the images and the voice. He grasped the card. As Mitch's shadow met the light in the doorway, Satyajit flipped the card over revealing two names scratched on the back. *Marci and Andrea.* Satyajit called out, "Who are Marci and Andrea?"

Mitch let go of the door handle. He sighed. "Andrea and Marci are two beautiful young women who came with me to see you. The guards would not allow them to come in."

Satyajit nodded. Biting his lip, he stared blankly at the stark, gray wall. Keeping his eyes wide open, he heard no voices, no cries of pain, no expressions of hope.

Mitch lingered on the doorknob as he slid out the door. *Why would a young man give his life for a crime he did not commit? What is he holding back?*

# CHAPTER 19

At the Rani Lodge
Wednesday, September 10, 2008

Marci whimsically waltzed into the restaurant. "You like my hair?"

Mitch smiled at the jostled mess. Her teasing smile and giggling eye-roll tempted him more than she would care to know. He inhaled every curve as she slid into her seat. Her figure melted his mind like steaming fudge. *Why are Christians so particular and prohibitive about sex?*

The fantasy faded as Andrea marched up beside him and slumped into a chair. Mitch tried to capture her eyes, but she stiffened and looked away.

Marci asked. "Mitch, why did you try to show me pictures from the fire?"

"I thought you would be curious. I thought you would want to know. I would want to know," said Mitch.

"Well, I wouldn't."

"Oh, that's right. You believe without knowing."

Andrea interrupted, dangling a classic Rolex in her outstretched hand.

Mitch patted his wrist and looked around as though searching. "Where did you find that?"

"Is this yours?"

Mitch nodded as he grabbed the watch.

"What if I hadn't given it to you, but instead asked, 'Where's your watch?' How would you have reacted," Andrea asked.

"I would have been upset, of course. It's a $3000 watch."

"But you weren't upset until just now."

Eyebrows awry, Mitch warily looked at Andrea. "I hadn't realized it was lost."

"Ok, but suppose, instead of giving you your watch, I told you I knew where it was. Would you believe me?"

"I would have no reason not to believe you," Mitch said.

Andrea tilted her head. "Is that a 'yes'?"

"Yes, I would believe you."

Marci jumped in. "So... you believe without knowing."

Andrea scowled. The moment was gone. *Thanks a lot, Marci. I'm trying to reach out to him, and you just want to be right.*

Andrea changed the subject to avoid an argument. "What did the suspect say?"

Mitch shook his head. *How naïve!* "Why do you insist on playing mind games? I don't hate you because you don't 'believe' the way I do. I don't burn your church or home. I don't rape your wives, or kill or even threaten. I'm a reporter because I want to know. I want to know when, where, what, whom, how, and most of all why. You want me to believe in a god I can't see or hear, but what I do see is people killing people in the name of faith. I'm here to try to understand why."

Marci tried to speak, but Mitch said, "Don't offer a defense. I'm in no mood to hear it right now." He fumed to boiling as he restrained his words. He kicked the chair rather than continue his tirade. With a long, deep sigh, he turned and left for his room.

* * *

Sitting on his bed, he reached into his backpack and pulled out a catalog of glossy feminine morsels. Perhaps fantasy would ease his mind. Page after page of perfect skin, proud chests and enticing eyes seemed empty. Anger rose as he tried to fixate on one youthful vixen. He could not get his mind off Marci's warm smile and sensual hair. As he remembered her fragrance, he remembered the tender words of Andrea.

Pursing his lips and forcing an exhale, he blocked out all thoughts except for the glossy temptress before him. He heard a soft rapping on the outer door as he released his tensions and passion. He sat perturbed and slightly guilty. Putting himself together and disposing of his magazine, he shuffled out of the bathroom and opened the door. "Andrea! Won't you come in?"

Andrea shook her head. "How about joining me in the lobby? There's a quiet sitting area." She recognized a guilty flush in his cheeks.

To his surprise, Andrea gently wrapped her arm around his as though he was leading her. Sitting beside him, she placed her hand on his knee, and said, "Mitch, I'm sorry. I would love for you to believe what I believe, but I don't want you to feel attacked or judged. I would love to be able to just sit down with you and honestly and openly talk about what we believe."

For the first time in his life, Mitch actually found himself liking a Christian. "In 48 years, I have never met a Christian I could like or respect until now. Andrea, I suspect that if every Christian were like you, there would be a hell of a lot... a lot more Christians. If we're going to be honest and open, I must add that it will take quite a bit more than one perfect Christian to convince me, and yes, I know you're not perfect, so save it. I've heard it all."

Andrea smiled. "Can I add one more stipulation to the open, honest thing? Overlook Marci's little jabs and sarcasm."

Mitch snickered. "Agreed."

"Now, will you join us for supper?"

# CHAPTER 20

Vishal at Home
Wednesday Night, September 10, 2008

Vishal placed his wife's Bible on the bed and tucked the photograph into his pocket. His room had grown dark as the sun faded. He felt no motivation to turn on a light. Everything that ever mattered to him was gone, and he was alone. His home, once beautifully adorned, a welcome respite for friends and family, had faded with neglect. The stark walls begged for memories long since removed.

He trudged into his kitchen. He grasped a knife, rolling it in his fingers. Cradling the blade, he stared at the threatening edge. He braced himself against the sink, poised to impale his own chest. His hands shook as he swallowed. He closed his eyes and took a deep breath. He pressed the edge of the blade between his ribs.

At once, the unrelenting voice rang through his mind. *"Jeevan sadaiva."* He could not escape those words. He shook uncontrollably and threw the knife into the sink. It glanced back and pierced his hand. Blood spewed until he wrapped his hand with a rag. He held pressure until the bleeding stopped.

*Why did they take me to a Christian hospital? Why didn't they let me die?*

Tears streamed as he stared at his bloodied hand. He plucked the photo from his pocket. He choked as he took one last glance. *Perhaps I will have the will tomorrow.*

# CHAPTER 21

Rani Lodge
Thursday morning, September 11, 2008

"Wow! These eggs are delicious," Marci said with a mouthful.

"I had to convince the cook his green chilies would not be too hot," said Mitch.

Andrea was glued to the newspaper. "Can you believe this? They are going to pin this whole thing on that one suspect. There had to have been over twenty men."

"They don't care," Mitch said. "The Hindus believe the Christians are getting what they deserve. They see India as a Hindu nation. Anyone who doesn't agree is free to leave, convert, or die."

Andrea bowed her head in silence.

Marci said, "The Hindus want to kill the Christians. The Muslims want to kill everyone, and…"

"And the Christians want to send everyone else to Hell." Mitch couldn't help himself.

Andrea met his eyes with a deep ache in her heart.

Marci glared at Andrea and pointed at Mitch. "Can I say anything without some comment from Mr…?"

Andrea repeated her hand over Marci's mouth routine and looked at Mitch. "Please cut her some slack."

Mitch ruffled the newspaper. "It says here, they will be moving the prisoner to the Central Jail pending his trial. Perhaps you and Marci could go with me to visit him at the jail."

# CHAPTER 22

Vishal's Home
Thursday Morning, September 11, 2008

While sipping his tea, Vishal heard a familiar thud on the door. He pushed aside his breakfast and answered the door.

"Palash, what are you doing here?"

His old friend grinned and laughed. "Vishal, my friend, we thought you were dead. I am so glad you are alive." Palash tossed his newspaper on the table. "They have arrested this poor fool who was not even with us. What good luck. I cannot believe it."

Vishal stared at the headline. He quickly downed his tea and rushed out.

"Where are you going?"

"To the jail. That boy does not deserve my punishment."

Palash grabbed his arm. "Don't be a fool. It's a death sentence."

Vishal calmly pulled free. "It's my death sentence, not his. He has done nothing wrong. He was not even with us. I will be his chance to live. I am ready to die anyway."

Palash protested. "You are a fool, but if you insist on going, let me drive."

*If I let you drive, I'm sure it will be a quicker execution.* "No thanks. I'll walk. I need to clear my head anyway."

"Central Jail is five kilometers from here."

"Good-bye Palash."

\* \* \*

As Vishal approached the jail, he recognized Andrea and Marci waiting to enter. He gasped as Palash ushered them inside. A wave of fear set Vishal running toward the jail. When he entered, Andrea and Marci were nowhere to be found, but there sat Palash, smugly grinning behind a desk.

"Vishal, what a surprise! Why are you here?"

"Palash, you know why I am here!"

Palash stood. He scowled and leaned into Vishal. "The judge will know you were not working alone."

"Don't worry. I will say nothing. They have no evidence against you, but I cannot let this young man die. He was not even involved."

"Pfff, when did you develop a conscience? We left you, because we thought you were dead. What a mistake. How unfortunate that we were wrong."

Vishal clenched his teeth. "You, or someone else, shoved me into that fire."

"You were staring at Singh like a stunned fool, and now you are proving it."

"I am a fool because I don't want an innocent boy to die for my crime?" Vishal was amazed at his friend's callous demeanor.

"When did it become a crime to kill a Christian?"

Vishal slammed the desk. "I demand to speak with the judge."

Palash nodded to another guard. "Take him. He wants to wait for the judge."

Vishal stumbled as Palash shoved him toward the guard. He blindly followed the guard to a blank room with a table and two chairs. He stepped into the dusky room as the guard flicked on the light.

"Wait here. The judge will come when he is ready."

# CHAPTER 23

Satyajit in Jail
Thursday, September 11, 2008

Satyajit stared at the stone walls. Dried blood spatter screamed as he imagined the beatings and the tears. *How did I get in such trouble?*

*Natraj!*

*"Satyajit, come try this."* Natraj, I never imagined being your friend would be my death sentence. All the times we got into trouble but never anything serious. You said no one would investigate. "No one cares about Pahireju." Now I am going to die a criminal's death.*

He felt his life sinking in a flood of kerosene with flames rising and all of Orissa watching. *I do not want to die this way. I would rather hang myself?*

His pulse quickened as he heard footsteps.

Keys jangling, a twist of the lock, and the door creaked open. A bristly guard sneered. "Visitors for you." He stepped aside, revealing three very out-of-place foreigners.

"Mitch Hawkins, reporter from *The London Times*. We met at the police station. These lovely ladies are Marci Beaufort and Andrea Widener. We would like to help."

"There is nothing you can do. They have already decided my destiny."

Andrea stepped forward. "You believe in destiny?"

"I believe in karma."

Andrea continued. "Why do you suppose we are here?"

Words, like flames, shot out of his mouth, "To interfere with my destiny." Satyajit turned away.

Mitch grabbed his arm. "She is only trying to help."

"Help me? She doesn't even know me or anything about me."

Andrea's pulse quickened at the fear in his eyes. Her lips trembled as she spoke. "You are not meant to die here." *What are you hiding?* "You are meant for more."

Satyajit gazed into her deep blue eyes. He felt them searching his soul. His mind flashed back to the deep, leering eyes of Jeevan Joseph. Her eyes had the same reach, staring through his flesh, scouring his emotions. He turned his gaze to Mitch and Marci.

Andrea motioned for Mitch and Marci to step out and leave them alone.

With a gentle tug, Mitch led Marci out of the holding cell and whispered, "I think she has made a connection. I have a feeling he will tell her everything."

As they stepped into the corridor, Mitch intercepted the approaching guard. "Please allow her some time with him, alone. She may be able to get valuable information."

The guard nodded with feigned understanding.

Andrea sat on the floor facing Satyajit. "Why did you come to Sambalpur? You were looking for something?"

Guilt steered his eyes toward the floor. "I was part of a gang that burned homes and killed a Christian pastor and his family." He lifted his gaze to the soft brunette. *Who is this girl? Why does she care? She looks so pure, so innocent. How can I tell her what I've done? How can I tell anyone?*

"Please go on."

He drew a great sigh and closed his eyes. "I helped douse Pastor Joseph in kerosene, while he was still alive." He opened his eyes and stared blankly. "He watched us torture and kill his wife, then we tossed him into his burning church and burned him alive. His last words were a prayer." Satyajit melted into tears.

"Do you remember what he said?" Andrea felt a strange mix of compassion and fear. *I'm in a foreign prison talking to a confessed murderer who hates everything Christian, but his eyes reveal such pain. God, help me help him.*

Satyajit's brown-green eyes could not contain his tears. "In his dying prayer, the pastor said, 'God, send your mercies to my father.'"

"Was his father in the village?"

"I don't think so. I did not know this man or his father. I only knew that he was a Christian. We hate the Christians, and even more, we hate their pastors and priests. I killed a man I did not know only because of what he believed and taught."

Andrea studied his face, his eyes, and his every movement. *He is hiding something.* As she watched intently, the voice within spoke. "Satyajit, there is more. You were not running away. You were running after something."

"I don't expect you to believe me. I'm not sure I believe it myself. The night before we killed the pastor, I had a dream." Satyajit wiped his tears and looked into Andrea's eyes. "I saw a man walking through fire. He was surrounded by flames, but he was not burning. Two goddesses walked on either side. The man looked into my eyes. He said nothing, but I heard a voice telling me to go to Sambalpur. The next day as Jeevan Joseph looked into my eyes, I recognized his eyes from my dream. He said nothing to me, but again I heard that voice. The voice said, 'Go find them for me. Bring them here.'"

"Bring who?"

Satyajit expressed his surprise. "The two goddesses." Andrea's furrowed brow and lip nibbling disappointed Satyajit. He hoped she would understand his dream.

Andrea interrupted his disappointment and pressed him. "Describe the two goddesses."

Satyajit closed his eyes. His mind took him back to Pahireju. As usual the dream played over and over - the flames, the voice, and the disheartening, pleading eyes. He could see the man boldly stepping into and through the inferno. The crackling and snapping of sparks and the hiss of steaming sap grew deafening. The three were standing in the church as he had envisioned so many times before. Satyajit lost himself completely in his dream. He no longer had any sense he was in a prison, or anyone was with him. He was in Pahireju consumed by his dream.

Andrea shook and fell back as Satyajit began to convulse and drool. His eyes were white. Though he was shaking, he remained sitting, fully entranced. Her heart pounded wildly. In fear, she grasped his arm.

Andrea's firm hold was not enough to yield a response. *Satyajit, where are you?* She shook him and pinched him.

Satyajit was in Pahireju focused on the three glowing figures in the church. A surge of warmth and light engulfed him and whirled around him. Jeevan Joseph stood before him, spotless and gleaming in shadowless light. *How are you here? You were in the church!*

Satyajit's eyes flashed back to the three in the church. He rushed toward the man in the center. He recognized those thoughtful brownish-green eyes, the smooth youthful face and slender frame. The goddesses he had never seen until that day— a stunning brown-eyed beauty with auburn hair and olive skin, a petite brunette with mesmerizing blue eyes, a captivating smile. They were beaming with light.

Andrea startled as Satyajit open his eyes abruptly. He looked through her, still transfixed. Andrea did not mean to jerk, nor did she mean to gasp, but she could not restrain her surprise as Satyajit spoke.

"I am looking at one of them." Satyajit blinked and softened as he looked directly at Andrea. "I don't understand the dream. I thought the man was Jeevan Joseph... but I am the man standing in the church, and you and Marci are with me."

He released a sigh of agony as he realized destiny was calling him back to Pahireju. "How can I go back to Pahireju after what I have done? And how would I escape this prison?" *Oh, if I could cleanse myself in the Ganges.*

The door creaked. The guard stuck his head around the door. He pointed to Satyajit. "You must come, and you, also."

Andrea did a quick search as they stepped into the hall. Marci and Mitch were nowhere to be found. In silence, she and Satyajit followed the guard down the long corridor to a familiar room.

Satyajit paused in the doorway as the guard motioned him to enter. "May she come with me?"

The guard shrugged his approval.

"Why would they bring you back here?"

Satyajit shook his head and covered his face. His stomach lurched at the sound of footsteps. A decorated officer entered and handed Satyajit a paper. "You are free to go."

Satyajit slowly stood. Puzzled, he said, "I don't understand."

"You were not involved. You are free to go," said the officer.

Satyajit stared at the document. *It's that simple? What happened? No one has said anything to me.*

"I said you are free to go. The leader of the gang has confessed to the crime. He accepts full responsibility for inciting a mob of drunken youths and setting the car on fire."

# CHAPTER 24

Leaving the Jail
Thursday, September 11, 2008

Sunlight peered through the open doorway, welcoming Satyajit back into the world. As he walked the long corridor, he passed a man in handcuffs. As their eyes met, Satyajit felt a wave of nausea mixed with gratitude. *He must be the one who confessed.* His dry throat tightened and he failed to speak.

Andrea stood silently watching the solemn exchange of one life for another. Her heart melted in the weary eyes of Vishal. His handcuffs were all the confession she needed. Her eyes followed him down the hall.

Leaving Marci and Mitch, she pressed past Satyajit and the guard. "I need to speak to Vishal."

The guard asked Vishal, "You know this woman?"

Vishal nodded. The night before, he thought of killing himself. That day he decided to let the government do it for him. He had no will to live, no perceivable reason to live. Nothing was important to him anymore. His life was over. If he spoke to anyone or spoke to no one, it did not matter to him.

The officer ushered them into the same familiar room. "You have two minutes." He closed the door behind them.

"Vishal, you can't accept responsibility for killing the pastor and his family. I was there. You froze. You did not participate in starting the fire. Your friends pushed you into the flames and left you to die."

Vishal scowled. "You were not there. My friends did not leave me. They cast me onto the wagon behind us. I struck my head on a stone. They thought I was dead. They were fleeing the crime."

"Vishal, I was the stone you struck. I was hiding under the canvas with Mitch and Marci. When the mob began climbing on the wagon, I prayed God would make us like stones. He protected us, and he sent you to us."

"You are a Christian. I don't want to talk to you. Christians killed my son and stole my family, and now those terrorists have murdered our respected leader." His back turned, arms folded, heart broken, and thoughts whirling, Vishal never felt more alone.

Andrea struggled to find the right words. Her heart was furiously engaged in prayer, her mind chasing after some magic phrase to calm his restless soul. No words came. She wanted to reach for him, to place her hand on his shoulder, but fear stifled her. She was once again in a locked room with a confessed killer who openly hated Christians. Her blood chilled. Her stomach knotted. She swallowed a salty brash. *I feel like such a failure.*

Looking up, she noticed Vishal was holding something in his lap. She strained to see what it was. Rising from her seat and tip-toeing toward him, she could see a photograph of a young family. "Is that your son and his family?"

Vishal had no strength or passion for anger. His tears were spent, eyes dry. Hoarse from swallowing his sorrow, he stared blankly as the door creaked open.

As the guard stretched his foot through the door, Vishal discarded the photo, the last remnant of his past, all that was left of his world. The tender, forgotten family slid across the cold lifeless table toward Andrea.

Andrea welled with tears at Vishal's discarded memories. A handsome, slender father, smiled at her through pained eyes. Olive eyes and smooth dark skin matched the delicate beauty of the wife's ornate dress. Husband and wife stood as watchful towers, embracing five precious smiles, three sons and two daughters. *This must be his son and his family.*

Vishal turned in the doorway. "It's no one."

Andrea tasted bitter tears as she bit her lip and blew an exhausted sigh. She wiped her tears from the beautiful woman in the picture. *She seems so happy. What could have happened to shatter such peace?* A tingling chill wrapped around Andrea. What turned Vishal into such a monster, and what stopped him?

A voice within whispered, *"Our struggle is not with flesh and blood."*

*Vishal is not my enemy.*

Andrea listened as Vishal's footsteps faded. *He is a vanishing soul, a fire burnt to a smoldering crisp, steaming from a good dousing, the warmth of the flame long since forgotten. A mind without a spark.*

Kneeling on the dusty stone floor, Andrea prayed. "Dear God, protect Vishal and soften his heart, and give me the courage and wisdom to help him." She scraped herself off the floor and picked up the photograph. When she retrieved her backpack from the guard, she carefully stuck the picture in her Bible.

\* \* \*

Andrea left the jail behind and stepped into the sun. She heaved a great sigh at the sight of Marci, Mitch, and Satyajit.

"What took you so long?" asked Marci.

Andrea cast Marci a frosty glare. "Vishal confessed to the car-burning and confirmed that Satyajit had no part in it."

"Well, that's great. Satyajit will go free after all."

Andrea stuttered through her tears. "Yes, but Vishal will die."

Mitch said, "I'll never understand Christians. I mean, you guys just don't make sense. Here's a guy who was one of the leaders of the group that tortured and murdered one of your pastors and his whole family. If you believe in capital punishment, he clearly deserves to die, and he's not the only one. What is it that goes through your head? If there were no religion, what would be left to fight over?"

"Mitch, did you see Pastor Singh fighting? Or his wife, or what about his two children? Were they fighting? Vishal was burned and left to die because he dropped his hands and would not participate. He said he watched Pastor Singh's wife calm her husband. Then he watched the two of them offer prayers as, one-by-one they looked at each of the men who were intent on burning them alive. What kind of fighting is that?"

If it had been one of those random, hypothetical, sit-around-the-coffee-table discussions, Mitch would have lashed out with a derogatory comeback. He relished the slaying of Christians in the Coliseum of the College Café, but Sambalpur was not hypothetical. It was real. *I don't want your flimsy phony faith*, he remembered saying at one such Starbucks roundtable. *I need something that's real, something I can taste, savor, something I can feel, like this coffee that I grip. I can feel its warmth. I can smell the aroma. I can taste and know that it's coffee. That's real.*

It all seemed arrogant and shallow as he stood before this young woman living her faith. His calloused lack of emotion was jealous for her tears and the passion in her face. He gently touched her cheek. With his thumb, he brushed a drizzling bead of sorrow and felt an unfamiliar chill rush up his arm. He denied the thought, but deep down he knew that the elusive notion of faith was genuinely embodied in this tiny girl from Upland,

# Indiana.

# CHAPTER 25

Lunch on Thursday Afternoon
September 11, 2008

Mitch folded the newspaper and plopped it on the table. "Well, today marks the seventh anniversary of 9/11. Bush is dedicating a memorial at the Pentagon."

"I had a friend who worked in the Twin Towers," said Marci. "He was in Tower Two when the first plane hit. He worked with a guy who was there during the bombing in '93. The two of them didn't waste any time leaving."

Mitch sneered. "So, Satyajit, do you remember 9/11?"

"I was 10 years old. I heard about it at school. We were all quite angry."

"Why were you angry?" Marci asked.

"Those Muslims, they make no sense. They just want to kill everyone, especially Jews and Americans. They have no regard for anyone but themselves."

Mitch stepped on a dangerous line. "Does that not seem hypocritical? I mean, you admitted to your part in a gang killing of a Christian pastor and his family and the burning of their church."

Satyajit tried to defend himself. "We do not kill Christians only because they are Christians. Pastor Joseph was deceiving people and bribing them to convert. Christians reject their families, their traditions, and Hinduism. He was warned many times."

Mitch shrugged and smiled. "What about his children? Were they forcing people to renounce their beliefs? The other Christians in Pahireju, were they all offering bribes and coercing people to convert?" Satyajit's downward stare was permission to deliver the death blow. Mitch opened fire, "You are no different than the Muslim terrorists who killed 3,000 innocent people seven years ago. The only difference is the number, the location, and the nationality of the victims. You may as well have been flying one of those planes. Oh, but wait, there's one more difference. None of you planned on sacrificing yourselves. You could say the 9/11 terrorists had a dedication that you did not."

Andrea pounded her fist on the newspaper. "That's more than enough. Satyajit is not a terrorist. He was following a mob."

"No, he is right. I am no different except that I was a coward."

"You are not a coward..." said Marci.

Satyajit glared at her patronizing hand on his shoulder. "I was a coward. I wanted to be like my friend Natraj and the others, but I was afraid."

Mitch unloaded. "So, you killed innocent children because you were afraid?"

Satyajit's hands over his face could not quell the flow of emotion. "I was afraid of what would happen to me if I did not go along with Natraj and the others. They would think I was a coward, and they might have hurt me or..."

"Either way, you are a coward." Mitch was feasting.

Andrea called for a ceasefire. "Please. Fighting isn't helping anyone."

"It's ok. I know I was a coward." Looking into Andrea's knowing eyes, Satyajit continued. "But I am ready to face my fears. I will stand before the judge, but first I would like to go to Pahireju."

Mitch sneered. *You would like to buy some time so you can figure your way out of this mess.*

Satyajit stood. Stepping back from the table, he looked at Andrea and shook his head.

Andrea asked, "May I tell them?" As Satyajit closed his eyes and nodded, Andrea grasped Marci's hand. Looking Mitch squarely in the eye, she said, "Mitch Hawkins, you are going to experience God today. Satyajit, who is not a believer, has heard the voice of God, calling him to Pahireju. I don't know what we are going to uncover, but I know God is calling."

Mitch restrained himself, but inside he was laughing pathetically.

Marci elbowed him as she caught the sarcasm in his fake smile.

\* \* \*

On the Road to Pahireju
1:30 PM, Thursday, September 11, 2008

"Satyajit, Are you sure you know how to get there?" Mitch questioned.

"I have a good idea, but there are mostly dirt roads."

Mitch brought up satellite images of Pahireju on his laptop. "It looks like Pahireju is about 140 km from here."

"Oh, that's not so bad. We should get there in what, two hours?" said Marci.

"A minimum of three hours. We drive about 75 km south from here to Sonepur, and that's the end of the line for paved roads." Tracing the dirt roads between Pahireju and Sonepur, Mitch marked the key waypoints and uploaded the data to his phone. "So, we need to get there, do whatever we need to do, and get out. We do not want to risk driving at night."

\* \* \*

### 3:15 PM

The tiny car stirred a wake of dust. Even south of Sonepur, they could not escape the occasional wandering cow or women toting baskets on their heads. They passed two young goat herders and strode off-road to avoid an oncoming bus.

Marci dropped her jaw. "Did I just see a family of five riding a bicycle? No child of mine will ever complain about being cramped in the back seat."

Andrea stared, unaware. *Why am I here, God? My heart is pounding. My stomach is churning. What am I going to see, and what can I possibly do to help?*

"I think we have lost Andrea. How much longer, Mitch?"

"Not too much further. I wish I had a videographer."

Marci said, "I wish had a warm shower."

Satyajit sighed. *I wish I could wake up and forget his horrid dream.*

"...and mocha latte," Marci added.

\* \* \*

"Pahireju."

"Or what's left of it," Mitch said.

Clubs, bandanas, and debris riddled the road winding to village. The smoldering embers had disintegrated into ashes and rubble.

Mitch stopped the car at the edge of the village. He mounted his video camera on a tripod, framed a wide shot, and pressed Record. *Lifetimes reduced to seconds.*

He captured Marci walking into the village. As though on cue, she turned, hand on hip and waved for Andrea to catch up.

Mitch grabbed Satyajit's arm. "You should stay out of the camera and the audio. This video could be used as evidence against you."

"What you say is true, but only my own words can associate me with this crime... and I plan to confess."

Mitch shook his head and zoomed in on Marci walking by house after house, all burned to the ground. *She has seen more harsh reality than she ever dreamed.*

Marci turned toward Andrea and the camera. "It seems so philosophical and far away, when we talk about it at home, but here we are in the middle of real life-and-death persecution."

"It's hard not get angry."

As Marci walked up to one particular home, Satyajit ran toward her. He stretched out to stop her as she knocked in what was left of the door. Satyajit covered his mouth and bowed his head. His body twisted and writhed as Marci shrieked.

Andrea rushed up behind her. The scorched door collapsed and she startled at the gruesome site and screamed. "Children! Satyajit, children?"

"Oh GOD!" Andrea and Marci cried.

Andrea wretched on the charred dirt. Her mind spinning,

she braced her hands on her knees and leered at Satyajit. Shouting, she scorched her throat. "How could you? Trapped! Burned alive! Children!"

Mitch stepped away from the camera. Reaching into his pocket for his remote, he quickened his pace to match Marci's sprint toward Satyajit. As she drew back her hand to unload a fierce slap, Mitch clutched her arm. "He's not your enemy! Isn't that what you said?" He spit the words through gritted teeth. "That's what you said! 'Our struggle is not with flesh and blood... blah, blah, blah.' Do you still think he is not your enemy?" *I am so sick of these religious fools. Where is this god?*

Marci's anger turned to sobs. She wrestled free from Mitch, staring at Satyajit. Hate dissolved as she watched him trembling with tears streaming.

"I'm so sorry. I did not know what I was doing. I'm sorry."

Marci held her hand to his mouth. *Don't say anything.* Her mind flashed to memories of Sunday school and Jesus on the cross crying, "Father forgive them for they know not what they do." She stepped toward Satyajit. Without a word, she wrapped her arms around him. Tears turned to shaking and uncontrollable sobbing, and they collapsed in the dust.

Andrea braced herself in the doorway, unable to fight her tears.

Mitch adjusted his camera to catch the unexpected embrace. He zoomed in, pressing the eye of the world into the eyes of forgiveness.

Mitch turned toward Andrea. He faced the camera and clicked the remote. "We are in the tiny village of Pahireju, where three nights past, a mob of Hindu extremists stormed the village. They burned homes previously marked by a red cross such as this one, and..."

Andrea closed her eyes, shook her head, and shrugged. She stood and walked away to avoid the camera. She entered what was left of the home and tried to feel some connection with the victims. The disquieting eyes of Christ stared at her from a dried and singed portrait.

She felt the Mitch's footsteps behind her. She smiled to thank him for leaving his camera outside. Unable to speak, she stretched out her arms as if to show him the room: dirt floor, a broken kerosene lamp, scattered pages of Hindi script (presumably a Bible), but none of it mattered in the least, compared to the lives that were trapped and destroyed by blind hatred.

Andrea's quivering lips and pallor invited Mitch's arms. He squeezed her trembling frame. He felt a strange strength, meaning in an otherwise empty and tragic moment. Andrea was a puzzle piece he had not realized he was missing. As he watched her eyes browsing the carnage, he felt these children and families were not random, meaningless and forgotten. He felt something bigger, a much larger story. *Who are these two girls that they would travel 10,000 miles to mourn dead people they had never known?*

"Mitch," Andrea caught his eyes. She squeezed his hand to emphasize her words. "I weep for these children. There is no doubt about that, but my tears are more. You know that I believe what I say I believe."

Mitch nodded.

Andrea loosened her hug. "I cry more for the brutality of their deaths. This slaughter could only come from a blinded hate. I believe the men who led this mob will never know, or at least never admit to knowing, the truth."

Mitch's feeling of tenderness and hope faded as Andrea spoke. He couldn't stop the words that erupted. "You think they're all going to hell." He held her at arm's length. *Why can't you look at me?* His frustration boiled at the tears in her averted eyes, her face swollen from crying. "You think I'm going to hell, too." *I think we're living in it right here.*

Her eyes gripped his. "No. No, I do not." *God, he's like a little boy stumbling in the dark. Give me words.* "Mitch, I think deep down you want to believe, but you suppress your deepest longings. I believe when you are ready to honestly seek God, you will find Him and know Him. You see Christians as rule keepers and judges, but what saves is not a list of rules, but knowing Christ."

Mitch shrugged. *Well, it didn't do much to save this family.*

Andrea followed his eyes around the harsh reality. "This family is together in Heaven, but what about the families of their killers? Even if it was all some elaborate, multi-millennial, multi-ethnic, global conspiracy, do you really think the ones full of hate and covered in innocent blood are better off? This isn't philosophy 101. It's real. It's you and me and this crazy world."

Marci stuck her head through the door. "Andrea, Mitch, you ok? Are you coming? We need to check out the church before it gets late."

"Where's Satyajit?"

"I think he's seen all he can handle. I'll go look for him," Marci said.

Mitch shuffled after her, trying not to jostle his camera. "Marci, wait." He followed the dirt road as it curved through the town. Mitch chuckled as he met Marci blushing. "So, you found Satyajit? What was he doing?"

"Oh, nothing really. He was performing a common... custom of Indian men."

Satyajit walked out from behind a large tree zipping his

trousers.

The four of them stood staring at each other until Mitch broke the awkward silence. "Let's move on."

Rounding a jacaranda tree and a few more houses, they could see the remnants of a church at the edge of town.

Andrea wanted to run to the church, but she froze at the gruesome sight. *Dear God! That poor woman!* A disheveled and decaying mass of flesh lay in the street, covered with a small sari, her shredded dress nearby.

*What intricate lace.* Andrea almost chuckled at how she could admire such a detail amid such horror. *Wait! That's the dress from Vishal's photo. Pastor Joseph's wife!* As she stared at the bloated remains, she felt the eyes of scattered onlookers. She turned and studied the faces of the Hindu villagers who were spared. She tried to speak, but the words stuck in her dry throat. *You left his wife to rot in the street?* She waved her hands through the hovering cloud of flies.

"There is nothing you can do," Mitch said.

Andrea turned to him and her hand over his lens. "Please don't. Please."

Mitch lowered his camera.

Andrea ran to the nearest house. No blankets or sheets had survived. She found a tarp and a shovel behind the house. She covered the body with the tarp. "That will do for now, but we," handing the shovel to Satyajit, "need to dig some graves."

Satyajit found some softer ground behind the house. He began digging and grumbling. *Why can't they burn the dead?* Mitch found another shovel and joined Satyajit.

"At this rate, there is no chance of returning to the hotel before dark," Mitch said.

An elderly woman quietly swept her porch, pushing emotion away with the dust. She studied the unexpected visitors. Her eyes shifted as one of them approached. She pretended not to notice, but as the young stranger began walking toward her, she could no longer stifle her grief and guilt. She choked on her tears. *I watched my neighbors suffer and die. How could I ignore...* As approaching footsteps stirred the dust, she stiffened, clutching her broom.

Andrea sighed and prayed for boldness as she met aged hollow eyes. "Namaste." She motioned with her hands as she continued. "Could I please borrow a shovel to bury the dead?"

The woman dropped her broom. Her arms shaking, she ran into the house and came out with a shovel. She shouted instructions to her children who ran to the other homes to gather shovels and helpers.

Shortly, a dozen villagers had dug enough graves to receive all the dead. The women wrapped the remains in cloths and sprinkled them with fragrance. Young women shook with tears of guilt and sorrow as they helped carry the dead. They buried some of the families together, fourteen graves in all.

When they had finished, Andrea urged them to pause for a moment. "I will pray." Even Mitch bowed his head as Andrea poured herself out before God. "Our Father, You are everywhere, in all things, seeing all of our actions, knowing all of our thoughts. Your name is holy, unique, and distinguished above all other gods. May your kingdom fill the earth as it fills heaven. You give us today what we need for today. Trusting you for today is enough. Forgive us as we forgive those who would harm us, stifle us, or kill us. Let us follow where you lead. Deliver us from evil. We thank you for these precious lives. May their memory be cherished, and may their deaths change many lives, drawing them closer to you. Bless Pahireju and forgive those who harmed your children. I pray in the Holy Name of Jesus

Christ, Amen."

Andrea opened her eyes to see men and women on their knees, weeping. Children stood bewildered at the tears of their parents and grandparents.

Mitch Hawkins climbed up from his knees. *Are these the same villagers? What just happened here?* He walked over to his tripod. Turning the camera away from the graves, he panned across the village. Through stalwart trees, he zoomed in on the ruined church. His lens captured the unfettered cross leaning on the collapsed roof. As he widened the angle, Marci and Satyajit entered the picture, giving perspective. Andrea was close behind.

"What do you hope to find?" asked Marci.

Satyajit glanced at her, saying nothing. He climbed over debris to the place where they cast Jeevan Joseph. He bent down, scouring through rubble, tossing pieces of roof and brick. "He is not here!"

Marci blurted, "What do you mean, 'He is not here?'"

"His body is turned to ashes. The fire must have…"

Marci swung her arm out straight with a halting wave. "That's enough. I don't want to hear any more."

Oblivious to Marci and Satyajit, Andrea was transfixed by the unblemished cross on the far wall. Climbing and crawling over rubble, she noticed an open door near the left corner. Somehow the entire back wall remained intact, including the door. Stumbling into the wall, Andrea caught herself. She pressed her hands against the wall. Reaching upward she grasped the cross. Swollen with emotion, her heart emptied beneath the cross. *Oh, Jesus. I don't want to imagine the suffering that took place here, but I know that Jeevan Joseph died this way because he knew what life is all about. Your suffering on the cross, took on the sins of the world. No horror we suffer could ever compare.*

Tears flooded her cheeks.

As she was bent in prayer, the faint words of Satyajit clicked in her mind. *'He is not here... All I can see are ashes...'* What *if he somehow survived? What if he's alive?*

Startled by her thoughts, she dashed through the back door. Desperate eyes scoured the landscape. Sniffling and wiping her tears, she heard a more subtle sound, a faint gasp. Jerking to look over her shoulder, Andrea caught the eyes of a frightened young girl crouching against the church.

Digging in her heels, the shaken and filth-covered child began scooting away from Andrea. Feeling a safe distance, she flipped on to her knees, and hopped into a run.

Andrea darted toward her, grabbed her ragged dress and wrapped her in her arms. She held the trembling child despite the thrashing arms and kicking. Andrea remained calm and spoke in her most soothing voice. "You are safe. No one is going to hurt you anymore."

The kicking stopped though the heart continued racing, gradually slowing as Andrea held her gently. She cuddled the frightened child like a newborn and caressed her hair. *What terror you have seen? God, bless this child.* Andrea held her close while she stared at a cluster of teak trees behind the church.

*How could they be so indifferent? Those villagers stood, unmoved like these trees and watched their neighbors... How could they just stand there... gawking... doing nothing, and then days later... What happened here today, God? Why all of a sudden? It was like a light turned on or something. They just came together and helped... and they genuinely mourned. Father, flood this village with your presence. Breathe your Spirit upon them. Be the difference that overcomes their indifference.*

The exhausted child fell asleep in her arms. *Who is this child? She must have been one that slipped away, avoiding the mob. No doubt she has lost her parents. She was probably too frightened to go to anyone in the village.* Andrea saw the beauty beneath the dust-covered black hair, arms streaked with dirt, and feet caked with soil. The once lovely green dress was torn and wreaked of smoke. Andrea thought, *I'm going to need a long bath.*

Marci bolted through the door. "Andrea!" The startled shriek of the child caught her attention. "Andrea? Are you ok? Who is this?" Lovely brown-green eyes captivated Marci. Kneeling down, she said, "I'm sorry I frightened you. We are here to help."

"Where is my family?" the girl asked.

Andrea held her tight, exhausting her remaining tears.

"What are there names?" Marci asked.

"My mother is Pushpa. My father's name was... Ahhh!" She screamed and clung to Andrea as Satyajit rushed out of the church.

Andrea halted Satyajit with one hand, embracing the terrified child with the other. "Your father was Jeevan Joseph?"

The whimpering child nodded.

"And what is your name?" asked Marci.

"I am Indu." Her voice, like her body, was weak from three days of eating only scavenged scraps. Finding water was even more difficult. The village had no well. Her family was accustomed to treading three miles to the nearest well. Water was precious and scarcely wasted, but Indu had managed to steal a few sips here-and-there.

Andrea struggled to find a way to tell the poor girl what she already knew. As she opened her mouth to speak, Indu grew pale and fainted in her arms. Indu easily aroused, but drifted in and out of consciousness. "Marci, hand me a water bottle from your backpack." As she tipped small sips into Indu's mouth, Andrea felt a thready pulse.

Mitch walked up behind them and planted his tripod. "She is severely dehydrated. We need to get her to a hospital. Perhaps there is one in Sonepur?"

Satyajit shook his head. "She needs to go to All Saints Hospital in Sambalpur. The government hospital will do nothing for her. If we stayed with her, she might receive fluids, but nothing more."

\* \* \*

6:30 PM

Mitch knew they had about two hours of daylight to get back to Sambalpur. Driving dirt roads in India after dark would be like driving in pouring rain without windshield wipers. He drove as fast as he reasonably could.

Marci held on for dear life. The rumbling and bouncing reminded her of the mechanical bull at the South Carolina State Fair, except the bull ride only lasted two minutes. She endured the thumping and lurching on the dirt highway for over an hour. She groaned when they finally reached pavement. "It's a river of potholes." Her knees crashing into the seat as the tiny SUV turned upstream weaving between, around, and through the maze of pavement crumbs.

Andrea ignored the jostling, her eyes fixed on Indu collapsed on her lap. She cradled the sleeping child, exhausted and dehydrated. Andrea gently stroked her cheek and coursed her fingers through her hair. *I could see her mother doing this... just loving her... watching her face... imagining her dreams.* Andrea's pensive eyes absorbed the stained innocence and besmirched beauty of the cradled child. *I hope her dreams are beautiful. I hope she sees her mother glimmering white, surrounded by angels, dancing in an endless field of flowers. I hope she is unafraid.*

The injured angel awakened and felt the cool trickle of water through her lips. Through misty eyes, she saw Andrea's silhouette and tried to smile. She lacked the strength or the will to keep her eyes open. Resting in warm, loving arms, Indu drifted into a valley of flowers. Golden light bathed tranquil fields. The air sweet and fresh. The sky a crisp blue. No clouds. No sun. No shadows. Light encompassed her world.

She waltzed through the flowers casting no shadows and leaving no footprints. Light grew unimaginably intense, engulfing her. Despite brilliance greater than ten suns, her eyes never blinked nor did she squint. Her mother's smile pierced the light. Though she spoke not a word, Indu heard all her thoughts.

Her fears vanished.

\* \* \*

9:15 PM

Twilight turned daunting shadows into blankets of grey and black. The thin rim of daylight cowered behind the distant hills. The deep blue of night stretched across the sky chasing the fading light. Pinholes of glory speckled the expanse. Moonlight, almost full, caressed the gaunt cheek of Indu as the SUV rolled to a stop in front of the hospital.

Andrea groaned as she tried to stand. *I can hardly move let alone carry this poor girl.* She waited for Satyajit to offer his help. Streams of reflection marred his face in the moonlight. Andrea lifted her arms passing Indu's fragile life into his arms. *How much has changed in just days. God, I see you working in Satyajit's heart even now.*

Andrea followed as Satyajit carried the limp angel through the doorway. A nurse directed them down the corridor and into the procedure room. Chandrika's familiar voice calmed Andrea's fluttering heart.

"Bring her here." Chandrika's smile evaporated as she struggled to find a faint pulse. "This child is profoundly dehydrated." She scrambled to start an IV. "What happened to her?"

Andrea heaved a sigh. "Marci."

Marci gripped Andrea's hand. "Her family was killed early Monday morning. Extremists burned their village. She escaped, but she has been alone, without food or water, except for what she could scavenge."

Satyajit sat in silence, his eyes glued to the rhythmic drip of the IV. Each tiny splash crashed against his guilty soul. *Please don't die.*

Mitch stepped out of the room. He checked into his own world, emptying his thoughts into his laptop. Facts and photos could not bury his emotions. He sighed at the gravity of the images he had captured. As he listened to Andrea and Marci muttering their prayers, he cast one of his own. *Please don't die.*

Andrea lost herself in the tiny patient's gray face. *Please don't die.*

Chandrika stood close. She studied the IV drip and felt a strengthening pulse. "She is going to live." The moon lit Chandrika's deep eyes as she dimmed the light.

Indu shifted in her bed. She opened her eyes and reflected the hopeful, welcoming smiles. She smiled at the nurse who checked her pulse.

The nurse leaned toward her and said, "My name is Chandrika."

The small but certain voice answered, "My name is Indulala. My mother called me Indu."

"Indu – how pretty. You know your name means moonlight and so does mine."

Indu smiled and tried to swallow but her mouth was dry.

*She must be hungry.* Chandrika left her briefly and soon returned with fresh Pakhala.

Indu inhaled the fermented mix of rice, water, and yogurt. She sighed deeply and stared at the empty dish.

"Indu, you need to rest now." Chandrika gently motioned Andrea and the others to leave the room.

Indu closed her eyes and squeezed Chandrika's hand. A tear trickled down her cheek as she opened her eyes and faced Chandrika. "I am the only one left. My mother and father, my brothers, and my sister were all killed by those men. I was afraid, so I ran." Unable to contain her tears, her words sputtered. "I should be with my mother. Why did I run? Why did I run?" *Who will be my mother? What will I do? I have no family...*

Chandrika's strong, gentle hands stilled Indu's trembling shoulders. "Your father was a pastor?"

Eyes averted, Indu nodded.

Chandrika lifted Indu's chin and met her eyes. "Indu, every Christian is part of your family. There are many people that love you, even people who have never met you. God is hearing their prayers for you. He will take care of you." Chandrika whispered soothing words until Indu found sleep.

Chandrika slowly and gently withdrew her hand. She stood and tip-toed backward toward the door. Stepping into the dim hallway, Chandrika bumped into Andrea who was silently pacing. "Andrea, would you sit with her? I must check on a few other patients. I will be back."

Andrea nodded. "I will stay here with Indu. Please tell Mitch he can take Satyajit and Marci back to the hotel without me."

# CHAPTER 26

At Rani Lodge
Thursday Night, September 11, 2008

Mitch assumed his serious face. "Satyajit, you can sleep with Marci since Andrea is not with us." Maintaining a stern face, Mitch belly-laughed inside at Marci's dropped-jaw and wide-eyed gasp. "Oh, oh I'm sorry. I don't know what I was thinking. That would be inappropriate. Satyajit, you can sleep in my room, and I'll sleep with Marci."

Marci stretched a knowing smile and loaded her back-hand, feigning a slap across Mitch's smile. Her repulsion of Mitch Hawkins had long since vanished. Over 20 years her senior, he bore a well-rounded, beer-loving tub. Despite his appearance, his sarcasm and candor, Marci saw a genuine human being, a restless man, skeptically denying truth, yet cautiously hoping, deep-down wishing he could recapture the wonder of his youth. *I wonder what happened to him.*

Marci bounced back with her own sarcasm. "Mitch, you can sleep in my room. I brought plenty of duct tape for such an emergency. I'll tape your mouth shut and strap you to a chair, where you can listen to me talk until I am ready for bed. Then I'll plug your ears with my favorite tunes, so you can enjoy Christian music all night. I will feel so secure with a man in my room."

Satyajit stood somewhat bewildered. *I must keep an eye on Marci.* He imagined himself bound with duct tape and gagged.

Marci wheeled around. As she toted her backpack and helped Mitch with his camera bag, she searched the blank stare on Satyajit's face. "Mitch, look at him." Marci slowly walked toward the daydreaming Satyajit, calling out in a sing-song voice, "Satyajit, hello. Earth to Satyajit. Kssshhhksshh. Houston we have a problem."

Roaring laughter jolted Satyajit. He shook his head. *I will never understand Americans, especially the women. 'Houston, we have a problem?' What does she mean?* Having no bags to carry, no toiletries, no change of clothes, nothing, he stepped toward Marci and took Mitch's camera bag and tripod. "Let me help."

"Well, it's nice to have you back. Did you enjoy your orbit?"

A quick elbow from Mitch told Marci to lay off with the dumb jokes. "He'll never understand what you're saying. He already thinks you're a freak. Stop making it worse."

Satyajit was relieved that Mitch at least knew Marci was hard to understand, but he remained puzzled. "I do not think you are a freak," Satyajit said.

Marci returned the elbow, adding a childish 'so there' look. "Hmmpf. See, I'm not a freak."

"I will never know." Mitch groaned as he received yet another elbow to the gut.

"Whoa! I almost lost my arm on that one."

"I used to weigh 400 pounds until I went on *The Biggest Loser*."

"Oh, that's right. Didn't they name that show after you?"

Satyajit followed the laughing duo toward Marci's room, muttering and shaking his head. *Marci is a freak and Mitch is the biggest loser? What did he lose?* He bumped into Mitch as they stopped at Marci's door.

"Goodnight boys." Marci closed her door behind her.

Mitch stared at the door handle and sighed. "Come on Satyajit." He nudged opened their door. "Satyajit, why don't you shower first?" *Three plus days of accumulated filth. I really don't want you to sit on anything, and how you smell.*

Mitch prodded Satyajit toward the bathroom and handed him a bottle of Old Spice shower gel. "Here. Use this." Mitch demonstrated as Satyajit stared bewildered. "You squeeze the bottle like this, rub it in your hands and then all over your body. *Use it all if you have to.* Then rinse."

Mitch flipped open his laptop and began logging the day's events. As the moments passed, He didn't hear any water running. He didn't hear any noise at all. He inched open the bathroom door. "Satyajit? Are you o... whoa," He spied a naked Satyajit, smeared head-to-toe with soap, dipping his hand in the toilet to bathe himself. "What are you doing? Why aren't you using the shower?"

Satyajit had no inkling to cover himself or be embarrassed. "What is the shower?"

Mitch pushed him aside. Reaching across the tub, he twisted the knob, turning on the water. "You adjust the temperature like this. This way is hotter. This way is colder. You stand under it to wash your whole body. It will run until you turn it off like this."

Satyajit smiled like a kindergartner who had not been listening. He stepped into the shower, smiling as he felt the warm water bouncing off his chest and spraying all over the bathroom.

Mitch screamed and drew the curtain to halt his own, unexpected shower.

Satyajit had no idea how filthy he was. He had never used

nor seen a shower. All of his life he had only bathed in lakes and rivers, and only rarely. The warm, clean water felt like new life washing over him.

Mitch stuck his head back into the bathroom. "Rub some of that soap on your head as well to wash your hair. Make sure you rinse off all the soap and then dry with a clean towel. Mitch gathered Satyajit's clothes and tossed them into the trash. *He can borrow some of my clothes tonight. We'll buy him something new tomorrow.*

* * *

Marci savored her warm shower, but, staring at the ceiling, she struggled to enjoy her bed. She felt guilt-ridden for leaving Andrea. *My mother would kill me if she knew that I left Andrea and went to a hotel with a man I met only four days ago. I can just hear her. 'What are you thinking, Marci?'*

*Oh, and dad would chime in, 'That's just it, she's not thinking. Why did we let her go over there in the first place?'*

*'Well, she is 23 years old, dear.'*

Marci watched the ceiling fan slowly turning. *What am I doing here?* She propped her head with an extra pillow and tried to read her Bible. Skimming, she flipped to Leviticus. *Well, this would put me to sleep.* She turned to the New Testament and landed in Hebrews: "Let us draw near to God with a sincere heart in full assurance of faith, having our hearts sprinkled to cleanse us from a guilty conscience and having our bodies washed with pure water. Let us hold unswervingly to the hope we profess, for He who promised is faithful."

*"He who promised is faithful." God, why can't Mitch see it? What can I do to help him, to help him know You?* She heard his shower kick on for the second time. When the water stopped, she waited a few minutes, then rapped on their door.

Mitch opened with a "Shhh."

Marci peeked in to see Satyajit asleep. She whispered. "I can't sleep. Do you mind if we find a place to talk?"

"Marci, I would love to talk." *Or do anything else you might desire.* If not for her golden-brown eyes and alluring scent, he would have preferred a date with his lonely bed.

Mitch followed her to a cozy nook overlooking the street. The inviting sofa and soft glow of a nearby lamp enticed and welcomed the two unlikely friends. Marci's charming innocence captivated him. Her eyes spoke volumes as they sat in awkward silence almost too tired to speak.

"You wanted to talk. What would you like to talk about?"

"What were you like as a boy?"

"Is this small talk or do you really want to know?"

"I want to know. What were you like as a boy?"

"Well, unless something's changed, I'm still a boy."

"Ugh! You know what I mean. What were you like as a child?"

Mitch could not help himself. Kidding was a way for him to enjoy the moments of life, but it was also a defense, a way to avoid going deeper. "I was your typical gullible child. I believed my parents, and I believed my teachers" *until I could prove them wrong.*

"Go on."

"Oh, I grew up in a Christian home. My father was a minister. I went to a private school where the Bible was part of my curriculum until I was in ninth grade."

"When did you lose faith?"

"There really was not any one time when the light came on and I said, 'Aha.' It was more a process of doubt upon doubt eventually building into a solid wall of skepticism. There were too many questions."

"For instance?"

"For instance, how can you believe God created the Earth in six days, especially when geological evidence refutes the account of Genesis in a multiplicity of ways? How can you accept the Bible as divine revelation when it is loaded with contradiction, not to mention the fact that it was written by scattered writers, many of whom wrote decades after Christ's death? And perhaps most of all, how can you worship a god who allows so much evil in the world?"

Instead of a snapping comeback, Marci met him with kindness and a gentle touch. "Mitch, I respect your intelligence. You are thoughtful and unafraid to follow logic where it leads. We could spend hours debating, bouncing ideas, arguing, tracing the steps of our best reasoning, but if we walk the wrong path, we would never reach our destination. I don't expect you to do this right now, but sometime, when you are alone, I want you to take your picture of the world and turn it sideways. Look at it from a different angle. To me, when you ask, 'If there is a God, why does he allow so much evil in the world?' you are confining God to your own notions. If there is a real, true, living Creator God, He is defined relative only to Himself. We did not invent Him."

"So you're saying we should discard reason, and simply believe because God is bigger than any of us can understand?"

"I am saying it is a mistake to trust our finite reasoning. In other words, when you reach the limits of your capacity to reason, you once again make a reasoned choice."

"Example?"

"When you ask, 'If there is a God, why does he allow so much evil in the world?' Are you not also implying there is good in the world?"

Mitch struggled not to argue. Andrea had convinced him to try to reason with an open mind. "Of course I'm implying there is good. Not everything is evil."

Marci tried not to smile. "If there is good and evil, does that not imply a moral law?"

"I suppose. There have to be some rules of right and wrong."

"Who determines right and wrong?"

"Well you certainly don't need any god to tell you the difference. Understanding and desire for the common good help us set standards and determine right and wrong. Marci, I think we should talk about something else. You and I both know that this discussion will eventually boil into an argument."

Marci sighed and nodded, somewhat defeated. "Mitch, I just don't get it. If I believed life was the result of billions of mindless, purposeless, random, chance events, then, when you look at all the crap that goes on, I would have to ask myself, 'What's the point?' I honestly think, if I believed what you believe, I might just shoot myself to get it over with."

"Now Marci, it's you who needs to turn the picture around. If you believed like I believe, we would be up in my room together and Satyajit would be rotting in jail. If there's no purpose, no meaning, then there are no rules."

"But you said, if there is evil, there must also be good."

"So I did, but you were asking in the context of your God-centered worldview. From my point of view, there is no good, nor is there any evil. When there is no meaning, it's all the same."

"I've seen the way you look at me. If there are no rules what keeps you from forcing yourself on me?"

"Marci, don't degrade yourself or me!"

"What! If there are no rules, there are no measures of regard. How could I degrade something as meaningless as you? Tell me this, would sex with me be better if I were willing or if you forced it on me and I resisted?"

Mitch stood and glared. "You are treading a dangerous path. You would call me a post-modern relativist. That means decisions, moral choices if you will, are relative, so I would prefer consensual sex because it feels better, and because there are no unwanted consequences like prison."

*What is it going to take, God, to get him to see?*

Marci heard a voice within. *"To see what? To see things your way? Or My way?"*

Marci slowly stood. Biting her lip and swallowing trickles of emotion, she stared into his eyes searching for a soul.

She pressed closer. Her soft warm breath and overwhelming femininity consumed the sensually parched Mitch Hawkins. To his surprise she tightly embraced him.

When his arms reached to reciprocate, she pushed away. "As long as you believe nothing has meaning, love will mean nothing to you, and you will never know love." Tears in her eyes and trembling, she slipped from his dwindling grasp and walked briskly to her room. Feelings of failure followed her.

Mitch stood dumbfounded. His feelings of victory disintegrated. Cracking like a shell, his pride shattered on the ornate rug. *'...never know love.'* Somehow, he knew she was right. He had no intimate attachments, no lover, no close friends, and not really even any distant friends. He had numerous interesting associations, people with whom he could banter challenging thoughts and hypothetical puzzles, favorite lonely women, preferred call girls, business associates, but no real friends, none... until now.

Mitch gulped as he realized these two girls were his friends because they saw innate value and meaning in his life. *They see more in me than I do.* As he eased his way toward his room, uncertainty and frustration followed.

He lay in bed thinking. *Marci can't be right. I know what love is.* His deepest thoughts remained buried, but his tough shell was softening. Reckless lust had faded. Marci had started to mean something.

# CHAPTER 27

All Saints Hospital
Before Dawn
Friday, September 12, 2008

Indu was awake but silent. Having seen more death than life, her youthful eyes stared through the ceiling, far beyond the clouds. She heard gentle breathing as Andrea slept at her bedside. The soft tapping of footsteps drew her eyes toward Chandrika peeking around the door.

Chandrika whispered to avoid waking Andrea. "After the doctor sees you, you should be able to go."

Indu's tender smile turned to fear. *But where... where do I go?*

Chandrika's heart melted. *She has nowhere to go. Oh Lord, I did not mean to scare this child.* Chandrika wrapped her in her arms. "Indu, there are people who love you. I will make sure you are always with someone who loves you."

12 hours at the hospital had taken their toll, but limp hair and tired eyes could not suppress Chandrika's smile. "I will come back after I get some sleep." She waved a gentle good-bye. "Namaste, Indu."

"Jai Masih Ki."

Chandrika left the room, stunned at the tiny giant of faith. *'Jai Masih Ki?' She just lost her whole family and yet 'Praise the Lord' is her 'good-bye.' Oh Lord, that my faith could be so strong!*

For Indu, the room was calm and quiet. She tried not to move. She did not want to wake Andrea. *What an awkward position! She must be so tired. Why is she still here? Andrea, who are you? Why did you come to my village, and why do you care so much for me?*

Indu adored her gentle face. *She is lovely.* She was beautiful even with her half-opened mouth and extruding drool. Her hair, disheveled and jumbled, looked silky smooth to Indu. She resisted the urge to touch her hair, letting her sleep.

Indu noticed Andrea's Bible on the small table beside her. *She must have been reading her Bible while I slept.* Picking it up, she adored the fine leather. Nine years old, she could read very little English, but she flipped through the pages. Post-it notes, pictures, a birthday card. Indu found favorite passages underlined or high-lighted. As she skimmed through to find the maps, she flipped past a startling photo. *What was that?* She turned back a few pages and found it again, a serene family dressed in their best: husband and wife, three sons, and two daughters. She studied the picture, reflecting on every detail. No longer in the hospital, she was in the photo, walking around the room, inspecting the children, measuring the love in the eyes of the mother and father. She was intent on the picture as if nothing else mattered, as if nothing else existed.

Andrea awakened. "I see you found my Bible."

Indu did not hear a word. She was lost in thought, her gaze fixed on the photograph.

Andrea hunched over, trying to make eye contact. She heard a suppressed sniffle, and noticed tears and trembling. "Indu, are you ok?" *I can't believe I just asked that question. She lost her family. Of course, she's not okay.*

A numb face with blank eyes reflected Andrea's tears. Indu plopped the photograph in her lap and clasped her hands on the top of her head.

Andrea picked up the photo. "Indu? This picture was in my Bible. Do you know these people?"

Indu's whole face squinted, squeezing out the last few tears. Indu nodded, and then stuttered through her sniffling and choking. She pointed to the older girl in the delicate white dress with frilly socks and lady-like shoes. The smiling girl had a lovely flower in her hair. Everything was perfect and in its place.

The strained look in Indu's eyes made it plain to Andrea that everything was out of place. She watched in amazement as Indu retrieved the picture and held it next to her face, so Andrea could see it.

"It's you. Isn't it?" Andrea said. "The older girl is you?"

Indu blinked away a tear and offered a subtle nod.

"These are your parents, your brothers and your sister?"

"Yes. They are all gone, but I know they are with Jesus. I wish I had not escaped. I wish I was with them."

Andrea hugged her firmly. "Indu, I am so sorry. God must have wanted you here for a good reason." *God, surely you have a good reason.*

Andrea studied the photo intently. *This is Indu's family. Jeevan was her father. That means... Vishal is her grandfather. Dear God, her parents are dead, and her only living relative is facing a death sentence.*

Andrea could not bring herself to say anything to Indu about Vishal. *She has already lost her family. Now she is going to lose the grandfather she never knew. I have to speak to Vishal.*

# CHAPTER 28

Invitation to Violence
Friday Morning, September 12, 2008

"Natraj, where is your friend?"

"Oh, Satyajit? I don't know. I have not seen him since Pahireju."

"You should look for him. We need as many devotees as we can find. Here, take a stack of these. Give one to everyone you know, everyone you can trust. We will go to Gourpali on Sunday. We will surprise the Christians while they worship."

Natraj eyed the pamphlets, each a death sentence for Christians. The Hindi script translated, "In order to make it a grand success, you all are requested to please come and join the rally with all your traditional weapons."

*  *  *

Breakfast at The Rani Lodge

With a washed out stare, Satyajit handed Marci a crumpled piece of paper.

Marci asked, "Where have you been?" She crinkled her brow at the scrawled Hindi script. "I can't read this! What does it say?"

"A stranger gave it to me. It is from Natraj. They are ridding the district of Christians one village at a time."

Marci's eyes widened. "We have to do something! Where

are they planning to attack?"

"It does not say, but I was told Gourpali, a small village east of here. Their plan is to attack during the worship."

Marci looked around for Mitch. "We have to warn them!" Walking back through the hotel, she spied a police officer. "We should let the police know."

Satyajit grabbed her arm and whispered. "The police already know and they plan to do nothing. If they come, they will arrive at least two hours after the attack. The crowd will disperse, and no one will be arrested. The church will continue to burn, and my friends will have killed every Christian in the village."

"What the police do with the information is up to them, but I am compelled to tell them. They need to know that I know."

Satyajit squeezed tighter. "You must not tell them. If the extremists know that you know, they will change the attack, and they would target you. Trust me, the police already know more than enough."

\* \* \*

Mitch was sitting alone in the dining area. *What is taking Marci so long?* He felt alone without his laptop. He left it in his room. He wanted no distractions since he had Marci alone for breakfast, but there he sat by himself. He halfway rose out of his chair, peeking over the potted plants to look for her. He saw the top of her head in the foyer. *Whew! What is she doing?*

A policeman brushed past Mitch and gave him a wary glance. The officer walked over to the front desk and whispered something to the clerk. Shifting his assault rifle on his shoulder, he looked around to insure no one was watching. The clerk appeared to be reading something below the counter.

Mitch felt a strange chill as he spied Satyajit clutching Marci's arm and whispering. *What is going on here?*

Satyajit and Marci retreated to a table in the far corner of the foyer. Marci motioned for Mitch to come closer. She held the startling notice inside her opened journal. She smiled innocently when the police officer cast a leery eye.

With his back to the policeman, Satyajit whispered the translation to Mitch.

On hearing the distressing news, Mitch quickly turned and walked toward the front desk. As he approached, he nodded to the officer and addressed the clerk, "Excuse me."

The policeman took his cue and left.

Mitch rapped his knuckles on the counter. "May we have two clean towels in room 107?"

"Certainly, Mr. Hawkins."

When the clerk left the desk, Mitch wheeled around the counter. Scouring everything with his eyes, he discovered a crinkled ball of yellow paper. He unfolded it enough to confirm that it was the same notice Marci had shown him. He crunched it once again into a ball and carefully returned it to its spot.

Hearing footsteps, Mitch tossed his pen on the floor and bent down to retrieve it just in time to be witnessed by the clerk.

"The maid will deliver your towels promptly." The clerk glanced behind the counter. "Did you find what you were looking for?"

Mitch waved his pen and smiled. "Yes, thank you."

The clerk spotted the wadded notice. *It's still there.* His wary eyes followed Mitch.

Mitch patted Satyajit on the shoulder. "We have fresh towels. Satyajit, why don't you take your shower first while Marci and I eat breakfast?"

\* \* \*

Satyajit had never taken bathed two days in a row. *I have never felt so clean. I smell like Mr. Hawkins.* He gazed at himself in the mirror. The crisp, clean reflection did not look like the Satyajit he remembered. He was no longer the boy he remembered from his grandmother's hazy mirror. Who is that man?

He gasped and looked away as the mirror reflected the pleading eyes of Jeevan Joseph. He tried to think of anything else, but those eyes pursued him. He recalled the same pleading stare from Indu. *I killed her sister and brothers.*

No amount of bathing or cologne could mask the stench he felt in himself. *Why am I here? What have I done to deserve to live? I must be here for a reason.* He glanced at the mirror one more time. *Why do I see Jeevan Joseph in my eyes?*

His mind running wildly, he could not escape his thoughts. He tried to command his memory, focusing on his mother cooking over an open flame, but his thoughts drew him to the fire, to the burnt church in Pahireju. His heart resurrected Pastor Joseph's prayer, "God, send your mercies to my father." Satyajit slumped to the floor as the prayer played over and over in his mind.

Casting aside generations of tradition, he called out to a god he had never known but had rejected. "Oh God, I don't know who you are or if you are real, but I know your believers are willing to die for their belief. I offer you this: if you lead me to Jeevan's father, I will deliver whatever mercy you send." *What am I doing? I don't know if this god even exists?*

With a deep sigh, Satyajit turned away from the mirror.

He opened the wardrobe to discover a tidy pile of new clothes and a note. *Satyajit, I thought you could use these. I asked the maid where I could buy some men's clothes. She offered to do it for me, so if you don't like them blame her. Your friend, Marci.*

*Who are these people?* After he buttoned his new shirt, he left the room, and walked down the hall toward the dining area.

\* \* \*

Andrea entered the hotel. She recognized Marci's distinctive laugh and marched toward her. Seeing Satyajit in the corner of her eye, she waited, prompted by a subtle urge deep within. She stepped toward Satyajit. Stopping him with her hand on his chest, she said, "Vishal is Jeevan Joseph's father." She could not understand her compulsion to tell him before Marci and Mitch. "I must go to Vishal and tell him about his granddaughter Indu."

Satyajit stood speechless. *Who is this God? I pray and a moment later the answer to my prayer walks through the door.*

Andrea's voice brought him back to the moment, "Satyajit, are you ok?

"Hmm. Oh, yes. Yes, I'm fine," Satyajit answered. As Andrea turned to walk toward Marci and Mitch, he said, "Wait! You cannot see Vishal. With a death sentence, he is not allowed visitors."

Almost crying, Andrea protested. "But I have to see him. He needs to know that his granddaughter is alive."

"You cannot see him, but I can. I know a way."

"But you said..."

Satyajit grinned. "No visitors... but another prisoner...." He mused at Andrea's puzzled look. "I will commit a small offense, enough to get thrown in jail for three days, more than enough time to find Vishal and give him the message."

Still chewing on his words, Andrea could no longer suppress her hunger. She walked into the dining area with Satyajit following. She sat down with Mitch and Marci.

"You look good," said Mitch sarcastically.

Andrea cringed as she scrunched her unsettled hair. *I must be quite a sight. Oh well, I'm too tired to worry about it and too hungry to care.* She plunked into one of two empty seats. She looked at Mitch. She had no toothbrush at the hospital, and her devious side wanted to feign a kiss and breathe into his face. *I couldn't do that to Mitch.*

"Andrea, you seem pensive?"

"Well, Mr. Hawkins, I was devising a plan to torment you..."

"Sounds interesting."

"But I can't bring myself to it." Andrea did not stop fiddling with her hair.

Satyajit slid into the open seat. "Andrea told me Indu is the granddaughter of Vishal."

"How do you figure?" asked Marci.

"When I met Vishal at the prison, he was holding a photograph of a young family. When they took him away, he left it on the table. He discarded it, really. I looked at the picture and stuck it in my Bible. This morning Indu found the photo while I was asleep. She found herself, standing in her best dress with her family. Don't you see...?"

Mitch finished the thought. "Jeevan Joseph was Vishal's son."

"I don't get it," Marci said.

"Jeevan grew up Hindu. When a Hindu converts to Christianity, his family disowns him and mourns his death. In more hostile, fundamentalist families, they actually kill the convert. Vishal most likely only knew his adult son through that photograph. He has probably never seen Indu except in the picture."

Satyajit stood abruptly. "I have something to say." He swallowed hard as six startled eyes fixed on his somber face. "God has brought me to Sambalpur. I have not known him as you do," he said, nodding to Marci and Andrea. He looked at Mitch. "But I know He is real. I prayed this morning that He would fulfill the dying prayer of Pastor Joseph through me."

"What was his dying prayer?"

"He prayed 'God, send your mercies to my father.' I prayed to God, 'If you lead me to Jeevan's father, I will deliver whatever mercy you send.' When I finished praying, I left the room and then immediately met Andrea who told me Vishal was Jeevan's father."

"You must go to him," Marci said.

*Well, it makes a nice story.* Mitch drew into his tight shell, withdrawing his emotions. *I have to know. This metaphysical mumbo jumbo does not work for me.*

Andrea's gentle touch disrupted his retreat. "You should go with him, Mitch."

"Satyajit does not need me. He doesn't need my help."

Andrea could no longer see the distant vagrant soul she met in Amsterdam. She saw a frightened child, afraid to know the truth. *God, give me the words to say. Spirit, speak through me.* "Mitch, you are right. Satyajit does not need you to go, but you do. The Spirit is but metaphysical mumbo jumbo to you. You need to know. Go with Satyajit, please."

*Metaphysical mumbo jumbo? Did she just say that? Is she reading my mind?* "Andrea, I don't understand your faith, but you are right. I need to know. I will go with Satyajit, but you need to get cleaned up and go back to the hospital. They will probably release Indu this morning. You should be there."

# CHAPTER 29

Early Morning
All Saints Hospital
Friday, September 12, 2008

Dr. David eyed the growing crowd outside the hospital: mothers cradling hope, villagers with cracked and blistered feet, *too much work for three doctors*. He did his best to ignore the clock as he moved from one patient to the next. Finally, he grasped the chart of his last patient.

"Dr. David, you saved the cutest patient for last."

"Namaste," He nodded and smiled. "I am Dr. David and your name is…"

"Indu," she giggled.

"Well, Miss Indu, you do not seem very sick. I see Chandrika took care of you through the night. You were dehydrated, but you have recovered well, and now you are ready to…"

Indu's nurse, Naomi grasped his arm and whispered. "She has no home. She is from Pahireju. Her home was burned, and her parents and siblings were killed."

Dr. David placed his stethoscope on Indu's chest. "Take a deep breath, again… Your lungs are clear." He examined her ears and throat. He felt her neck. "Lie down." He examined her belly. "You are a very healthy young lady. Naomi has told me what happened to your family. Do you have grandparents or an aunt or uncle, any family you could live with?"

Indu shook her head. She knew no family but her own. *Where will they send me? I wish Andrea was here. I wish my mother was here.* Indu looked out the window. She could see the rising flood of patients and their families filling the yard around the hospital. She spotted a lonely girl. *She looks like me.* The little girl wore a faded green dress. She weaved aimlessly, in and out, between, and around the infirmed who were waiting. Her wandering turned to whimsical spinning and hopping. What is she doing? As the girl hopped once more, she stretched her arms high above her head and softly clapped her hands. *Oh, now I see the butterfly.*

The spry child could not be suppressed. She gaily chased the butterfly as it danced on the air.

*I wish I was chasing butterflies.*

The little girl turned around, responding to the voice of her mother. She waved good-bye to the butterfly and skipped back toward her mother.

"I need to find a family," Indu said.

Naomi's heart wrenched. *How can we possibly find her a family this quickly? She will undoubtedly have to go to the children's home, at least for awhile.*

Knock! Knock! Knock!

Dr. David turned toward the door. He saw a smiling Chandrika. "What are you smiling about, and why are you here? Did you not work all night?"

Chandrika walked toward Indu. "I cared for this angel through the night." Facing Naomi and Dr. David, she continued in a lower voice. "Indu lost her parents in much the same way I did. I needed a mother." Folding her hands, she pleaded through a whisper. "I would like to take her home and raise her as my own. I would love her and care for her."

The thoughtful and patient doctor knew Chandrika's heart. *There is no one more innocent and pure than Chandrika, except perhaps Indu herself.* He knew that Chandrika would make a wonderful mother, but was she ready? Was she offering for the right reasons? *I can't say, "No."*

Dr. David placed his right hand on Chandrika's shoulder and leaned past her, hovering over Indu's bed. "The decision is not entirely mine."

Indu said, "I would like to go home with Chandrika." *Her smile reminds me of my mother, and I know she will love me.*

\* \* \*

As they left the ward, Naomi warned Dr. David. "It would be best if we did not alert the authorities. They would insist she go to a children's home."

"Or worse," Dr. David added, "they could force her to live with a Hindu family. We will tell no one."

"What about the Americans who rescued her? What if they come back? What do we say?"

"We tell them what they need to know. 'She went to a Christian family.' That would be enough to allay their fears."

\* \* \*

Late Friday Morning

All Saints Hospital

September 12, 2008

Andrea stepped over a man lying on the sidewalk. She hurried to get back to Indu, but compassion gripped her. She turned around and knelt beside the suffering man. An older woman, sitting beside him, began pleading with her. Andrea understood very little Hindi, but she could not recognize the woman's dialect. She understood from her motions that this man had been coughing for quite some time.

Andrea had no medical skills whatsoever, but she laid her head on his chest. As she listened to his wispy gasps for air, she prayed, "Lord, thank you for the kinship that you give to your children. I don't even know this man. I cannot understand him or speak to him, but I can see that he is dying. Dear Jesus, please rid his lungs of disease and protect him from persecution."

The old woman clasped her hands, saying "Dhanyvād."

*Thank you... I understand that.* "Jai Masih Ki," Andrea replied.

The wrinkled mother smiled through a veil of tears.

Many others reached out to Andrea as she passed through the growing crowd.

*What it must have been like when Jesus walked through the crowds! How could he feel that woman touch his robe?*

\* \* \*

As she entered the hospital, Naomi greeted her with a smile. "You must be Andrea."

"Yes."

"Indu told me about you. You are a brave woman to leave your family and come to such a troubled land."

Somewhat embarrassed, Andrea smiled and asked, "May I see Indu?"

Naomi stretched out her hand, touching Andrea's arm. "I'm pleased to tell you she has been adopted by a Christian family."

"She's not here?" Andrea's face flushed with disappointment. "I'm glad she found a family. I feel so bad for her. I can't imagine losing my father or mother, let alone, my whole family. What cruelty she has endured."

Naomi nodded her agreement. "Suffering is difficult, but our burdens are light compared to the cross."

Andrea felt a sense of calm. "Do you know where this family lives?

Naomi answered, "No. I'm not sure exactly where Indu will be living, but I know her new mother, parents will cherish her and raise her as their own."

# CHAPTER 30

The Prison
Friday, September 12, 2008

Arriving at the prison, Mitch squeezed the tiny car between two others and said, "Here we are. So, how do you plan to...WHOA!" Mitch was startled at Satyajit urinating at the feet of a policeman.

The officer grabbed Satyajit's shoulders and whirled him around. The wild spray splattered across his trousers. He scowled and thrust his knee into Satyajit's back. "You are under arrest."

Mitch stood dumbfounded as Satyajit zipped his pants. He winced as the officer thrust his club into Satyajit's back and shoved him toward the prison but chuckled as Satyajit waved a smiling good-bye.

*What is he doing? I can't leave without knowing.* Mitch shuffled across the street, carrying his camera and notebook.

He stopped at the entrance, blocked by a scrawny guard with a formidable weapon.

The guard asked, "What are you doing here?"

"I am here to find out what happened to the young man who came in a moment ago."

"He committed a crime. He has been arrested."

Mitch tried to think quickly. "Sir, can you tell me the penalty for urinating in front of a police officer?"

"Ha, ha, ha!" The guard could not stop laughing. "So, that's what was all over his boots." Turning back toward Mitch, the convulsing guard laughed. "Ha, ha, it is three days in jail and… ha, ha, 150 rupees."

*So, it's about three bucks. He's a clever little…*

The guard interrupted his thought. "After he is processed, he is allowed one visitor each day that he is here. Ha ha ha… He may have to buy my friend some new boots."

Laughter trailed behind Mitch as he walked to the visitor's waiting area. He sat for two hours, but Satyajit never came. He had scratched all the notes he cared to write. Without his laptop or Wi-Fi, he was wasting his time if he stayed any longer. He approached the guard once more.

"Come back later," said the guard, laughing once again. "Perhaps he is embarrassed because he had to change his pants."

Mitch rolled his eyes and smirked as he left the prison.

\* \* \*

Late Friday Morning

Rani Lodge

September 12, 2008

Marci finished her coffee alone. *Well, it's not Starbucks, but it's not bad. I wonder what that little spice is.* The warm mug in her hands and the familiar aroma reminded her of the times she shared with her mother. Coffee was a bridge that brought them together. They shared many a story over a cup of coffee. Heartaches, joys, celebrations, dreams and aspirations.

Thinking about her mother, Marci glanced at the time. *It's about 10:40. I wonder what mom is doing right now. Ha, well I guess she's asleep. It's just after midnight in Goose Creek.*

A polite voice disrupted her daydreaming. "Did you enjoy your breakfast?"

Marci looked up at the waiter. "Oh, yes. Thank you." She admired his pleasant manner and his immaculate uniform. As he walked away, her thoughts followed him. *He just wants to live his life in peace. I wish we could all have that, but I don't see much of it around here.*

The waiter paused, turned and bowed. "I apologize. I presumed you were finished. May I offer you anything else?"

"There is one thing. Is there an internet café in Sambalpur?"

# CHAPTER 31

3619 Palmetto Lane
Goose Creek, South Carolina
12:10 AM, Friday, September 12, 2008

"Leena, are you still awake?" After 29 years, Ashton Beaufort could feel the emptiness in his bed without his wife, and he knew when she was crying. Raising his head and propping himself on his elbow, he could see her silhouette against the computer monitor.

The shadowy figure of his wife turned around to face him. "Oh Ash, Marci hasn't posted anything on her blog in five days, and she hasn't called."

Ashton crawled out of bed and stood beside her, gently placing his hand on her shoulder. "You are a mother and you have a right to worry, but I don't think worry is going to help."

Leena Beaufort leaned into him, embracing him tightly. She held him, shaking, fighting tears. His warm arms gave her strength but not comfort. She dreamed of holding her daughter, looking into her eyes, and knowing she was safe and home.

She loosened her hold. "Ash, you should go back to bed. I'm not going to be able to sleep anyway, and you have to get up for work in a few hours." She kissed his cheek and pressed his hand against her face. "I'm going to pray for her and Andrea and post my motherly comments."

* * *

Marci was ten-and-a-half hours ahead of her mother and

halfway around the world as she logged into her blog. *Where do I even start?* She opened Facebook in a new window and began uploading photos of herself and Andrea. *How do I explain Mitch... and Satyajit?*

A familiar tone and pop-up alerted her to an instant message from her mother. "Where are you? Are you ok?"

Marci fired back. "Sambalpur. Ok."

Marci waited for what seemed like 10 minutes for her mother to type a complete sentence. "Your father and I have been worried. We are praying for you."

*Wow, Mom, you type so slow.* The two Beauforts volleyed messages for almost an hour. Marci loved being able to touch her mother from 10,000 miles away.

Leena Beaufort hated not being able to touch her daughter. *I just wish I could hold her.* Mrs. Beaufort signed off. "Please call when you get a chance. Call anytime. We will continue our constant prayers for you. I love you. Give Andrea my love."

"I love you too, Mom. Please pray for the people of Orissa. Pray for our friends: Vishal, Mitch, Satyajit, and especially Indu."

\* \* \*

2:30 AM, Friday, September 12, 2008

Goose Creek, South Carolina

Marci's Blog: You think you know what life is about. You think you know Jesus. I'm not saying you don't, but I'm not sure how well I did. A week ago I was worried about making my hair appointment and if I have enough clothes packed for our trip. I had this patronizing fantasy about how I was going to change the world, as though the poor Christians in India somehow needed me. I was all concerned for them in their poverty and suffering. No doubt they are suffering, but I'm not so sure they are the ones without hope. At home we feel like we've got everything we need, but we're trapped with expectations of what we're supposed to make of our lives. Our self-made lives have a way of stealing our joy. We bind ourselves with debts. Busyness pulls us away from family and friends. I imagine myself working away paying bills, trying to meet the mortgage payment, squeezing kids in somewhere only to find that they've grown up while I was pursuing the dream.

I hope you don't think I'm preaching. Let me be the audience. I am preaching to me, Marci. I want to live life. I want to live life for Christ. The Christians in Orissa don't need me one tenth as much as I need them. We found this nine-year-old girl in the village of Pahireju. She lost her whole family to an attack by Hindu extremists, but she could still praise the Lord, even in her pain.

We heard about a pastor and his family who were burned alive in their car. The pastor and his wife were praying for their murderers as their car roared in flames. I can't even pray for the guy who cuts me off in traffic. These people are living a New Testament, Book-of-Acts kind of faith. Please pray for them, but while you're praying, get down on your knees and pray for yourself.

We are in a spiritual war, and I feel like we are out-flanked, distracted, and unaware of the raging battle. The enemies of the cross are not flesh and bone. Instead they are the powers of darkness that prey on human souls, confounding them with ignorance and hate, jealousy and contempt. Orissa is burning. Hindu extremists follow the confusion of their hearts and their lust for vengeance. Christ is dragged through the streets and beaten. His bride is soaked in kerosene and torched. Her torn flesh is paraded proudly and recklessly discarded. His house is burned to ash and rubble. Bewildered unbelievers watch in disbelief without affection. As He is carried through the town, He cries for those who abuse Him. They do not know what they are doing.

My heart breaks for India. Hinduism claims to believe karma defines one's destiny, but humanity defies such belief by seizing destiny and directing karma with fists and clubs. If Christ were a false god or just one of millions of gods, then leave Him to fade into obscurity. Reality affirms His deity and sovereignty because He is a threat to all other notions of faith. He is either who He claimed to be, namely the Creator God, the Lord and Savior of humanity, or He is a lunatic or a liar. If He were a lunatic, none would persist in following. If He were a liar, then His message would have died with Him. If He is Lord, then we must decide to follow or rebel.

India is in the fire. Can you walk in the flames and not be burned? Christ called to Peter to come to Him on the water, and Peter stepped out of the boat and walked on water. Christ is calling our brothers and sisters in India to walk through fire. Can we trust Him? Pulpits around the world accuse Peter of doubting, losing faith, taking his eyes off Christ. Peter did not sink for a lack of faith any more than his faith alone could make him walk on water. He knew that he was able only because Christ enabled him. He also knew that he was sinking because Christ let him sink. When Jesus questioned his faith, it was as though He was saying, "Do you think I am going to let you drown?"

I can hear my Christian brother in India saying, "I trust you, Christ. If I am called to walk through the fire, then so be it."

Thank you for your prayers and support for Andrea and me. We are praying for you as well.

Marci Beaufort
September 13, 2008

Through tears of worry mixed with sorrow and joy, Leena Beaufort finished reading her daughter's blog. "Ash, you've got to read this. Marci is writing from the front lines. She is our little spiritual soldier. I'm so proud."

* * *

Halfway around the world, the Internet café in Sambalpur was a burgeoning hub of activity. Marci Beaufort was the only American. A tall blond Swede, a tiny Nepali man, a dozen Indian men all wearing the same tan pants and white shirt, and a German couple filled the connected microcosm.

Marci sat in a puddle of tears in front of a PC, unaware of the bewildered stares of those around her. She raised her head and looked around. As eyes shifted away from her, she sniffed and wiped her tears. Realizing that everyone had been watching her, she thought, *oh, I must have been sobbing.*

As Marci's eyes traveled the room, she imagined people connecting all over the world. The tall blonde chatted with her boyfriend in Ronneby, Sweden. The Indian men conducted business with Bangalore, Mumbai, and Delhi. The German couple connected with each other over a cup of Garam Chai. Marci felt herself starting to think like Andrea. *All of us are so connected all over the world, but how many are truly connected to God?* Her heart went out to all those who shared the moment with her in that café.

She logged off and left.

# CHAPTER 32

The Prison
Afternoon, Friday, September 12, 2008

Vishal was not alone, even though he was confined. He was not still, even though he was frozen on his floor mat. Surrounded by unforgiving memories of a life wasted, he realized nothing remained that he had ever loved. Everything he had held dear was gone, destroyed by his own hate. His thoughts raced wildly, bouncing about in his 4 x 8 cell. Regret, bitterness and emptiness filled his personal prison.

*My life is already over. I hope they end it soon.* Vishal did not hear Satyajit's footsteps or his nervous whistling. Only the forceful rattling of the bars alerted him. "What do you want, and why are you here?"

Satyajit pressed his face between the bars. "I have something important to tell you."

"Important enough to get yourself thrown into prison? *There is nothing I would care to know.*

Satyajit trembled as he tried to speak. "I saw your son..."

"My son is dead! Gurdeep died at the hands of Christians."

Satyajit continued. "...in a vision. I saw him in a vision."

"Go on." Vishal sat up on his mat and folded his arms around his knees as Satyajit spoke. It did not matter what was said. Vishal could only hear the voice of Pastor Singh crying. "Jeevan sadaiva."

The voice waned as Satyajit's words grew in pitch and intensity. *He saw my son?*

"He was standing in his church. He spoke to me."

Vishal interrupted. "My son? You know where he is? Pleading turned to unrepressed screaming. "My son! You know where he is! Is he alive?" *Or has hate killed him, too?*

"Vishal, I was there when extremists killed your son and his family."

Foaming, Vishal sputtered. "Could you not help him?"

Satyajit swallowed hard. "I was one of them. I handed our leader the kerosene. I am haunted by his eyes. He looked straight at me before we burned him."

Overwrought with agony at losing his son twice, Vishal yelled. "You came here solely to torment me with news that my son, who was dead, was alive, but you killed him? You killed him and his family. Why did you come here? Why?"

As Vishal shook with tears as Satyajit's words rang, overpowering his thoughts. *"I handed our leader the kerosene to douse Jeevan... Jeevan... Jeevan?"* His thoughts quickly turned to the Pastor Singh's face mouthing, *"Jeevan sadaiva."*

Vishal fixed his eyes on Satyajit. "Did you say Jeevan?"

Satyajit could hardly speak through his tears. "Jeevan. Your son changed his name to Jeevan Joseph.

Vishal stood slowly and walked toward the bars and squeezed them. "I still do not understand why you came? Why could you not let me die in ignorance?"

Satyajit reached his hands through the bars, placing them on Vishal's shoulders. "God sent his mercies to you through Andrea and Marci. If they had not been there Tuesday night, you would have died alone, who knows where, and I would be in that cell, taking your punishment.

"What has any of that to do with my son?"

"Vishal, before Jeevan was burned, he shook free. He did not run. He did not beg for his life. He turned and faced each one of us. He looked into my soul as he cried his last prayer. 'God, send your mercies to my father.'"

Loud footsteps and an angry voice disrupted them. "What are you doing here? It's time to go to your own cell, unless you want to trade places with him."

Satyajit needed no prodding, but he jolted at the guard's stick in his back. As he marched toward his cell, a deeper pain reminded him he was not through with Vishal.

* * *

Satyajit stopped when he no longer felt the guard's prodding. The guard strongly nudged him into his new home. On the cruel stone floor of the cramped cell, an elderly man knelt in prayer. Satyajit stumbled, falling on the man who was calling out to Jesus.

The old man continued his prayers through the loud protest of the guard. "Shut up, old fool. Have you forgotten why you are here?" The guard cursed in anger as he heard the man's prayer for him. He slammed the cell closed and marched off.

"I'm sorry," Satyajit said, as he climbed off of the old man. "I didn't mean to disturb your prayers."

"In this land, prayers are the only act that cannot be disturbed. When I pray, I am no longer part of this world. For that moment, I am alone with our Creator and Savior. What could possibly disturb such a union of peace?"

Satyajit responded with humble silence. *What can I say to*

*that?* He felt awkward, even looking at the man. He could not help but notice that his feet and knuckles were badly swollen.

The old man read his face. "You look troubled." *God, I know you brought this man to my cell for a reason. Give me the wisdom I need to help him, and please soften his heart to the truth.* An inner voice spoke to the old man. *"Close your eyes."* With his eyes closed, he saw a flurry of images: a burning car, a burning house, a burning church, and a man walking in flames. His mind shot back to the brief image of the car. He remembered the newspaper photo. It was the same car.

"Where are you from?" the old man asked.

Satyajit answered blandly. "It doesn't matter.

"Right you are. What matters is where you are and where you are going."

"I don't really see myself going anywhere.

A smile stretched across the old man's face. "You feel lost and without purpose because you have been following the plans of others. I believe God has brought you to this place. I believe He brought you to me."

"Who are you, and why are you here?"

The old man started to answer, but Satyajit interrupted. "...And who are you to tell me how to live?"

"I can see that you need to know, but you are afraid. Do I seem afraid to you? Look at me." Years of rejection etched in the scars across his face and neck. "Look at my hands." The old man held out bruised and swollen mitts. "Look at my feet." Their warm effusions screamed.

Satyajit stared at his cracked and bleeding soles, calloused, mottled and bruised. *How can I stand, let alone walk?*

The old man watched his new cellmate's eyes. "These are not the marks of fear. I have nothing left to fear. Nothing more can be done to me, and nothing more can be taken from me. My family have all gone to Heaven. As I sit here in prison, I asked God why He insists on keeping this old man alive. As I prayed this prayer, your footsteps brought the answer. You thought you came here for some other important reason, but God brought you to me."

Not knowing quite what to think, Satyajit studied the old man's smile. *How can he smile? Life has beaten him and rejected him. He will likely draw his last breath in this cell. Despite his pain, he smiles.* The old man's warm eyes blended with his smile and caught Satyajit by surprise. "You remind me of a friend. I see the same light in her eyes."

"What is her name?"

"Andrea."

"Andrea? Where is she from?"

"She is from America."

Shaking his head, the old man puzzled. "And she came to Orissa?"

"She says God called her to Orissa."

Tears met the old man's resilient smile. *We are not alone. You send your angels to protect us and comfort us. Thank you, God. Bless and protect Andrea.* "I have no doubt your friend was sent here by God, and God has somehow used her to bring you to me. Your friend is a Christian?"

"Yes, Andrea is a Christian."

"But you are Hindu. How is it that you are friends?"

"I would rather not talk about it."

The old man chuckled. "I don't know what you've done to get yourself thrown in prison, but you have at least three days to share this little world with me, and I think you need to talk about it. You remind me of a younger me: full of energy, impulsive, idealistic, ready to take on the world, but I was blinded by tradition and driven by hate. As a young man, I made crime my occupation and pastime. I took special pride in crimes against Christians. I had no Christian friends, so tell me, how is it that you have a young Christian friend from America?"

Satyajit opened his heart. "I have two friends from America: Andrea and Marci; and a friend from London named Mitch. Andrea and Marci are Christians. I am certain Mitch is not. He is a journalist accompanying them. He seems to be waiting for something dreadful to happen so he can be there to report it. Andrea and Marci are here to help people who have been hurt by extremists and to encourage other Christians."

The old man interrupted. "You are Hindu, aren't you?"

"Yes."

"You still have not told me how you are their friend."

Satyajit could not look him in the eyes. He swallowed hard. "I cannot say I am their friend, but they have been friends to me." Satyajit choked on his tears and shook as he spilled the whole story, including his dream, burning the homes and churches in Pahireju, and killing Jeevan Joseph.

As he spoke of wrongfully going to jail for burning Pastor Singh, he noticed the old man was shaken with tears streaming. "Are you alright? I'm sorry I upset you."

Robust eyes pressed through the flood of tears. The old man stood on his blistered feet and hobbled to the back of the cell. He stared out the tiny barred window at the dusty blue sky, void of clouds. *How much longer, God, before I stand in your presence?*

A silent whisper from within quieted his impatience. *"Are you not in my presence now?"*

The elder saint turned around and faced Satyajit. He could not suppress his tears. "I am Jai Singh. The one you call Pastor Singh is my son, Chetan."

"Please, Mr. Singh, know that I had nothing to do with his death."

"Of course you didn't, but even if you had, I could not hold it against you. I committed even worse crimes in my youth, yet God has forgiven me." He looked at the young eyes of Satyajit. "The only difference between you and me is that I was Muslim. We hated Christians and Hindus. Crimes against non-Muslims were not crimes at all. They were games, and I was good at them. My passions grew restless. Small thefts grew into larger heists and more elaborate schemes. Hatred grew into beatings, rape, and even murder. I eventually earned my living as contract killer. I killed men, men I never knew, unbelievers who did not deserve to live. That is how I used to think.

One night after I had fulfilled a contract, I discovered a gang had been hired to kill me. I did not go home that night. They burned my home, destroyed all my things. I was not yet married and my parents lived elsewhere, so no one was hurt. I lived with a friend for a few days, but again, this gang discovered where I was hiding. I did not want to endanger my friend so I fled.

Six men pursued me. When they spotted me, I ran. Darkness fell, making it easy to hide but harder to run. I saw a church building with a crowd outside. I hid behind some houses and then ducked into the church. I sat on the floor beside an older woman and draped my head with her dupatta. I waited until the service was over. I knew the gang would not follow me into the crowded church, so I sat and listened.

I had always believed Christians were hate-mongers. I was taught they ate Muslim babies, they drank blood and ate flesh in their worship. As I listened to the preacher, he spoke about the son of a wealthy landowner. The son wanted to get the most out of life, all that he could afford. He did not want to wait for his father's death to inherit his share. His father granted the son his portion, and the son went away and squandered his wealth. Years later the foolish son was feeding pigs when he realized the pigs ate better than he did. He got down on his knees next to the swine and began to eat their food. Overwhelmed with sadness, he thought, 'What a wasted life! My father's servants live better than this. I will go back to my father and beg his mercy. I will ask him if I can become one of his servants.' Do you know the story?"

"I've never heard it."

"What do you think happened to the son?"

"I'm not sure, but I would be surprised if the father accepted his request. The young man was a fool. He got what he deserved."

Jai nodded. "That is what I thought as well, but when the young man returned home, his father saw him in the distance. I imagine him, going out to his porch everyday or on the roof, scanning the road as far as he could see, hoping and waiting, until finally the day came when his son returned. As soon as the father saw his son, he ran to him. He wrapped the smelly pig-farmer in his arms. He called for his servants to bring him a new robe, then he placed a ring on his finger. That night they celebrated the return of their lost son. All was forgiven and forgotten."

Jai set his hand on the young man's shoulder. "I have told you my name, but you have not told me yours."

"I am Satyajit."

"Your name means the truth is unconquerable. I pray that you would come to know the truth. Should I finish my story?"

Satyajit nodded.

Jai continued. "As I sat in that church, I felt a chill. I saw myself as that lost son, but for the moment I remained lost. I was more concerned with staying alive. I left the church, hidden within the mass of people. Through the dark streets, I managed to sneak out of town on the train. I felt awkward and guilty each time I stole after that night. I was unsettled, searching for fulfillment and meaning, not to mention food and a place to live.

Finally, I made my home in a small village. After a few months that same preacher came into my village. Everyone gathered to hear him. He said God is a God of love. 'God so loved the world, that He sent His one and only son, that whoever believes in Him should not die but live forever.' I had always believed in God, for as long as I can remember, but the God I knew made few promises and his love was for those who love him. In my Muslim faith, a wrong was met with vengeance. We made things right with violence. We converted the unbeliever with fear and force. I did not know forgiveness, and I would never have offered forgiveness to anyone. The idea that God loves everyone seemed very strange. I wrestled with that thought, but I could feel the Spirit of God urging me to believe. As much as I wanted to deny it, in my heart, I knew it was true."

Jai folded his hands and pressed them to his lips. Satyajit marveled at the passion and emotion in Jai's eyes. "Satyajit, I accepted Jesus Christ as my Savior and Lord."

Satyajit shook his head. *I'm not ready.*

"I was not ready at all, but the news eventually made its way to my family. I was unaware that my brothers proclaimed a fatwa against me, a call for my death as a religious duty.

I happened to see my youngest brother in Delhi. I was afraid to tell him I had accepted Christ, knowing he would not accept me if I told him. I told myself that praying for him would be enough. My brother met with me a few times but mostly watched me from a distance, until one day when all of my brothers came to my village.

They dragged me out of my home, threw me onto a truck and drove me to our home town. They wanted to kill me in front of everyone. They beat me with fists and sticks. My oldest brother pulled me up by the shirt, shaking me violently and slapping my face. He asked me, 'Jai, tell me, before I kill you, what is the difference between Mohammed and your Christ? What is different between Islam and Christianity?'

I looked intently at each of my brothers. I could taste my own blood. My eyes stung with tears and sweat, but my heart was broken for my brothers. They could not see the unconquerable truth. I said, 'Let me ask you this: have you seen a difference in me?'

They answered, 'Absolutely, you are as different as night and day. You are not the same person that you were before you accepted Christ. You are completely changed, like a new man.'

I replied, 'That is the difference between Mohammed and Christ.' One by one, my brothers let go of me, then stepped back, began walking, and then ran from me. My youngest brother paused to look back. Even from a distance, I could see his tears. Although they have not yet accepted Christ, they let me live because they could see Christ in me."

*They could see Christ in me. Dear God, you see this boy with his heavy heart. Speak to him through my words. I can see the desire for hope in his eyes.*

\* \* \*

Satyajit laid awake staring at the stone ceiling. He watched rare flickers of light dance across the mottled gray. A thin rim of moonlight painted each of the iron bars. The street noise had all but died. Inside the prison, the occasional clanking of bars broke the silence.

Finally, all was quiet, except for Satyajit's mind. *"God, send your mercies to my father."* Jeevan Joseph's prayer played in his mind. Satyajit dared not close his eyes. He knew all he would see were visions of that fateful day and those unyielding eyes.

*Why did Natraj drag me into such evil? How could I have followed so blindly?* Guilt and confusion engulfed Satyajit.

\* \* \*

Across the cell, Jai Singh prayerfully meditated. *God, please give me words to awaken his soul.* He startled his young cellmate with a break in the silence. "Satyajit, this prison is only bricks and mortar. Though my body is bound by this cell, my soul is free."

Satyajit questioned, "How can your soul be free? You are in prison."

"Satyajit, you are held captive by doubts and worries. Your thoughts are slaves to fear and guilt. I have no such doubt or fear. My thoughts are free." Jai restrained his answer as he heard subtle, distant footsteps. He raised his hand and motioned for silence. Neither he nor Satyajit made a sound until the guard passed and the footsteps faded.

When all they could hear was silence, Jai continued. "Despite these walls, Christ has taken my doubt and fear. He has set me free. You remember the eyes of Jeevan."

Even in the darkness of their cell, Satyajit could not hide

the truth. His breathing betrayed his fear and his pulse was audible. He smacked his lips and tried to swallow because his mouth was so dry.

Jeevan Joseph owned his memory. In the cramped darkness, he felt a swollen and battered hand on his shoulder.

Jai's voice crackled. "The eyes of Jeevan Joseph, did they show any fear?"

*No, they showed peace and resolve.*

"Did his eyes reveal hate or a desire for vengeance?"

*No, they were full of love.*

"And what did he pray?"

Unable to escape the cry of Jeevan, Satyajit answered, "God, send your mercies to my father."

"His father had rejected him, disowned him, and even buried his memory, but Jeevan's dying prayer was for mercy for his father." Jai moaned with pain. "Satyajit, I believe God has chosen you to deliver Jeevan's father. If only we knew who he is. Jeevan had changed his name."

Satyajit interrupted. "His name was Gurdeep. His father is Vishal."

"You know him?"

"He is the reason I am in prison." Satyajit stood and walked toward the tiny window. Saying nothing, he stared at the blank sky. *How do I tell him?*

Jai was puzzled by his silence. "Satyajit, what did he do to cause you to go to prison?"

"He did nothing that affected me. I wanted to visit him, but he is allowed no visitors since he was arrested for a capital crime. I had to be arrested to see him. I am here to bring him mercy. He needs to know that his son remembered him in his dying prayer, and he needs to know that his granddaughter is alive."

"I am confused," Jai said. "What did he do to deserve death?"

Satyajit muttered toward the window. "He is here for killing your son."

"What did you say?"

"Mr. Singh, I'm very sorry. Vishal confessed to leading the mob that killed your son."

Tears erupted. "My son! My son!" He envisioned the terrified eyes of his son, the flames engulfing the car, the screams of his children. Anger and grief raged through his mind, but a strange sense of calm seized him like a gentle hand. He felt himself drawn into his daughter-in-law's prayer, familiar words, words spoken from the Cross, words that understand and transcend. "Father, forgive them for they know not what they do."

Jai felt his words echo through heaven and across time. He collapsed on the floor of his cell, coughing and choking on tears. He could not feel the hands of Satyajit reaching to help him. He did not feel the crushing pain of the hard floor as he fell. He could not feel anything. He was drifting away. His cold hand and his life slipped from earth's grasp. I see my son and his wife. I see my grandchildren. *I see Jeevan. His eyes do call for mercy. If Jeevan could forgive, so must I.*

"Mr. Singh?"

"Satyajit, tell him, I forgive..."

# CHAPTER 33

Late Friday Evening, September 12, 2008
Internet Café

Mitch sat alone. The light of his narrow world was a 17-inch screen. As he pressed the keys furiously, he failed to hear the approaching footsteps of authority.

A timid young voice pleaded. "Sir, we are closing. You must go."

Mitch sighed and forced a smile. "Just logging off." He tossed his coffee in the trash, unfazed by the stern face, stiff black boots and AK-47 standing behind the weary young clerk. Reaching into his pocket, he handed the clerk two crumpled bills.

100 rupees. The weary face brightened. "Thank you, sir."

Mitch patted the clerk's shoulder, and nodded to the officer. "Thank you for letting me stay a little later."

As he retraced his steps back to the Rani Lodge, his thoughts whirled. *What am I doing here? I come to these far-off places. Do I come to escape reality? Do I come to discover, to find something real? Or do I come to write my own story?* Choking on the fading smoke from Power and Steel, he trudged alone.

He stepped over the occasional slumbering beggar as he waded through the dwindling stream of humanity and livestock. The dust and smoke combined to produce a deep orange haze. The deep blue of midnight was fast approaching. From a distant doorway, a splash of light reminded him of home. He could hear the faint memory of his mother's call. *"Mitchell, it's time to come home, son. It's getting dark."* It's getting dark.

* * *

### Mitch Hawkins' Flat
### London
### Friday Evening, September 12, 2008

Only one light shone in the back of the loft, nothing stirring, not a sound. Crawford Hawkins rapped on the door with his knobby fist. "I told you he wouldn't be home, and we should call before stopping by."

Margaret Hawkins' knowing eyes peered over her wiry specks. "Crawford, you should know better after 54 years. Something is wrong, terribly wrong. When I feel it, I know it, and you should know it's true."

Mrs. Hawkins was not a worrier. She was a devout woman of faith. Lacking the words to persuade her son, but she never lacked discernment.

Mr. Hawkins recognized her stubborn look of unwavering conviction from decades of peering through the windows of her deep and tranquil soul. He knew she was right, but this dreary night, her look was different. He could see uncertainty and dread.

Margaret peered through the etched glass. *It's getting dark, Mitchell. Where are you?*

Crawford wrestled his keys from his pocket and twisted the lock. He entered the lonely flat with his wife close behind him. The floor creaked as he marched down the dark corridor. "Margaret, would you turn the light?"

Nothing special about the flat, their son was, indeed, utilitarian and practical to a fault. The cramped kitchen had a small table with one chair.

"He surely can't call this a kitchen."

"He has an icebox and a microwave," her husband said.

Off the kitchen was a small study with a cozy oak desk, a sturdy recliner, cluttered shelves, an overflowing waste can, and the hum of Mitch's snoozing desktop.

"What is that hum?"

Crawford bent to look beneath the desk. "Well, he's left his computer running." As he rose, his hand inadvertently depressed the space bar. The hum became a whir. The monitor came to life. "Margaret, come and see. It's Mitchell's internet page."

\* \* \*

The Skeptic Sole
Mitch Hawkins' Blog

Mitch Hawkins here, beating a path across the dust of Orissa, India. What is it that stirs the human emotion, causing one person to disregard another? In this dry, "God-forsaken" land, it is religion that scorches the mind, sucking even the tiniest vestiges of reason. Hindu Devotees pretend to rely on their millions of deities. They put their faith in flames and fists, using violence to annihilate Christianity. The weary and impoverished Dalit Christians confound reason by retreating into the jungles and hills to find refuge, or, worse yet, they succumb to the extremist vendetta, becoming martyrs of their faith.

Faith in what? What kind of faith causes one to hang all hope on an unseen, unhearing, unkind, unbelievable god who blithely ignores the pain of his followers? If this god is all-knowing, all-seeing, and all-powerful, then he must apathetically disregard the cries of his children...

\* \* \*

Heartache drizzled down Margaret Hawkins' face. "I can't read anymore. Crawford, what has happened to our son? What did we do wrong?" His gentle face melted through her veil of tears.

Crawford placed his sturdy hand on her shoulder. "Margie, do you believe those words? Is your God all-knowing but uncaring?" His eyes spoke to her heart. "No, of course you don't. God reads those words as well. He is Mitch's father just as He is yours and mine. He brought you here to read them. If you know and see those painful cries of your son and if those words pierce your heart, think about our Father in heaven, how those words must pierce Him."

Margaret's eyes gleamed. "He wanted me to see and know. He does hear the soul-stirring cry of our son." *He hears the cries Mitchell screams in silence.* "Crawford, I know that Mitchell will know the truth one day."

"And the truth will set him free."

"Crawford, can I communicate with Mitchell somehow through this machine?"

Crawford chuckled. "Of course. *'Comment.'* Click. There you are, my dear. Type to your heart's content."

Margaret entered the portal to Mitch's world. As she typed, she spoke to God. Prayer emitted like a luscious fragrance from her lips. She caressed the heart of God with deeply felt words. Her hands cradled her tears as she begged God for wisdom. "Father, give me the words."

*Forget about words, let your heart speak; let it scream like a mother who has given her son to God.*

Her fingers flew across the keys as she began to type.

# CHAPTER 34

Early Morning, Saturday, September 13, 2008
Rani Lodge, Sambalpur

Mitch opened his tired eyes in frustration. The flat, white ceiling looked the same as it had the hour before and the hour before that. Shadowed with a rare glint of light, the lines between the tiles numbed his mind. *Why can't I sleep? What is wrong with me? None of this should be getting to me.* Mitch could not escape the continual replay of Andrea's words. *"I believe, Mitch, that when you are ready to honestly seek God, you will find Him and know Him."*

*Why do I need to seek God, if God is so great, why doesn't he just reveal Himself to me? I don't want to seek God.*

A faint, almost imperceptible voice within him said, *"You don't want to seek God, because you are running from Him."*

Disregarding the thought, Mitch bolted out of bed and flipped on his laptop. He had done his work at the Internet Café to avoid any intrusions from Andrea and Marci, but in his room, in the middle of the night, he was alone. There was no Satyajit, no all-seeing God, and no mother to scold him or tuck him in bed. *It's just me and Miss Flavor of my whatever mood.*

As his mind began to burn through fantasyland, his screen woke up where he left it, on his blog. *Comment? Wow, somebody has already hit my blog.*

\* \* \*

Comment

Mitchell, it may seem to you that God is uncaring, distant, and apathetic. You could think the same about me. I seem like I am a world away, here in London, but I read your words. I see your photographs. I can even watch your videos, but unless you read my words, you do not even know that I am here, but you know me, and you know that I care for you deeply, and I respect you, even when we can't agree. You are my son. I love you, no matter what. No matter where you are or what you are doing, I love you. What do you need to touch, see, or hear to know that I love you? You just know, don't you? You know that I love you. I have always loved you, and I will forever love you.

Margaret Hawkins, your mother

\* \* \*

Mitch slammed shut his laptop and plopped on the bed, staring in disbelief. He tried to silence his mind and fall into the trance of tracing the ceiling tiles. It was no use. His mind took flight, dashing wildly through every time his mother had been right. He knew she loved him. She always loved him.

*She's right.* He tried to stifle the thought, but her words kept pressing. The ceiling tiles were no help. They were too ordered just as she was. He could not focus on the ceiling tiles. He shifted his thoughts to Marci. He cast aside any inhibitions imagining her luscious form and her sweet smile, but the girl in his mind kept nodding her head.

*She's right.* The thought was screaming, pounding through his skull like footsteps in pursuit of his soul.

*I've got to get out of here.* He turned to the window. *It's too dark yet. There is no way I'm going out there.* He popped a sleeping pill. *Maybe I can make those tiles look like sheep.* He smirked in the darkness. *If I were a Christian, I would pray for sleep.*

# CHAPTER 35

Dawn on Saturday, September 13, 2008
Rani Lodge

A golden halo grew around the curtain. The sunlight awakened Marci. She looked at Andrea resting peacefully. *How does she sleep so soundly with so much distress around us?* Marci quietly slipped out of bed. Drawn to the sunlight, she peered out the window.

*Such a peaceful garden in such a hostile world.* The bougainvillea drew a smile. Their petals bursting. Papaya and mango seemed to ripen before her eyes.

*Life goes on.* Marci shook her head in wonder. As she opened the window, she heard the familiar dissonance of horns and motors. Her heart burst as she anticipated the violence to come. She imagined everyone knowing, but doing nothing. *We've got to stop it. We've got to do something.*

Marci turned to discover Andrea rousing slowly. "You're awake."

Andrea squinted. "Marci, we have to warn the Christians in Gourpali."

"How in the world? Do we just walk into town and start telling people they are in danger? Do we shout 'Hey, extremists are coming tomorrow to steal, burn your church, and drive you out of your town.'?"

Andrea's eyes shifted back and forth across the marble floor. *No, we can't just walk into town. Not everyone in that town*

163

*is Christian. The extremists would, no doubt, get tipped off.* "Marci, we've got to know who the Christians are. If we go into that village and start spouting off about an attack, the extremists would find out and simply attack on a different day."

"If only Satyajit wasn't in jail, he could pose as an extremist youth, scouting the village. Instead of finding the Christians, we would discover their betrayers."

"That sounds great, but Satyajit's got two more days behind bars."

"Wait, Andrea, we've got to get back to the hospital. Surely someone there will know a way to get word to the Christians in Gourpali."

# CHAPTER 36

Saturday Morning
September 13, 2008
Gourpali

A loving caress awakened Indu. She welcomed the smile of her new mother, Chandrika. Her morning could not be brighter. The sunlight on Chandrika's face softened her heartache. She smiled at the gentle kiss on her cheek but frowned as Chandrika stood and backed away, picking up her bag.

"Where are you going?"

"I must go to the hospital, Indu. Anila is here. She will stay with you. Don't be afraid." *We are so close to Sambalpur. Surely our village is safe.*

Chandrika's adopted mother Anila shuffled into the room. The sun and the years had not been kind. Once a radiant beauty, her flesh was withered and bent. Despite her troubles, her heart pulsed with love.

Anila's children abandoned her when she became a Christian, but she found a new family with Chandrika. Love healed her fractured life. Her crinkled face and hazy eyes bore a fearless smile.

Her smooth leathery hand patted Chandrika's cheek. "Don't worry. Indu will be safe with me." Her smile widened as she gazed on her new granddaughter.

Indu's eyes followed Chandrika through the doorway. She froze with her eyes glued to the empty door, and her heart imprisoned by empty memories. She blinked at the gentle touch of Anila. "Why does she have to go?"

"She must go for you. You are the daughter she has prayed for."

# CHAPTER 37

Saturday Morning, September 13, 2008
The Road to All Saints Hospital

The sun followed her bus from Gourpali to Sambalpur. Chandrika walked to the main road each day to wait for the bus. She would squeeze into the mass of people trying to force their way through life. A hot, sticky and boldly aromatic ride was not the best for a nurse, but it was the best she could do. The twenty-kilometer commute took almost a full hour.

Unaffected by the tiresome journey, she popped out of the tight bus like a seed escaping an overstuffed pod. As she bounded down the lane toward the hospital, she heard foot-steps and two familiar voices growing closer behind her.

Recognizing the voices as Marci and Andrea, she stopped and whirled around to meet their smiles. Instead she saw meas-urable tension in their faces. "Andrea, what's wrong? Why are you going back to the hospital?"

Andrea clutched Chandrika's arm. She glanced up and back along the lane, waiting for people to pass by. She pulled her aside and leaned in closely. "Chandrika, something terrible is about to happen. Extremists are planning to attack Gourpali tomorrow during worship. Do you know any Christians in Gour-pali? We have to warn them."

Streams of sadness revealed Chandrika's answer. *Why did I think we would be safe? Will this bitter land always steal my joy?* Her eyes stared beyond Andrea and Marci. "I live in Gourpali."

Andrea's heart leapt with fear, but she clung tightly to unwavering hope. "Chandrika, God brought us to this moment. If we failed to reach you, how could we warn the believers in your village? Marci and I could not walk into town and tell them. We don't know who the Christians are, we would certainly alert the extremists, but you, you know the Christians, and you can warn them."

Like a waxing moon, joy returned to Chandrika's face. She gulped and nodded, thwarting tears and almost laughing a smile. *Lord, thank you for bringing these angels to protect me, and to protect Indu and Anila.* "I know all the Christians in Gourpali. I must warn them now." Chandrika turned to head back toward the main road.

Andrea asked, "Chandrika, what about the hospital? Won't they worry when you don't show up for work?"

Chandrika stopped. Looking back down the lane toward the hospital, she said, "I'm not sure I will be able to work all day, feeling as I do, but you are right. I must work as though nothing is wrong, and then warn them this evening, but I am so worried for Indu and Anila. I wish I could warn them now."

Indu? Andrea's heart stopped at the sound. "Chandrika, do you mean Pastor Joseph's daughter?"

"Yes, I have taken her home to live with Anila and me."

"Anila?"

"She is like a mother to me. I have lived with her since my parents were killed."

Marci interrupted. "Forget about the hospital. You should go to her, and -."

"No. No, Marci! Andrea is right. If I do not work as scheduled, who knows what suspicions may be raised? You pray for Indu and Anila, and please pray for me as well. Now I must go. I will warn the others this evening after my shift. May God bless and protect you."

# CHAPTER 38

Saturday Noon, September 13, 2008
Rani Lodge

Mitch awakened late after his restless night. He lay on his bed staring at the ceiling tiles. *What detailed etching. It's amazing what you can see in the right light.* His brief insight disappeared into sclerotic skepticism.

He mechanically rose to face another pointless day. He suppressed his mother's words. The distant voice within screamed like a child ten miles away, unheard and ignored, as though non-existent. For one brief moment, the child in the hollow of his soul tried to whisper, I love you too, mum. But his embittered, stiffened ears failed to hear.

As he sat up, his eyes begrudged the sleeping laptop on his desk. *Why did she have to read my blog? I am a grown man, yet my mother is still watching and listening. How did she read my blog so soon?* The thought struck him, *she doesn't even own a computer. She must have gone to my flat. She was using my computer. I must have left my webpage open, but why would she go to my house on a Friday night?*

The unshaven face of Mitch Hawkins reflected dissatisfaction and puzzled distraction as he studied his own eyes. His skeptic's shell was beginning to crack, though he remained unaware, unbelieving. Foam, mixed with black and gray stubble, plopped into the sink as life returned to his face.

# CHAPTER 39

Vishal's prison cell

No mirror could reflect the grief from Vishal's stubbled face. With nothing and no one to comfort him, he slowly sank into despair. Worn and weary, his heart already broken, his tears spent, he slumped in the corner of his cell.

He did not hear the distant clanging of bars, nor the shuffling of steps. When the footsteps halted, the guard rapped on the bars. "You did not eat your supper or your breakfast."

Vishal lifted his head and stared with indifference. He closed his eyes and dropped his head without the least utterance.

The guard rebuffed his shallow disregard. "Are you wishing to die? You need to eat."

"I am already dead. Food has no value to a dead man, so leave me alone. Let me rest in peace."

"You may wish you were dead, but you are not dead. Your judgment is not final until it is carried out, so I will not leave you in peace. I will stay here until you have eaten."

Vishal nudged his bowl. "Stay as long as you like, but I will not eat."

# CHAPTER 40

Saturday, September 13, 2008
Road to Gourpali

*What a long day!* Chandrika couldn't remember a single patient from her shift. Her mind focused on Indu and Anila and nothing else. She trembled as she walked toward her bus stop. Tears swelled as she sniffled and swallowed, trying to suppress her fears. She was more heart-broken than afraid. The threat of violence awakened every painful memory of that day when her parents were taken from her forever. *I can't let that happen to Indu. I can't.*

Waiting for the bus, Chandrika was covered in a mix of dust and sweat, her face drizzled with tears. She stood amid the usual crowd at her usual stop, but she felt unusually alone. She did not feel the pushing and prodding as people packed into the bus. She did not feel their stares. She floated like a stick in a stream and slumped into a window seat.

The ride seemed to last for hours, although it was no longer than usual. Her face pressed against the jaded window, Chandrika could see the feeble hints of her village. The thought of walking the rest of the way home seemed insufferable under the weight of her fear. *Oh, God, please protect Indu and Anila.*

The bus groaned to a stop. Numb to her surroundings, Chandrika marched off the bus along with many others from her village. The clanky diesel sputtered its black smoke, marring the orange horizon. As the bus rambled away, Chandrika stood alone and empty, despite the small crowd about her. Through her brooding stare, she imagined her village roaring with flames. She imagined sparks dusting the sky, clouds retreating from their heat, and a mixed chorus of cries and jeers ringing through the fields.

Her morbid thoughts fizzled with the flames dying in her mind. She clenched her teeth, set her eyes on Gourpali, and began her march home.

# CHAPTER 41

Saturday, September 13, 2008
Internet Café, Sambalpur

*Well, it's not Starbucks,* Andrea mused as she waded through the stream of people crowding the tiny café. Spiced chai and incense created an overwhelming but welcome alternative to any other fragrance in such a tight space. She elbowed and wiggled toward an open PC.

She browsed a few favorites, and then clicked into Marci's blog. She read the most recent post and perused the four trailing comments. *Oh, where do I start?* Her heart was swollen with emotion and teetering on the edge of exhaustion. She clicked on the comment from her former youth pastor.

"Marci and Andrea, what are you guys thinking? India? Wow! I'm so proud of you. I always knew that God had great plans for you. I am praying for you, for God's protection over you, and that he would bless our brothers and sisters in India through you."

As Andrea reflected on his words of encouragement, she began to ardently type her own comments. As her thoughts unfolded, hurried reflections darted across her monitor and growing shadows encroached. The tiny café emptied quickly except for the stiff black boots surrounding her. Andrea abruptly ended her thought and clicked, "submit." As the page loaded, she felt a firm grip around her arm.

A trio of policemen surrounded her. "You must come with us." They curtly escorted her through the vacated café and out the door. They hurried her into their police car and sped away.

Andrea knew enough to remain silent. *God, I know you are with me. Give me today what I need to make it through this day. I don't know what that is, but I have to trust you. I can't do this.* Life blurred as the world rushed past her window. She could not fix her eyes or her thoughts on any one thing.

Andrea puzzled as the police car slowed for a herd of cows crowding the road. *The jail is the other way. Oh, Dear Jesus, where are they taking me?* Fear pounded through her heart as Sambalpur slipped away.

The officer in the passenger's seat turned around and stretched a wicked smile. "Do you want to know where we are taking you?"

Andrea bowed her head without a word. She suppressed the rolling nausea and hid her fear behind closed eyes.

The officer mocked her resolve. "Ha! You think you are under arrest. No, no, of course not. We are simply taking you to meet some of your friends."

*Oh, God! What have they done with Marci and Mitch?* When the car turned eastward out of Sambalpur, Andrea realized the painful truth. *Gourpali. They're taking me to Gourpali.* She imagined herself thrown into an unsuspecting crowd of worshippers and set ablaze.

As the car stopped, whirls of dust swept past her window. The two officers in front climbed out of the vehicle, leaving Andrea and the other officer in the car.

Andrea glanced at his fidgety hands. *He is trembling and so young.*

While watching the other two officers arguing, Andrea

mustered the courage to speak. She strained the words, "May I..."

The young officer brusquely silenced her with his hand over her mouth. "Shh. I am trying to listen."

Andrea watched through the shadowed wood as the two arguing officers drew closer. Their Hindi meant nothing to Andrea, but their anger was palpable and needed no translation.

The officer beside her, warned. "You are a Christian, an American? India is Hindu. We have no place for you here. You should not have come." The night compounded the gloom in his eyes. A steel blue glow outlined his threatening stare. "Your only chance to leave this place is if you apologize for bribing these poor people into conversion."

Andrea protested. "But I've never been here."

"No, but I know you have been to Pahireju." His disturbing eyes pressed her, looking for fear. "We thought we had killed all the Christians there until you came. Now, most all who are left have converted. We blame you, and you will pay for what you have done."

Fear and doubt churned within Andrea's heart, testing her resolve. She doused the pesky flames of uncertainty with prayer. *Oh, Lord, help me. Give me the words. Speak through me. Guide my steps, and protect me. Somehow get me out of this.*

She faced the police officer. "I don't understand. I have not bribed anyone. I did go to Pahireju, but all we did was help clean up the mess and bury the dead."

The officer grabbed her arm and pulled her out of the car. Almost dragging her, he plodded into the silent darkness. Rare flickers of light through the trees failed to guide his steps.

Andrea pleaded, "Don't you have a light or something?"

15,000 candle-power and an instant headache interrupted her sarcasm.

She could not see anything for several minutes as she stumbled along under the officer's control. She could not tell when he had turned off his flashlight. Her complete loss of control and disorientation only added to her fear. Each step felt like a thunderous jolt to her pounding head. The ripples of each tiny earthquake shook within, awakening her stomach to join in the fight.

She jumped with a start at the lead officer's piercing voice.

"We found them. Leave your light off, and come with us."

Andrea's headache diminished as the four of them continued their journey in darkness. She felt thankful for the stillness of night. As she walked, distant specks of light slowly grew into focus. She shed unseen, silent tears as she gazed at the starry expanse. Despite her circumstance, she could not escape the wonder of her Creator. *None can measure your greatness, oh God! You are God, no matter what. I trust you for every step in this dark world.*

She could not see her feet beneath her. She followed the young officer's tugging grasp. As the rare lights grew nearer, their troupe walked more slowly, almost without a sound. Andrea could see the faint hints of tiny houses. An eerie feeling of looming death swept over her as they entered into the humble village. Most of the tiny homes were completely black. The wafting aroma of smoldering incense grew as they softly strode down the dirt street. She collided with two of the officers as they stopped in front of her.

The first officer leaned into Andrea. Nose-to-nose, he whispered tersely, spraying his breath in her face. "This will be your home for tonight. We will be watching you. If you try to leave, this night will become your last."

# CHAPTER 42

Saturday, September 13, 2008
11:30 PM
Rani Lodge

Mitch walked into the dining area to see Marci sitting alone, studying her napkin and wringing her thumbs. "Where's Andrea?"

Marci startled. She shook her head and choked on her tears. "I don't know."

Mitch was struck by the fear in her eyes. "What do you mean, you don't know?"

"She left for the Internet Café over three hours ago." Marci's eyes glazed with dread. Her further attempt to speak collapsed into muttering sobs. She felt Mitch beside her. His hand on her shoulder gave her strength to continue. "I left to go check on her. I had a bad feeling. I don't know why I ever let her go by herself."

"Go on." Mitch gently stroked her hair, lifting it over her ear to reveal her face.

Marci composed herself. "As I neared the Internet Café, I saw a policeman standing watch outside. When I noticed the café was dark, I panicked. It apparently closed early, but I could not see Andrea anywhere."

Mitch pressed her. "Did you see anything else?" He watched the wheels turning as she mentally retraced her steps.

Marci gasped and swallowed. "As I walked closer, I kept back from the street, hiding in the shadows. I remember a police car driving past. I thought nothing of it at the time, but its headlights were off." She looked at Mitch. "There was no one in the passenger's seat, but I saw an officer in the back seat. Oh, Mitch! What if Andrea was with them?"

Mitch's thoughts raced with Marci's. *Oh, god, they've taken Andrea.* Deep in his thoughts, he had known these two naïve girls would bring him his story. He knew they would fall into serious trouble, completely unprepared and unaware. That knowledge drove him to join them in their journey, but he had never dreamed he would grow so close to them, so fond of them, so in love with what they had that he did not. If he had a faith, it would have been shaken. As it was, he felt numb, stunned by his surprise and fear at Andrea's presumed abduction.

Once again, life became more to him than momentary and meaningless. Andrea meant something to him. Marci's tears meant something to him. He could not acknowledge the voice within, but something deep in his repressed soul screamed, "You were meant to live for so much more."

Marci could see the drowning soul in his eyes, but she fixed her mind on Andrea. She continued to recount her past hour. "I know it's not unusual to see several cars at night with their lights off, but not a police car."

Uncharacteristically, Mitch drew Marci into his arms to calm her.

She drenched him with tears. "Mitch, I'm scared. I'm afraid something terrible has happened. I know they've taken Andrea. Oh, God! I hope she's all right."

"We should go to the jail to see what has happened."

Marci pushed him back to see his face. "But you said we

could not trust the police."

"Right you are, but, even though they will surely deny any knowledge, we must let them know that we know, and we must make them aware that your embassy has been informed."

"But we haven't informed anyone."

"Not yet. We must do it now before we go."

Mitch led Marci by the hand to his room. He relished the way she grasped his hand. She was more enticing than ever. He knew she needed him, and for the first time in a long time, he felt like he needed someone as well. His self-reliance was melting in her palm.

Opening the door, he paused as he noticed his laptop slightly askew. Mitch Hawkins was a classic artist: creative genius, disorganized, full of ideas and arrogance, starting many projects, finishing only those that grow and come together, discarding the rest, but pathologically organized about his personal items. In particular, he prized none more than his cameras and his computers. He knew, when he saw his laptop slightly rotated, that someone had been in his room, on his computer. He combed the room, looking for any other disturbances.

Marci asked, "What is it? What's wrong?"

"Someone has been in my room."

Mitch grabbed her hand once again, and took her to her room. Her door was open. Nothing seemed amiss inside.

"Mitch, we never ever leave our door open."

Mitch pressed his lips to her ear and whispered urgently. "Get your things, and Andrea's! We have to leave now!"

"Where are we going?"

"The only place we know is safe - the hospital."

Mitch had never packed so quickly in his life. He led Marci toward the stairs. From the stairwell, he could hear the desk clerk. Peeking around the stairway, he recognized the patented boots and beige of the police. Wheeling around he pulled Marci back down the hallway toward the side entrance. Coming down the stairs, he spied a policeman outside the door. His heart skipped a beat. Sweat beaded on his face. "Back up. Back up the stairs. We have to sneak out a window. As quickly as you can, take only what you can fit into your backpack. Strap it on tightly. We will climb down the side of the hotel."

As Marci rearranged her things, she felt like she was saying goodbye to the things she was leaving. *I will never see this room again.* She stuffed her Bible and her journal into her already overstuffed bag.

While she scrambled to repack, Mitch tied sheets together. He fixed one end to the hand crank on the window. As he finished, they sighed and looked at each other.

As Mitch reached down for his bag, Marci grasped his face and met him eye-to-eye. She drew his face into hers and said, "I know we are going to make it. I know it."

Somehow, Mitch knew as well. Mitch Hawkins, who never accepted anything without "knowing," Mitch knew. *We are going to make it.* He surprised Marci with a kiss on the cheek and leaned through the window. "I'll go first."

Marci offered a quick, silent prayer for the hand crank as Mitch slid down the side of the hotel. Unlike Western hotels, there was no well-lit parking lot behind the Rani Lodge, only a garden of shadows.

As they tip-toed beyond the edge of the hotel yard, Mitch whispered. "We will have to keep walking. I don't really know what is going on, but I know we are in danger. We can't think about using our car. I'm sure they are watching it. Until we get back to Delhi, we would be wise to avoid using our credit cards as well." Mitch's nervous rambling failed to build confidence. "We honestly don't want to be seen anywhere. Hopefully, we can find Chandrika at the hospital. We know her. We can trust her."

# CHAPTER 43

All Saints Hospital
Sunday, September 14, 2008
1:00 AM

Parched, thirsty for sleep, and running on fumes, Mitch stood with Marci on the road near the hospital. "I don't trust this lane tonight. Let's continue to the north. We can cut back through some yards and alleys and weave our way back to the hospital."

Marci gripped his hand in silent agreement. She imagined a gang in the bushes, waiting to pounce on anyone going to the hospital during the night. Fear had grown into paranoia.

Their zigzagging maze eventually led them to the dimly lit hospital. They followed their fear around the side of the hospital. Clinging to shadows, Marci and Mitch approached All Saints from behind. Peering into an office window, they saw Naomi, a nurse whom they recognized.

Mitch crouched beneath the window. He gently tapped on the glass with no response. He tapped again. Spying over the windowsill, his eyes met the startled nurse, Naomi.

Naomi opened the window. "What's wrong?"

"Leave the window open, and turn off the light."

Mitch climbed through the window and lifted Marci behind him. Without a sound, he closed the window and the blinds.

Naomi switched on the lamp. "What is happening?"

Marci collapsed into a chair. "We believe the police have taken Andrea. They searched our rooms and waited for us to leave the hotel. We sneaked out a window and came here. We need your help."

Naomi crinkled her brow. "How can I help?"

Mitch asked, "Does the hospital have an internet connection?"

"Yes, but it's slow and not always reliable."

"We need to contact the American Embassy."

Naomi puzzled. "Why would the police take Andrea? Are you sure the police took her?"

Marci drew a huge sigh. "We discovered a flyer promoting an attack on Christians in Gourpali. The attack is going to take place during worship this morning. We think Andrea's disappearance is related."

"I do not understand. How would the police know?"

"Marci, someone must have overheard your conversation with Chandrika."

Fear swept Naomi's face. "You told Chandrika!"

"Andrea and I were on our way to the hospital to find her. We saw her walking from the bus stop. We told her about the attack. She said she would warn the Christians in Gourpali. We thought she would raise fewer suspicions than we would."

Marci gasped. "Oh my! Mitch you're right. Someone must have heard us. We were talking in the lane. People were passing by. I didn't notice anyone lingering or listening, but at one point, Chandrika looked past me. She pulled us close, and we softened our voices. I don't know who she saw, but I didn't think they could have heard anything."

Mitch paced while listening. He paused and placed both hands on Naomi's shoulders. "Chandrika lives in Gourpali, doesn't she?"

Naomi nodded.

"She must have seen someone she recognized, probably someone from her village."

Marci said, "A Hindu extremist? But how would they connect anything to Andrea? And why would they take her?"

Mitch gritted his teeth. *How did they make the connection?* He unleashed his frustrations on a loose sheet of paper from Naomi's desk.

Naomi cleared her throat. "Don't destroy that lab report!"

"Lab report! I'm sorry." Staring at the wad in his hand, his thoughts took him back to the front desk at the Rani Lodge and the crumpled flyer announcing the attack. "Naomi, I need to get on the internet."

She directed him to the nearest computer. She logged in and stepped aside.

Mitch googled. "Here it is! http://kolkata.usconsulate.gov."

# CHAPTER 44

Prison
Sunday, September 14, 2008
1:00 AM

The guard's metered march was followed by another pair of footsteps. "I've brought you a visitor." The guard almost laughed as he blinded Satyajit with his flashlight. "Is that him?"

"Yes, Palash, that is him."

Satyajit struggled to hold his stomach as he recognized the voice of Natraj.

"My friend, Satyajit." The ashen defeat in Satyajit's face brought a sardonic smile to Natraj.

"Why are you here?" Satyajit moaned.

"Oh, my friend, I am here to get you out of prison. You don't want to miss our party at Gourpali, do you? You know we are going to build a great fire. I thought perhaps you would like to pour the kerosene. You did so well in Pahireju."

Palash unlocked the door.

Natraj stepped proudly into the cell. "Everyone will be there... even your new friend, Andrea."

Satyajit collapsed. His mind flashed through the images of the past few days, how his whole world had turned upside down almost overnight. In his sickened terror, he wretched on the floor.

Palash thrust his boot into Satyajit's chest. "I do not know why your friend Natraj has a second thought for you. I would leave you here with this dying fool, but Natraj wants to find out who your real friends are."

Palash dragged Satyajit from the cell. "I am sure the judge will not mind if we end your sentence early."

Satyajit offered one last glance at Jai Singh. *He is free. He is at peace. God, I pray you are with me as you were with Mr. Singh.*

"No more thoughts for the old man." Palash grabbed his arm and yanked him out of the cell.

The door slammed shut, but Satyajit could hear the voice of Jai Singh. *Always trust Him, my son.*

# CHAPTER 45

Sunday, September 14, 2008
3:30 AM in India
5:00 PM, Saturday in Goose Creek, South Carolina

Marci's mother could not get home quickly enough. Pouncing on her computer, she brought up Marci's blog. *Hmm. There's no new post. Oh! But there is a new comment.*

\*\*\*

### Andrea's Comment

These past few days have swept around us like a whirl-wind. How could so much emotion and energy be stirred and spent in so little time? I will never forget the resolve and the stubborn joy of my Christian brothers and sisters in Orissa. These humble saints peacefully bear the cross of Christ, suffering with Him and for Him.

Despite their pain, they pray for us, and they pray for those who are persecuting them. I am writing to plead for your prayers as well. We have learned of an impending attack on a nearby village. The attack is set to take place during Sunday morning worship. The villagers are unaware. Please pray that we can alert them in time.

Someone is behind me

\*\*\*

Marci's mother sank in her chair. *Oh, dear God! Her message stopped so abruptly.* She fought the ensuing tears, held up her left hand, and waved for everything to stop. She covered her mouth to hide her trembling lips. "Something's terribly wrong. Andrea knows better than to leave us hanging like that. She would have gotten back online, or tried to call or email or something. Oh, dear God, please protect her!" Frazzled she realized, Andrea surely would have called her mother.

Leena scrambled through the prompts on her cell phone trying to find Andrea's home phone. The phone vibrated out of her trembling hands and hummed across her desk. *317! That's Indiana.*

"Hello."

"Mrs. Beaufort, this is Maureen Sturgis, Andrea's mother."

"I'm so glad you called. I am terribly worried about our girls."

"You must have read their blog as well. I have already called the State Department. I didn't have much luck there, but I have a friend in London who is very well connected and might be able to help us."

# CHAPTER 46

Sunday, September 14, 2008
3:30 AM
Vishal's Prison Cell

Vishal awakened to the quiet rattle of a guard opening a prison door. Shuffling of feet, muffled voices, and approaching footsteps could not stir his curiosity. He should have wondered why they would be moving a prisoner, but nothing mattered anymore. He heard but did not acknowledge.

The guard leading Satyajit, whispered to Natraj. "We will take him out the long way. The fewer who know, the better."

As the trio passed Vishal's cell, Satyajit paused and turned toward Vishal. He stood firm against the fierce poking in his back. "May I have a moment with this prisoner?"

Everything within the guard said, No! But his hands released him, and he heard himself say, "Yes, five minutes." The guard opened the door and nudged Satyajit into the cell. Closing the door, he stepped away, motioning Natraj to follow.

Natraj glared at the guard, puzzled. "What are you doing?"

"What can it hurt? They are both going to die."

Vishal sat in silence. He eyed Satyajit with contempt while Natraj and the guard walked further down the corridor. "You are wasting your time. I have nothing to say to you or anyone."

Satyajit opened his mouth, but Vishal interrupted, "My

life was already over before I met you, but I took your punishment in prison. I will die in your place, but that was not enough. You had to destroy all that was left of my heart by telling me about my son. You resurrected him in my mind, only to kill him once again. There is nothing more you can do to hurt me now."

"I am so sorry. I did not come to cause to pain. I came because of your son's dying prayer. His eyes still haunt me. I can still hear him, 'God, send your mercies to my father.'"

"How can you call this mercy?"

"Vishal, the other day, I was taken from you before I could tell you, your granddaughter survived the attack."

"My granddaughter?"

"Her name is Indu. She is beautiful. I can see her in your eyes. I pray that you will somehow be able to see her, and although your son is dead, you need to know he never forgot you." Satyajit spoke quickly as he heard Natraj and the guard approaching. "Even in his death, he cried his last words for you. How could I not answer that kind of devotion?"

Vishal sobbed. "I rejected my son when he accepted Christ, but even in his death, he remembered me. My wife..." His voice broke into a silent scream as the guard opened the cell door.

"Let's go."

\* \* \*

Silent footsteps led Satyajit out of the prison. He remained hushed, his hands bound with ropes. An occasional rap on the head guided him in the right direction.

As they rounded the street corner, the guard looked over his shoulder, watching the prison fade into shadow. When darkness replaced the prison, he signaled down the street with a flashlight.

Satyajit gasped as he was slowly surrounded by familiar eyes and bandana-covered faces. He shuddered as the guard disappeared toward the prison. A restless surge rose in his stomach, quickly followed Natraj's fist. One blow followed another, and unbridled pummeling ensued. Natraj's face faded to black.

The impassioned mob dragged his limp body to a small pick-up truck. Bloodied and disfigured, Satyajit was barely breathing as they slung him into the truck bed. "Why don't we just kill him and leave him?"

"Satyajit was my friend. I have something special planned for him."

# CHAPTER 47

Sunday, September 14, 2008
4:00 AM
Gourpali

Andrea sat in darkness in a strange house. She heard some-one breathing. She held her breath and listened. *It must be one of the officers. The other two must be outside.* A brief flash of head-lights swept the room. Andrea stiffened as the officer scrambled to the door. She slid to the glassless window and spied a flurry of shadows running toward the car, arms waving.

The lead officer grumbled. "What is that idiot doing? Turn off the headlights!"

As she stumbled in the shadows, one last gleam from the headlights revealed a photo on the wall. Her heart leapt at the glimpse of two smiles, *a mother and her daughter.* The picture drew her thoughts to Chandrika and Indu.

*Lord, please protect Chandrika and Indu. Watch over the Christians in this village.* Andrea stepped toward the darkened picture, but there was not enough light, and she lost the image in her shadow.

Andrea closed her eyes. Her thoughts raced, worrying over Marci and Mitch, wondering how Satyajit was handling prison, and hoping God would work a miracle and somehow save the Christians in Gourpali. She prayed until her thoughts tumbled over one another. *Oh, God, please protect Marci and Mitch, and give strength to Satyajit and Vishal.*

As Andrea prayed for Vishal, a chill overwhelmed her. She

was startled by a sudden, gripping fear. She imagined Vishal, alone in his cell. She shuddered at the image of his lifeless body suspended from the ceiling. Eyes wide open, she prayed aloud. "Dear God, please bring your light to Vishal." *It doesn't matter what happens to me. I know I will be with you no matter what, but I don't feel the same assurance for Vishal. I don't know his heart. I don't know what's going through his mind, but I know he needs you right now. Strengthen his weary soul with your peace. Draw him close, Oh God. Draw him close.*

The officer's flashlight cast a startling glare on the wall photo. Andrea could see the smiling mother and daughter. The gracious smiles and simple beauty seemed so out of place. The light flashed and faded. Footsteps shuffled from the window to the open door. Andrea turned to face the young officer.

He shone his light and said, "She was beautiful."

*Was?* Andrea felt heart-broken at his words. *I can't ask him who she was or what happened. He is dying to tell me. It's going to be brutal.*

Although she tried to resist, a voice within, prompted her to ask, "Did you know her?"

The smiling officer was caught off-guard by the question. He expected, "Who was she?" or "What happened to her?" not, "Did you know her?" His mind raced to his childhood days when he would sit on the ground with the other children. A beautiful goddess would speak strange words to them, words of love and compassion. *We must carry one another's burdens.* They would sing songs about hope and faith. She told the children stories about Jesus, and then, their reward for listening was a bag of rice and some vitamins. He loved those days. Her tender eyes enlightened and bedazzled him. He loved her soothing voice and the loving words that poured from her heart.

At home, he heard a different voice, consternation and

thankless acceptance. His father would lift the rice from his arms as though removing a burden. *Father, why are you so angry? He wondered, but dared not ask.*

One day the answer came. In an unguarded moment of delight, the young boy greeted his father, saying "Jai Masih Ki."

Rage swelled in his father's eyes, and his heart erupted. "These Christians bring their Western traditions, their lies and deceit into our country and our village. Our wells are dry and our crops fail because of them, and now they poison the minds of our children."

The beautiful woman vanished from his childhood. Never again was he allowed to return to see her. Occasionally, from a distance, he would catch her smile, but she and her husband had been warned. "Stay away from my son. You know what will happen if you don't."

Love and longing slowly turned to bitterness as he swallowed the words of his father. Hatred churned within, growing as he grew. *Did you know her?*

"Yes, I knew her." The young officer brushed past Andrea. He lifted the picture off the wall, his eyes caressing the enchanting smiles. Tears mixed with rage as he flung the picture against the far wall. The sudden fury and shattering of glass shook Andrea to her core.

Fear gripped its twisted spines around her throat. She choked as she tried to swallow. Andrea backed against the wall. Fear commanded her thoughts. *He is capable of anything.*

# CHAPTER 48

Sunday, September 14, 2008
4:30 AM
Vishal's Prison Cell

*"God, send your mercies to my father."*

Vishal clung to those words. He dug through the buried memories of his son. He paused on the memory of his son's family photo. He studied each face as he fought exhaustion. He imagined the daughter-in-law he had never known smiling at him. *She is so beautiful. She must have brought joy to my son.* His thoughts colored the photograph with a mix of love and despair.

He imagined himself alone in the interrogation room, staring at the photo. His weary eyes rested on the lovely white dress of his granddaughter. Tears that had run dry found a renewed source. *Indu. I did not even know her name.* Tears clouded his vision and showered the photograph. The young family seemed to dissolve in his hands.

Smoldering anger cleared sorrow's fog. The black-and-white image began to yellow under a growing heat. A darkening spot grew over his son's face, eroding his smile and bursting into flame. One by one, the fiery wisps of gold and white snuffed out each face. The glowing edges faded to black, leaving only the innocent, unmarred face of Indu.

Her tender face rested in a pile of ash. He saw himself at the table. He watched, paralyzed, as the Vishal in his dream left the discarded photo and walked out the door. *Why am I leav-*

*ing her?* He watched the door close as he saw himself leave the room.

His eyes quickly turned back to the table. The eternal smile of Indu once again captured his heart, but there were no burnt edges. The photo was whole. He reached toward the picture, but two pearly soft hands lifted it. *The young woman from the hospital.* Vishal followed the picture as those gentle hands slipped it into a Bible.

*Andrea!* Vishal awakened as he thought of the young woman who saved him. A sense of calm, like he had never known, rushed over him. *I was saved for a reason. I am here for more than to simply die in this prison.*

# CHAPTER 49

Sunday, September 14, 2008
4:30 AM
Gourpali

Chandrika lay motionless in her bed, emotions running furiously as she prayed for sleep. She found herself in a darkened wood. *Why am I running?* Twisting vines tangled her feet. She clawed her way through the trees. Her pace quickened as she felt a pursuing presence. She could see no one following her. She heard no footsteps but her own. A shadowed mist emerged from the mossy earth, growing into a fog, edging closer.

Panic lunged within her breast, pounding a deafening beat. Turning from the impending darkness, she pressed her lungs and legs to their limits.

Far ahead, light adorned a glowing meadow. Gusts of color burst across her path. A rich, calming warmth rushed toward her, flooding the woods in a sea of light. She squinted, shielding her eyes from the intense radiance.

Blinded in the shadowless wood, she could not see the lovely form before her. The tenderness of a familiar voice awakened something deep within her soul. "Chandrika."

Mother.

As she opened her eyes, the light was vanquished by a startling scream. No longer in a mysterious wood, she was in her pitch-black bedroom. The scream was quickly silenced, but she knew the voice. *Andrea. Oh, dear God, please!* Chandrika bolted from her bed. She wasted no time reaching for the light or fumbling in the dark to find her shoes. She launched out the door.

She was not alone. She joined the silhouettes and shouting filling the dusty street. Chandrika pressed through the growing crowd. *Andrea, where are you?*

An angry young police officer slid his AK-47 off his shoulder. "Go back to your homes!" He gripped his weapon and shouted, "We have everything under control. There is nothing for you to see."

Chandrika stood still as the crowd began to disperse. She cringed as the lead officer slapped the young policeman in the chest. Fighting her fear, she stepped toward the young officer as he shouldered his weapon.

Darkness shielded her eyes from the blood stains beneath her feet. She could barely define the form of a woman curled on the ground. *Andrea!*

The officer blocked her path. "You cannot be here. I told everyone to go home."

"I am a nurse. I heard screaming. I am here to help."

Chandrika leaned past the office. She saw a small pool of blood. She heaved a sigh at the gruesome site of Andrea holding her abdomen, blood oozing from her lips, even too faint to whimper.

Chandrika leaned toward her battered friend. *Andrea, what are you doing here?* She lost herself in Andrea's bludgeoned face.

Reality fractured her trance as the butt of an AK-47 quaked pain through her spine. The sudden wave of agony dropped her to her knees. Chandrika gasped and groaned uncontrollably. *I can't breathe.* Chandrika clutched her chest. She coughed, choking on her own blood.

The loud crack awakened Andrea. She blinked at the dust in her eyes as two knees crashed near her face. She moaned at the mix of blood and dirt. Her eyes strained to see the shadowed face above her.

Chandrika steadied herself. She braved a smile at Andrea's throaty moan. *Thank God, you're still alive.* She gripped her chest and prayed. *Lord, give me strength. Help me find a way to save my friend.* Chandrika struggled to her feet, and boldly stepped toward the policeman. "This woman needs help. What has she done that you are holding her?"

"We are not holding her. She is free to go."

"Then why will you not let me help her?"

The officer looked around to be sure none of the villagers were still watching. He raised his gun, and delivered a crushing blow, splitting her forehead, her limp body collapsing beside the American.

\* \* \*

The three policemen dragged Chandrika into the house. "Why did you strike her?"

"What does it matter? You know what's going to happen to her anyway." The young officer's insolence was met with a fist in his stomach.

"Fool. You are a policeman. No one can see you participate. We are not a part of this. Do you understand?"

Despite the pit in his stomach, the insolence persisted. "Who is going to live to tell?"

Disgusted, the lead officer left the room. He scavenged the kitchen with little success.

The second officer followed him. "What do we do now?

And what about the girl in the street?"

The lead officer pulled a solitary Pepsi off the shelf. "I think we've done more than enough. Our instruction was to bring the American here and make sure she stays until morning. We were supposed to remain out of sight and quiet."

\* \* \*

Andrea lay in the street. Beaten, bleeding, and reeling in pain, the last thing she wanted to do was move. Her mind raced, and her heart cried out to God. *Lord, give me strength!* Despite her prayer, everything within her surrendered to the overwhelming urge for sleep.

She had no restless dreams, no nightmares, only sleep. Eventually the terrible pain in her side awakened her. She could still feel the policeman's boot thrust into her ribs. Her head spinning and throbbing, she tried to move, but strength escaped her. She choked and coughed on the dust in her face. She stretched her arms and legs as though climbing the ground, but she could not even crawl.

Exhausted, she collapsed once again and slid into a restless dream. The hard dusty street became a wet wooden deck moving beneath her. Waves crashed about her in darkness. She puzzled at how she wound up in a sturdy wooden boat on a stormy sea. A handful of men scrambled about the deck. Two lowered the sail. Some bailed water. Others prayed. Some held tightly to the tossed vessel, but one was asleep at the stern. *These waves are so violent; the wind and the thunder, so threatening. These men are obviously frightened. Why does he sleep?*

As Andrea pondered the resting man, he smiled. Andrea felt a sudden chill. *He knows I'm watching. How could he know what I'm thinking? He's asleep.*

"Am I?" She heard his voice plainly, though he remained

still and his lips failed to move. "Why are you frightened?"

A bizarre combination of terror and comfort over-whelmed her. She seemed invisible to all the men on the boat except the one who was sleeping. A huge crushing wave smashed the side of the boat, raining down on all those on board. The sleeping man did not flinch. *He must be exhausted.*

"I don't tire easily." His words drifted through her mind like a whisper on the wind.

The ferocity of the storm was too much for the crew. One of the men clawed his way to the stern, shouting, "How can you sleep at time like this? Don't you care that we are going to drown?"

The man sat up smiling. He whispered something to the one who awakened him. As he stood, the boat ceased creaking. The thunder, still rumbled. The boat still tossed about. The man did not brace himself or hold on to anything.

He fixed his eyes on Andrea. He held her entranced in his tender gaze. Unaffected by the storm, he stood unwavering, completely aware and in control.

Standing in the stern, the man stretched out his hands. He glanced at the powerful waves, the whitecaps, the bending and twisting trees in the distance, the black rolling clouds, and the shimmer of lightning dancing within them. Before uttering a single word, he looked deep into the eyes of Andrea once more. His eyes and his outstretched arms spoke to her. *"Do you trust me, even in the storm?"*

As the man turned to face the wind, Andrea was thrown to the side of the boat. A wave of nausea swept over her. She coughed a mix of bile and blood and awakened, once more, in the street, alone. No sign of Chandrika. Stillness beneath the speckled night sky, the horizon a midnight blue, daylight would soon encroach.

Andrea reached deep within, mustering every ounce of remaining power. She crawled to the opposite side of the street and slid behind a tree. *Dear God, I've got to reach Mitch and Marci. Give me strength, and please protect Chandrika.*

Eyeing the tiny village, she cried. *Where do I go? God, how do I find the right house?* Her decision became easier when she saw the shadow of an elderly woman in an open doorway. Andrea could not see her face, but she caught a glimpse of a cross on the wall behind her. *That's the one.*

Andrea shuffled toward the woman in the doorway, straining with each movement. Her eyes captured a glance from the aged woman. She felt a glimmer of hope as two aging feet scurried toward her. Andrea lifted her hand and cautioned the woman to remain quiet. She felt strength from the woman's frail shoulders and tremulous hands.

In the tiny home, Andrea collapsed on a mat as the woman spoke feverishly in Oriya. Andrea sat dumbfounded, searching for strength. She could not understand a word, but she understood the name, Chandrika. *She is asking about Chandrika!*

Andrea smiled. *Thank you, God. I'm in the right house.* She sighed as she looked into the face etched with years and graced with tears and a smile.

The woman had very little to offer, but she gave Andrea a drink and a damp cloth. Pointing to herself, the old woman exclaimed, "Anila." Nodding, she said her name once again. "Anila."

Andrea wiped her face as she listened. The moist cloth on her face helped lift some of her exhaustion. The tepid water refreshed her and cleared her thoughts. As Anila spoke, Andrea remembered Chandrika had adopted Indu to live with her and

Anila.

*Indu!* Andrea gently grasped Anila's shoulder. "Indu! Where is Indu?" She followed Anila's eyes to a bedroom door. As Andrea stood, she heard tiny footsteps. Her heart melted at Indu's ear-to-ear smile. Andrea wrapped the child in her biggest hug. "Oh, Indu, I am so glad you are safe." Squeezing tightly, she forgot all of her pain.

Andrea's filthy, bleeding face was not lost on Indu. Growing up in Pahireju and meeting persecution face-to-face had taught Indu to expect the worst and hope for the best. "Where is my mother?" Indu quietly asked.

Andrea could not disguise the truth. "Chandrika has been hurt, but we know where she is and we are trusting God."

The perceptive Indu asked, "Where is Marci?"

"Marci and Mitch are safe. They will help us." *God, help us!*

Indu ran into the bedroom.

# CHAPTER 50

All Saints Hospital
Sunday, September 14, 2008
5:00 AM

Mitch Hawkins was glued to the boxy 15-inch monitor. He had not seen such slow internet service since he cancelled his dial-up connection. He drummed his fingers as Naomi refilled his tea. He mused at Marci shifting back and forth, pacing and praying.

Mitch drew a deep breath as the screen moved like a tortoise finally crossing the starting line. "Oh God! Finally! Sorry, Marci. Finally, an emergency phone number."

Dialing the number, Mitch realized, Wait a minute, *I can't use the hospital's phone. There are enough people in jeopardy already. He hung up the phone.*

"What are you doing?"

Mitch flashed his satellite phone. "Trust me. I need to use this phone in case someone is listening in on the hospital line."

"Wow, we really are paranoid." Marci nodded.

Before he punched the first number, the phone began ringing. *What the?* Mitch flipped it open and heard the frantic voice of Andrea Widener. "Andrea? How did you know this number?"

"Never mind!"

"Where are you?"

"I was abducted by the police and brought to this village. They were just holding me, like they were waiting for someone else. I realized they were going to turn me over to Hindu extremists, so I tried to sneak out. One of the officers tackled me in the street. I screamed to draw attention. I saw lights coming from some of the houses, so I screamed louder and longer. To silence me, they beat me into unconsciousness."

"How did you get to a phone?"

Andrea choked, holding back tears. "Chandrika." Her voice cracked. "She must have heard me screaming. She tried to help me... I didn't see what happened, but I know they beat her badly. I woke up when she collapsed beside me. She was moaning. One of them knocked her out with his gun. I couldn't move."

Mitch listened, imagining Andrea on the edge of life in a hostile land. *What is this girl doing so far from her home, her safe, comfortable home?*

Andrea's voice wavered. "Mitch, they took Chandrika and left me in the road. They thought I was dead. I knew my only hope was to get out of there and find you. I waited and then crawled away. We need to help Chandrika."

"Where are you now?"

"I'm in Gourpali, in Chandrika's house. I'm here with Indu and Anila."

Mitch's pulse quickened. "Andrea, you've got to get out of there?"

"Yes, but where do we go? I can't just go back down the street."

"Does Anila have a car?"

"Are you kidding? Chandrika has a bicycle, but that's

not going to help three people escape." Tears interrupted her thoughts.

"Andrea. Andrea, hold it together. Take the phone. Take Anila and Indu, and leave the village now. Go through the woods. Find some place to hide. I will...."

"Mitch, I'm scared."

*Scared? Where is your faith now? Why doesn't God save you?* Mitch Hawkins composed himself. Not an appropriate time for an intellectual attack.

"I'm scared, but I'm not scared. Mitch, I know you don't believe God is watching over us, but I do, and I know we will ride this storm no matter where it takes us. Peace is not in safety, but in knowing that God is in control no matter what."

Her words were too much for him. "Andrea, I don't want to argue with you in this moment, but I just can't hear anymore nonsense about God, not now."

"Mitch, I don't mean to frustrate you. I am telling you because I care about you, and I don't know that I will see you again."

Mitch was silent.

Andrea finished. "We need to get moving if we are going to beat the sunrise. Good-bye, Mitch. I'm praying for you. Tell Marci I love her. Make sure she gives my love to my mom and dad."

"Stop talking like that, Andrea."

"It's ok, Mitch. We will do our best to stay safe and hidden until I hear from you."

\*\*\*

Andrea flipped the phone shut, and placed a hand on Anila's shoulder. "We need to leave. We need to leave now."

Andrea slid her arm around the frail grandmother, embracing her and feeling the trembling of restrained tears. "We have to go. We can do nothing for Chandrika right now." *And we're no good to her dead.* "I must get you and Indu away from the village to a safe hiding place. Marci and Mitch are going to bring people to help Chandrika." *God, please help them bring someone.*

As Indu quickly gathered some food and water, Andrea watched in amazement. *She has done this before?* Andrea felt a wave of compassion in the pit of her stomach. "Indu, let me help you." She grabbed a satchel and peered through the doorway.

The unlikely trio slipped toward the edge of the village under the glow of the waxing moon. Andrea, Anila, and Indu set their minds on finding a place to hide. None of them dared to look back.

Moonbeams danced across the shimmering lentil fields, dusting light on their path.

Andrea pointed ahead. "Look past the fields. We can hide in that cluster of teak trees."

Marching through the knee-deep paddock, Andrea struggled to understand. She failed to restrain her tears. *This is not some movie. I'm living this. Tromping through fields in the middle of the night, 10,000 miles from home, with people I've never met, and running for my life. What have I gotten myself into?*

She stopped. Her eyes followed Indu gently leading Anila by the hand. Andrea's heart melted as Indu looked back toward the village.

Their eyes met. Though they kept walking, time seemed to stop.

Indu's eyes pleaded with Andrea. *Please don't let me lose another mother.*

Andrea held Indu's tender heart in her hands. Every step away from the village felt like she was tightening her grip. She heaved a canyon-sized sigh at her own words: *We can do nothing for Chandrika right now. Did I say that?*

Her eyes focused on Indu. *Oh, what your eyes have seen. God, no matter what, please bless this little girl. Protect her, and please protect Chandrika. Indu cannot lose another mother.*

Indu clutched Anila's hand a little tighter and the trio kept marching. The cluster of teak grew ever nearer, the village smaller. When Gourpali was out of sight, they felt a small measure of comfort as they disappeared into the tiny forest. Anila knelt to pray, still holding on to Indu.

Andrea stared. Her mind a blur, almost numb, she stood transfixed on the trees as though lost in a work of art. Light and shadow wisped around them. Splotches of moonlight on the ground reminded Andrea of the woods on her farm beneath a gentle dusting of snow.

As a young tomboy, she would often tromp into the woods. The trees were friends, her guardians in her quiet place. She would plop down on their mossy floor, lie on her back and gaze at the sky through the trees. Her thoughts would fly with the cloud creatures, the forest entrancing her with a chorus of birds and the seemingly senseless banter of squirrels. Alone in the woods, she would talk to God, sometimes with words. Her heart resonated with her Creator amid His creation.

Reality slowly gripped her mind as her eyes returned to the scene of Anila and Indu praying, but the image quickly faded. Exhausted, and a little dazed, Andrea collapsed.

The sudden thud startled Anila and Indu. Anila quickly

snatched a water bottle from her satchel and handed it to Indu.

Andrea failed to hear Indu's whispers or feel the tiny hand touching her cheek. In her slumber, she was entering the woods with Indu and Anila. Her mind flashed through her flight to India, the hotel in Delhi, meeting Mitch, the train, Pahireju, Satyajit, her abduction and beating, everything. As she began to awaken, she strained to keep her eyes shut. *Make it all go away. I want to wake up at home, safe, in my own bed.*

Andrea startled at the nudging voice within. *If you hadn't come, where do think Indu would be right now? Where do you think Mitch Hawkins would be heading?*

*Right here is where I'm supposed to be? Right now?*

"Andrea?" Indu's tiny voice begged to see her eyes.

Andrea opened her eyes and offered a feeble smile.

Indu thrust a strong hug around her neck to say, *I do not want to lose anyone else.*

The distant rumble of an engine disrupted their quiet moment. Andrea sat up. "Chandrika!" She turned and looked toward the village. Tiny reflections of moonlight revealed nothing. She could hear the engine, but saw no headlights or taillights. She rose to her feet, listening and hoping.

As the engine revved, she imagined the crunch of gravel spitting from the tires. By the fading of the sound, the car must have been going the other way. *They're leaving. I've got to go check on her.*

Andrea turned once more toward Indu and Anila. She called out to them. "You must stay here. These woods will protect you. I am going to see if I can help Chandrika." *Or see if they've taken her.*

\* \* \*

Mitch dialed 0-33-3984-2400. "Hello, I need to speak to the Duty Officer." He paced silently. "Yes, hello. My name is Mitch Hawkins. No, I am not a U.S. citizen. I am a journalist from London, but I am traveling with two American women, and one of them has run on a bit of serious trouble…. Yes, well you see, she has been abducted by rogue police officers and taken to a village…. No she hasn't committed any crime. She is an innocent bystander who has witnessed violence in Orissa. We intercepted written plans for an attack on Christians in Gour-pali…. It's near Sambalpur. That's where she was taken…. Yes, by the police…. I'm quite sure. I've spoken to her via cellular just recently…. Her name is Andrea Widener. She arrived in Delhi on Monday, September 8$^{th}$ with her friend Marci Beaufort…. No, Marci is safe with me…. What do I need from you! I am hoping for some kind of assistance…. I told you already, she has done nothing illegal or questionable…. Yes, I'm accusing the local police, or at least a few officers, of being crooked. They have wrongly held one of your citizens…. Well, it doesn't seem to me that you care at all…. Yes, I know I've awakened you out of a dead sleep. For that I am truly sorry, but this young woman's life is in danger. Can you please help us?"

Mitch fell silent. Disgust covered his face.

"What? What did they say? Are they going to help?"

Mitch glared at Marci, as if blaming all Americans. "The gentleman said he would call his superiors first thing in the morning."

"By then it could be too late."

"Exactly!"

Mitch scrolled through numbers on his phone. "I will call everyone I can think of. The more who know, the better our chances." He ran through his entire list of contacts: friends, other journalists, political officials, businessmen. Calling one after another, he fell victim to hang-ups, shouting, "I don't owe you any favors," endless ringing, and one meaningful communication.

# CHAPTER 51

Sunday, September 14, 2008
12:00 AM in London
The Home of Daniel Zweritt
Publishing Director of London World Magazine

"Who in the world is calling at midnight?"

Daniel Zweritt sat up abruptly. He flipped on the lamp and scrambled to find his phone. "Hello! Mitch? You sound addled. Is everything ok?"

Daniel's wife tried to sleep in vain. Stuffing her head under her pillow, she could not escape the muffled voice. Her husband's silence was all she needed to understand the gravity of the phone call.

"Mitch, I can't promise anything, but I'll do my best to help."

"Was that Mitch Hawkins? What so important for him to call in the middle of the night?"

"He's in some serious trouble this time, I'm afraid."

"Well, what does he expect you to do at this hour?"

"He is in India."

"And how are you supposed to help him in India?"

# CHAPTER 52

All Saints Hospital
Sunday, September 14, 2008
5:15 AM

Marci anxiously tapped her nails. "Who was that? Are they going to help us?"

"That was Daniel Zweritt, an old friend. He used to be my agent. Now he's a publisher, a big shot. He can't do anything to help us directly, but he knows everyone." Mitch looked Marci in the eye. "Daniel will get the word out. Someone will be listening who can help." Mitch was unsure if Daniel would even remember their conversation since he was a notoriously sound sleeper.

"Ok, so what do we do in the meantime?"

In the dimly lit office, Mitch paused on the soft glow of Marci's face. Her innocence was mildly jaded by the angst in her eyes. As Mitch examined her face, he could not judge her. He simply studied her. He was startled by the lingering thought in his mind. *I don't love her. I barely know her, and she's a child.* His heart leapt. *Of course, I don't love her.* Remembering their recent conversation, he thought, *how could I? I don't even know what love is!*

His mind went back to the moment he first saw her. He had been selectively studying his pre-flight reading materials when he felt her stare. He turned and glanced at her and then back to his magazine. He smirked within as he plotted to eye her once again. Standing in the airport gift store, he stared at the glossy vixen in his hands and then bent his gaze toward his momentary stalker, pausing long enough to let her know he was looking. When their eyes met, he very intentionally gave her a slow up-down and smugly reverted to Miss September, feigning complete boredom.

He felt uneasy in his stomach as he relived that first glance. This time was different. He remembered her guilty smile from their in-flight confrontation, a furtive glance on the hotel lawn in Delhi, her frustrated, stool-tainted smile on the train to Orissa. His eyes traced the tousled wave of her hair. He imagined the warmth of her smile, veiled by her silhouette. Despite the shadows, he knew her face. She was more beautiful than any fantasy he had ever known, and for the first time in his life, he saw a beautiful woman without undressing her in his mind.

Marci interrupted his "aha" moment. "What are you looking at? Are we going to do something or what?" She paused, amazed at his blank stare. "Mitch, come on!"

He shook his head as if to rattle the gears. "Of course. Here's what we need to do. Marci, you must promise me that you will stay here with Naomi, and please stay out of sight." He held up his hand to halt her protest as he turned to Naomi. "Is there a vehicle I may borrow?"

"I do not have a car, but we could take the ambulance. No one will give us any trouble if we are in the ambulance." Naomi glanced at Marci. "But I will have to go with you."

"And that will mean that Marci will need to go with us."

Naomi stuck her head out the door checking the dim corridor. Fighting emotion, she devised a plan. She stepped back into the office. She grasped Marci and Mitch and gently prodded them toward the window. "Climb out, and wait there until you hear me say, 'Hello, and good morning to you.' When you hear those words, you will know that my replacement has arrived. Then go to the west end of the hospital. After five minutes, I will meet you there with the ambulance."

Approaching footsteps disrupted their discussion.

Without a word, Marci grabbed her bag and one of Mitch's and hefted them onto the desk beneath the window. Sighing and grunting, she thrust open the rusted frame and leapt to the ground.

Naomi offered to help Mitch, as though he were an old man.

Without time for embarrassment, Mitch was thankful for the assistance. He climbed out the window, panting and already sweating through his clothes. *I must lose some weight. This is ridiculous.* He grabbed Marci's hand to diminish his clumsy jump.

They collapsed on the ground and waited for the magic words. When they knew Naomi was free to leave, they slid along the side of the hospital, crouching as they passed each window. They stepped quietly until they reached the west end of the building. Around the corner, they could see small numbers already approaching the hospital.

The two unlikely friends from different worlds waited, flanked by two great bougainvillea bushes. Five minutes turned into fifteen and seemed like two hours as Marci and Mitch silently ruminated over every what-if they could imagine. Mitch stared aimlessly at the backpack between his legs while Marci whispered a prayer.

Mitch felt no comfort in her prayer. *I've been all over the world. Been in hostile zones, taken fire, faced threats, jail, I've even been beaten. I've had more exotic diseases than I'd like to remember. I've done it on my own and my way. In all my journeys, I don't remember ever being as scared.* With his eyes tightly closed, he reached for Marci's hand and drew a shaky breath as though in pain.

Marci felt her fears dissolve with one look at Mitch's face. *He's not afraid for himself. He's been through too much. He's seen the world. He is afraid for us, for Andrea and me.* Marci lifted Mitch's hand to her lips and pressed a gentle kiss.

Mitch let down his steely guard and looked into her eyes. *Who is this girl who travels around the world following Jesus? That's crazy, yet adorable, adorable until it gets scary. Marci, how could you risk your life like this, and for what? And what about Andrea?*

Mitch heaved a sigh. Staring, he imagined Andrea climbing over a rocky hillside, twisting through trees and brush with Gourpali fading behind her. He envisioned her pausing on the hillside to watch the dying village. *What is she doing? No! No! No!* He pictured her leaving Anila and Indu to climb back down the hill toward the village.

*She is walking into the flames. They are going to kill her.* His heart skipped a beat as he caught himself mid-thought. He imagined the village burning around her, and himself crying out to God. "No!" He spoke aloud with a start.

"Shhh," Marci reprimanded as she lifted him from the ground and back to reality. She whispered, "Naomi is here with the ambulance."

Naomi backed the ambulance to the edge of the hospital. She dashed around the side, opening the back for Mitch and Marci. They climbed into the ancient VW microbus, a former reefer wagon painted white with a red cross on the side. "Lie down. We must leave before people gather around the ambulance."

Mitch glanced to see if there was a dream catcher or fluffy dice. He chuckled when he realized there was no rearview mirror.

# CHAPTER 53

Sunday, September 14, 2008
12:20 AM in London
The Home of Daniel Zweritt

"What's the matter, Joan?"

"I can't sleep."

"You're not worried about Mitch?"

"No. I keep thinking about a friend from college. You ever get one of those feelings?"

"Like something bad has happened?"

"Or is about to happen."

Daniel moaned and crawled out of bed. "I'll put on the coffee." *It looks to be a long night,* he thought as he trudged down the hall, rubbing his eyes. "Why did he have to call and stir up a fuss?" he muttered to himself. "There's not a thing I can do until morning."

He returned to the bedroom with two steaming cups of coffee. "Joan?" He flipped the light switch. "I didn't see you there. Were you praying?"

"I was. Is that so unusual."

"No. I suppose not, but I've never seen you do it outside of church."

"I can't explain it. When Mitch called and you said "India," I could not help but think of my friend Maureen. She so wanted to go to India, but she got pregnant and could not go. I hadn't thought of her in years.

The phone rang, interrupting her thought.

\* \* \*

"Hello, Joan?"

"Maureen? Oh, my goodness. Are you all right. I was just thinking of you, literally down on my knees praying for you. What's the matter?"

"You remember the baby I had in college."

"Andrea?"

"She is in serious trouble. She and a friend took a trip to India, just like the one you and I talked about."

"But you got pregnant."

"Yes, the best mistake I ever made. Andrea was blogging and got cut off. Her last entry read, 'Someone is behind me' and ended there. I have not heard from her. I am afraid she was abducted."

"Dear God, Maureen, I'm so sorry. You know I will do what I can to help."

# CHAPTER 54

Before Sunrise in Gourpali
Sunday, September 14, 2008
7:00 AM

A glint of midnight blue crested the horizon. Darkness slowly waned in the disquieted village. Chandrika lay still on the dirt floor. She dared not groan as she awakened to immense pain. Crying inside, she tried to move, but pain overwhelmed her. She could hear the ground rumble with voices and footsteps.

Chandrika cried out to God with her heart. *Dear God, please protect me!* She listened intently to every noise: their shuffling feet, knuckle popping, even their breathing. She dared not move. In her thoughts, she fled home. *Oh, God, save Indu and Anila, and please save Andrea.*

With her eyes closed tightly, she heard the youngest officer ask, "Is she dead?"

With a hushed, yet stern voice, the senior officer rebuked him. "Shut your mouth, you fool!" He pressed his finger into the young man's chest. "We were never here. Do you understand – never here?"

As though he did not hear, the young officer asked, "What about the American girl?"

"What about her?"

"Well, she is not here."

The lead officer glared at the insolent youth. He motioned him toward the police car, leaving the beaten and bloodied Chandrika for the gang that would soon arrive. "As I said, we were never here. I know nothing about any American girl or anyone else."

With headlights off, the car slowly and quietly rumbled away from the village.

# CHAPTER 55

In Gourpali
Sunday, September 14, 2008
7:55 AM

Chandrika drew a great sigh as she heard the police car slowly fading into the distance. *I've got to find Andrea and help her.* Opening her eyes, she could see nothing. The tiny house was dark. The crystal-clear moon glowed almost full. Pressing against the floor with all her might, Chandrika tried to rise on her hands and knees. *I can crawl, if I cannot stand.* Her ribs screamed with every movement. Nausea joined the pain as she heaved a mix of blood and bile. *Oh, dear God! Help me!*

She crawled to the doorway. Grabbing the door frame, she pulled as hard as she could. Searing pain quaked through her skull. As she raised her head, the moon seemed to melt into the whirl of spinning trees. The tiny house disappeared as darkness engulfed her. Chandrika lay silent and still, barely breathing and alone.

\*\*\*

Mitch glanced at his watch as the makeshift ambulance rambled along. *Almost 8:00 AM.* His heart pounded with the pistons. His thoughts stretched ahead to Gourpali. Mitch thought it safe to raise his head as they cleared the edge of town. There were no lights in the vehicle and no lights on the road. *No one can see me in here, now. It's too dark.*

Mitch spied the countryside. The golden-brown fields yielded a dusky grey in the moonlight. Even in the early morning, the road grew congested. Not so many cars or buses, but people. People walking, a boy driving goats, women carrying goods on their heads, men driving over-loaded tractors. Even before dawn, the flow of humanity began to swell. The scant light and shadows mimicked invisible obstacles.

A rumbling truck twisted sideways, barely missing an overloaded tractor. The buzz of a stunted motorcycle rang like an annoying alarm clock until the smack of the unbending truck silenced the noise with a crunch. In the darkness, the intoxicated bus driver barreled along, unaware and indifferent. The farmer leapt from his tractor to assess the damage.

Mitch recognized the farmer as their savior from car trouble on Tuesday. He stared, speechless, trying to grasp the reality and urgency around him. A quick head shake and Mitch grabbed his camera and clamored for the door.

Naomi protested. "What are you doing?"

"Someone is hurt. We need to help." *This is an ambulance isn't it?*

Naomi flipped on the emergency lights and hopped out of the van. "I don't think we are going to be able to do much. I suspect he's dead."

"He's alive!" The farmer shouted.

Mitch rushed toward the victim, shooting a few quick photos as he stood over the young man. *He needs help now!* He turned toward Naomi and Marci and shouted. "Come quickly! He's not going to last much longer." Mitch eyed the young man. Late teens, early twenties, before dusk on a motorcycle with no headlamp? What was he doing out here? *What a waste!* Turning to the peering eyes and gaping mouths, he shook his head. *A wasted life in a wasted country. If there were a god, this would surely be a god-forsaken place.*

Marci tugged his shirt. "Mitch, help us get him into the ambulance."

Naomi braced the victim's leg, wrapped it snugly, and looked up at Marci. "He will need surgery, or he will die."

Mitch approached with a stretcher and three smiling recruits. "Let's get him to the hospital."

Naomi shook her head as she motioned them into action. The four men not-so-gingerly plopped the patient on the stretcher and carried him to the ambulance. "This is not like America. I cannot call for a helicopter, and there is no surgeon to operate on him today." Naomi studied Marci's face. *She does not understand what I'm saying.* She clutched Marci's shoulder. "We cannot save his leg, but we can save his life. We must keep him from bleeding to death until the surgeon can remove his leg."

Marci buried her emotions. *I've felt all I can feel. I wish I was numb like one of those days when you're sick, in bed, watching TV until your brain is mush. I'm not sure how much more I can take.* Reality spat on her feet as the four men hauling the stretcher paused for the young man to wretch.

Mitch shrugged at the sight, remembering Marci's mishap on the train. *What a week! I just hope I live through it. I hope we all live through it,* he thought as he helped slide the stretcher into the microbus. He dispatched his volunteers with a smile and a handful of rupees. He watched the three, almost skipping as they left. He kept his eyes on them, but his mind was on the young stranger behind him in the ambulance. *I want it to matter,* he thought. *I want life to matter. I want there to be some meaning.*

Mitch gazed at the moon and stars. *I am a meaningless speck. Why can't life mean something? Believing feels good, but that is no reason to believe.* "I've got to know."

"Got to know what?" Marci asked, assuming Mitch was

talking to her.

*Did I say that aloud?* "I was merely thinking."

Mitch lurched as Marci engulfed him with a hug. He echoed the embrace, holding her tight. He felt as though she were drawing strength from him. "Don't you think it strange that one week ago you judged the very sight of me? Without knowing me, you utterly disdained me." He gently stroked her hair. "And now, here you are embracing me as a much-needed friend."

Marci lifted her head. Opening her eyes, she dove deep into the portals of his soul, searching his thoughts. She said nothing. She softly planted her cheek against his chest. "I'm sorry, Mitch. I will never be the judge again." *I know when Christ sees you, when He sees anyone, He loves. He didn't give His life to fulfill a dream of judgment, but to release the full measure of His undying love.*

Naomi interrupted their trance. "I need you lovers to stop hugging and give me a hand." She handed Marci a flashlight. "Mitch, hold him still while I start an IV."

# CHAPTER 56

Dawn in Gourpali
Sunday, September 14, 2008
8:15 AM

Natraj slapped his longtime friend across the back of the head. "Satyajit, my friend, are you ready?"

Satyajit was all too familiar with the scenario - an angry mob, shrouded in faith and bandanas, clutching sticks and clubs, while marching to the tune of hate. Satyajit could barely see through the bruised swollen pulp that used to be his eyes. He held his jaw stiff but open. Clenching his teeth sent a bone-shuddering pain through his ear and into his neck. His jaw swollen, he could not feel his cheek. As they shoved him from the bus, he clutched his friend Natraj to avoid falling.

Natraj glared at him through eyes of disgust and hate. *I can't wait to watch you burn,* he thought as he brushed off Satyajit's arm and thrust him facedown into the unyielding dirt.

Satyajit was briefly blinded by the jolt as he splayed across the road. He opened his eyes to a blur of sweat and dust. He lifted his head enough to catch a glimpse of approaching feet. One boot thrust into his face. His world faded instantly as searing pain racked through his skull.

"Why did you kick him, you fool? He needs to see this, and I want to watch him suffer." With a shove, Natraj commanded. "Get him up. If he can't walk, drag him."

Satyajit awakened to the jarring of his head and shoulders as he was dragged by his feet. Choking on dust, he coughed and sputtered. His feet dropped with a thud. Satyajit dared to glance at his former friend, even though he feared another boot in his face. He lacked the strength to moan or move. Every part of him was screaming in pain except his dust-coated throat.

Natraj stood over him, hands on his hips, waiting. Natraj grunted and motioned Satyajit to his feet.

Fear of another kick, prompted Satyajit to dig deep for enough strength to stand. He slowly rolled, pushing away the earth with his bloodied hands. On his knees, he tried to rise up.

Memories of the past few days roared through his mind like a whirlwind. Each face, every emotion, every heartache, all the excitement spun into a blur as horror quaked his soul. Panting and reeling in pain, he lifted his head. As his eyes met Natraj, he could not restrain his tears.

Natraj smirked. "What a pathetic display of weakness!" He wrapped his arm around Satyajit and lifted him. "Don't give up yet, my friend. You will want to see your new friends again, I'm sure."

Half-carried and shoeless, Satyajit plodded down the dirt street dripping blood with each painful step. He leaned on the strength of Natraj. With each agonizing step, he muttered prayers for his friend. "God, I did not know what I was doing when…" *You know that Natraj does not know what he is doing either. Please show him mercy.*

Natraj sneered. "Stop your blubbering, you fool."

One of his men asked, "Natraj, why did we come so close to this village and why so close to dawn?"

"It doesn't really matter. These villagers know we are coming. The police were reckless, alerting everyone with all their noise. They beat two women in the street. Don't worry. They will pay for their mistake."

"The police?"

"No. Of course not. The two women will pay. Our friend, Satyajit will pay, and any Christian foolish enough to remain in Gourpali will pay – with blood."

\* \* \*

Andrea looked behind her. She paused for one last glimpse of the distant wood that held Indu and Anila. She had almost reached the edge of Gourpali. The pit in her stomach rumbled. *I can't eat a thing, but why didn't I eat something. God, give me strength.*

The comfort of the moonlight faded as long streaks of sunlight burned through the trees, dispelling shadows. *I feel so exposed,* Andrea thought as she crept toward the waking village. She coursed along the north side of the village. She dared not go directly toward Chandrika. She slid between the teak and jacarandas and the tiny clay houses, staying out of sight, trying to find the best vantage point to spy the village and the house where Chandrika had been taken.

Startled by a scurrying chicken, she gasped and covered her mouth. She closed her tired eyes and listened, but her violent pulse drowned out her hearing. Sweat veiled her vision.

Sliding between two tiny homes, she leaned against a flimsy wall to catch her breath. Wiping her forehead, she wished for a tissue and realized she had left her purse. She had no money. She didn't even have her passport. Panic raged as she felt the weight of anonymity and the distance of 10,000 miles from home. *Get a hold of yourself, Andrea!*

A firm, yet gentle voice within, disrupted her fear. Like the comfort of being warmly tucked into bed, safe, loved, and fully at peace, the deep whisper calmed her soul. *You are not alone.* She didn't turn to look for the voice. She knew, without doubt, where and whom the voice came from. The hurricane around her did not matter. She stood with the One with power to command the wind. The voice continued. *Wipe your eyes and see what I will do.*

Hope overcame panic. Her heart pulsed in rhythm with the Spirit within. *God, my life is in your hands.* She sighed and smiled. *What are you going to do next?*

Andrea could not keep her thoughts on herself. *Oh, God, I know that Chandrika and Satyajit, Indu and Anila will be fine. No matter what happens here, they know You, but Mitch.* She prayed through her tears. *Please speak to him like you've spoken to me.*

# CHAPTER 57

At the Prison
Sunday, September 14, 2008
8:15 AM

Palash, the guard, smugly stared at Vishal through the bars. "What's the matter, my old friend? You seem upset." He chuckled.

Vishal said nothing.

Footsteps drew nearer, joined by shouts and jeers from inmates. Vishal could see very little. Palash turned toward the oncoming footsteps. "I guess I'll be going home now. Here comes my relief."

Palash gritted his teeth and kicked the bars of Vishal's cell. He shook his head. "Vishal, my old friend, how could you be such a fool? You have given up everything for nothing."

The footsteps halted. Palash stepped around the young officer as though inspecting his uniform. Nodding approval, he said, "Good morning, Manav."

"Good morning, sir." Manav stepped close to whisper, "Palash, there has been an escape!"

"No, there has been no escape." Palash stood stalwart.

"What happened to the new prisoner, Satyajit?"

Palash offered a sideways nod to draw the officer away from Vishal's cell.

As the two stepped away, Vishal shouted, "There was no escape."

The second officer, stopped abruptly. "What? What did he say?"

Palash ignored him. Glancing at his watch, he kept moving.

The officer marched up to Vishal. "What do you mean, there was no escape? We are missing a prisoner, and his cell mate is dead." The officer turned toward Palash, but he was not there.

Vishal stood and approached the bars. "Palash left because he took the prisoner out last night and turned him over to a gang of bandits."

"And you know this because?"

"They came by my cell, the guard, the prisoner, and a member of the gang."

"Tell me everything you know."

"Why should I tell you anything? I am facing execution. You can do nothing to me."

"You are right. I can do nothing to you, but perhaps there is someone else that I could help… or hurt. You tell me."

Vishal swallowed hard. "I have only one wish before I die."

"Go on!" The officer nodded.

"I have never seen my granddaughter. I would like to see her."

"You tell me everything first, and I'll see what I can do."

Vishal shrugged. "That's not good enough. I will tell you, and then you will disappear, and I will be stuck behind these bars."

The officer softened. "So, what do you propose?"

"You take me into your custody. Bring as many guards as you need. Take me to Gourpali, where my granddaughter lives. When I have seen her, I will tell you more than you would ever need to know."

The officer mulled over the notion as he reached for his keys and unlocked the cell. "Let's go!"

\* \* \*

Palash paced in the doorway, tapping his cell phone and watching the road. A wicked smile twisted across his lips at the familiar roar of a police car rounding the street corner. Tension faded from his face as three officers bounded from the vehicle and trotted toward the prison. Stepping outside, Palash squinted. "Is everything set?"

"We did our best. We were only able to find one of the Americans. She is there and the nurse from that hospital."

Palash was not fooled by their averted eyes and fidgeting. He stepped toward the youngest officer, "You, tell me what happened."

"She got away."

"She got away?" Shoving the senior officer, Palash pressed. "Who got away, and how did you let her do it?"

The senior officer confessed. "The nurse came to help the American girl. When we subdued her and took her into the house, the American slipped away. She was bleeding and unconscious when we left her. I don't know how she managed to escape."

Palash sighed in disgust. He stared at the officer in disbelief. As the officer cleared his throat and lifted his eyes, Palash whirled around to see Manav and the prisoner, Vishal. "What are you doing?"

Manav smiled. "I caught this man trying to escape with his young friend, Satyajit."

Vishal felt his stomach leap into his throat and his pulse rage.

# CHAPTER 58

The Prison
Sunday, September 14, 2008
8:30 AM

Palash smiled at their plot, but his heart was sick at the betrayal of his old friend Vishal. *How could you give yourself up and compromise all of us, you fool?* He stared at Vishal with disgust as Manav shoved him into the police car.

"Lie down!" ordered Manav.

The three sleep-deprived officers slid into the car, the younger next to Vishal. Eyes on the road, they sped away from the prison.

The younger officer questioned. "Why are we doing this?"

The senior officer rebuked him. "You fool. He is only going to get what he deserves."

"No, I mean, why are we doing this? We have been awake all night. We were supposed to end our shift at 7:00 AM."

The car screeched to a stop. The senior officer screamed. "Get out! You are no longer on duty. You can go! But I would hate for us to lose this prisoner."

The younger officer released the door handle and folded his arms with a sigh. The tires burned into the pavement and raced towards Gourpali.

Vishal slid toward the door, slowly avoiding any sudden movement. He knew better than to try to escape, but he wanted to lift his head enough to see where they were. The two officers in the front were talking while the younger beside him was asleep or trying to sleep. Vishal pressed up toward the window in time to feel the car slowing for traffic.

"It looks like an accident."

"We don't have time to stop. Keep going."

"But someone must have been hurt. There's an ambulance."

Vishal's pulse quickened at those words. Aware of the officers' distraction, he sat up, studying the ambulance as they passed. *Chandrika, please be there.* As he strained to see, he felt a smack across the back of his head.

"Stay down."

Vishal slunk into the seat, closing his eyes. The accident was strangely close to the place where his band had attacked Pastor Singh. He imagined the car ablaze. *That's what they will do to me, douse me and burn me alive.* Defying their orders, Vishal sat up.

"I told you to stay down."

Vishal stared through the officer. "I have no reason to listen to you. You are going to kill me anyway."

"I would certainly enjoy that, but I'm a police officer. I could never do such a thing, but we cannot be responsible for what others might do."

"So what is your plan for me?"

"We have no plan for you, but we have a friend who has planned a very special reunion for you and your American friend." Looking at the other two officers, he added, "Andrea, wasn't that her name?"

They nodded. "Yes, Andrea."

# CHAPTER 59

The Scene of the Accident
Sunday, September 14, 2008
8:40 AM
On the Road to Gourpali

"My first time to start an IV in the dark!" After Naomi secured the tape, the horizon began to glow. *The sunrise! Thank God! This road is no place to be at night.* She glanced at Mitch. "The IV is running. Let's go."

Marci stared at the blood-covered patient. "Will he be ok?"

Mitch gulped but could not swallow. His mouth was salty dry. The fifty-something world-traveler had "seen it all," but the heat, the smell, and the shrinking ambulance tested his resolve. He clutched Marci's shoulder. "We have to get to Gourpali soon, or more than just this man are going to die." He turned to Naomi. "How much further?"

"About six miles." Naomi climbed out and circled the ambulance. She halted as she noticed a police car.

Marci jumped as the car whirred past. "Do you think that was the police car that took Andrea?"

Mitch nodded. "I think I saw Vishal in the back seat." His eyes followed the police car until it disappeared into the menagerie of traffic. "I could swear it was Vishal."

"Vishal? He's in prison."

Mitch closed his eyes and sighed. "I have a dreadful feeling. I suspect the police are taking him to Gourpali. They will claim that he escaped to instigate further violence, and they will pin all the crimes on him."

As the ambulance rumbled toward Gourpali, the tremulous patient stared at crackled ceiling. He remained within himself, wide-eyed and silent.

# CHAPTER 60

Gourpali
Prelude to Worship
Sunday, September 14, 2008
8:50 AM

The sun streamed through the trees, casting shadows aside and flooding the village with light. The warm glow bathed the sleeping face of Chandrika. Like the fingers of a curious child, the sun pried open her eyes. She blinked to clear the film of dust and tears.

Every cell in her body screamed against moving. In her mind, Chandrika was trying to find Andrea, Indu, and Anila, but she lay still, bound by pain. She languished at the throbbing in her side. Every breath hurt. *I can't stay here. I have to move. I have to help Andrea.*

She grabbed the door frame and pulled herself close enough to prop up her head. The street was clear. *No people on a Sunday morning?* She would not allow her mind to go any further. *I don't want to know what they are doing to my village.* "Dear Jesus, please protect Indu."

Chandrika grit her teeth and mustered all her strength to sit up. Memories of the past week spun in her mind. *Indu, I hope you are safe. I want to hold you, but I cannot even stand.*

She closed her eyes and welcomed the sun on her face. Fighting exhaustion and nausea, she poured out her heart. "God, I need you now. I believe you are here. Please let me know you are here."

* * *

Andrea settled against a vacant house. She peered through the window and peeked around the side. *Where is everyone?* The words of one of her assailants stung in her mind. *"We will allow no Christians in this village. They will convert, leave, or die."*

"God, I need you now."

She felt a strange sense, even as the words left her lips. Warmth engulfed her as though God was speaking to her soul. *I am here. I know that you need me. Know that I need you.*

*God needs me?* Andrea lifted her eyes. Across the dusty street she watched the sun color the tiny home where she had been held and beaten. She strained as though trying to see through the walls. *I know Chandrika is in there.*

She glanced down the dusty road to her left and then back toward the house. Andrea's heart leapt at the sight of someone slumped against the doorframe. *Chandrika.* Ignoring her fear, she bolted across the road and slid to a stop beside Chandrika.

She glanced over her shoulder to inspect the street, and then she focused on Chandrika. Her head was a mangled mesh of dried blood, matted earth, and twisted hair. Her eyes were almost too weak to open. A dried rivulet of blood streaked from her nose to her left ear. Andrea cradled her friend and caressed her blood-matted hair.

With her lips dry, cracked and bruised, Chandrika tried to speak. "Indu?" she gasped.

"She is fine. She and Anila are hiding in the forest. They have food and water and your cell phone."

Chandrika sighed, unable to hide her smile. *Thank you, God!*

Andrea rushed through the house looking for water and a wash cloth. *No running water. I expected that, but there's no bottle, bucket, barrel, nothing.* Why did I not bring my backpack? "Chandrika, I can't find any wa—"

Her phrase died in the shadow of bandana-covered faces. Dark eyes stared through her soul like daggers of hate. They could not see Andrea but a lust for blood.

Andrea stood paralyzed. Nausea mixed with terror as she one of the officers said, "You had your chance to leave." Her heart was praying in overdrive, no words, just deep moans of the Spirit within her.

Her eyes drifted beyond the officers' silhouettes toward a growing mob. She trembled at the throbbing commotion as the mob pressed toward her. She shuttered at the horrific sight as the frenzied crowd spewed a beaten man through the door.

His hair was disheveled with sanguine dust, his eyes swollen almost shut, nose bent and dripping blood on the packed floor. Unrecognizable, he was wearing a stained bandana over his mouth, his hands behind his back.

*What is he going to do? He can't do anything. He can barely stand.* Her heart skipped a beat at the sight of tears squeezing through the swollen plumps on his face.

The man who had spoken drew a long knife. Reaching behind the bloodied young man, he cut the cords that bound him.

Andrea caught the rising emesis in her dry throat as she stepped toward the young man. "Satyajit." She intentionally left the bandana on his face as she pressed toward him. Embracing his wounded frame, she looked over his shoulder into the young faces drenched with rage. *Christ, give me patience. Give me compassion.*

A stinging grasp pierced her.

"Your moment is over. Our friend Satyajit would like to join you for worship. What a beautiful Sunday morning!"

# CHAPTER 61

Gourpali
Worship
Sunday, September 14, 2008
9:00 AM

No church bells pealed. No brisk handshakes. No smiles. No "Good morning." The tiny church's silhouette seemed austere and indifferent, like a god far away and unaware. The hate-filled mob pressed the shrunken remnant of the faithful toward the church.

One elderly saint crumpled to her knees in desperate prayer. None seemed brave enough or interested enough to abuse her. The throng simply flowed around her like a stream around a boulder.

Andrea watched, powerless as an impassioned cluster gathered around a young man, jabbing, slapping, spitting and threatening. Another group forced some villagers to kneel and recite some chant. Tears streaming, Andrea's thoughts raced to her mother as she watched these seemingly hopeless families. Those who were able grasped what little they had and sprinted away from the church and out of the village.

The pressing and shoving suddenly stopped. Andrea stood before the church, closed doors, no stained glass, no adornments, only a makeshift cross. To the mocking crowd, the petite church was a lost island in a dry sea, but to Andrea, the church was a bastion of hope. She studied the simple cross as she stood at the doorway between life and death.

The shadow of the church retreated before her, and the tiny cross grew in her mind. Entranced, she ignored the rising sun. The stark blue sky vanished from her mind as clouds of grey quaked with thunder. She found herself once again on the ship in the storm. She saw that warm and fearless face, ignoring the torrent, smiling; his hand stretching to hold hers. His calming voice spoke through his eyes. *Now you must choose.*

A wave of hands grasped and pulled her back into reality. The mix of Oriya and Hindi was intentionally broken as Natraj leaned over her and spoke with clear, enunciated English. He into her eyes, wanting her to hear and understand every word. "Now you must choose between life and death."

\* \* \*

The police car rounded the turn toward Gourpali and skidded to a stop.

"What are we doing?" asked the younger officer.

"We are waiting." The senior officer twisted around in his seat. "You heard his story. Our friend Vishal wants to see his granddaughter before he dies. We are going to help him."

Vishal tried to think of anything else, but his mind recoiled mercilessly between regrets. He stared out the rear window, muttering to himself. *My son, I am so sorry I rejected you. None of this would have happened if I had not let hate consume me. Now I've lost everything and everyone.* A startling warmth rush over him as a voice within said, *"Not everyone." Indu, my granddaughter! God, do not let me lose her.*

Vishal held his breath as the ambulance dusted around the corner, barely missing the police car.

\* \* \*

Mitch fired off a few photos of the police car, hoping to

catch a shot of Vishal. He struggled to maintain his balance at 50 miles an hour with a beat-up suspension bounding over a hole-infested road. He straddled the patient as he looked toward Naomi.

Naomi felt his eyes on the back of her head. "We have no time to stop, and they would probably detain us anyway."

\* \* \*

Andrea cowered at the oily, leathery fingers pilfering her innocence. Her stomach leapt into her throat as clamoring hands lifted her overhead, drawing her into the center of their hate and arousal. They tossed her on the ground next to Chandrika, hands still clinging to her, stretching and tearing her clothes.

Natraj stood over Chandrika. Speaking to his crowd, he shouted, "This one is too worn, beaten and filthy." He turned to Andrea. "But this one is fresh and so fair."

Pressing himself against the drawn and quartered Andrea, he sunk his talons into her waist. He forced his cheek against hers, drew the deepest breath, inhaling any fragrant remnants that hid beneath her stench. He dug his lips into her ear. "I've never been with an American girl." He tightened his jaw and his grip. "Until now." His nails climbed her back, and his winding fingers clenched her collar.

The forgotten Satyajit slapped him from behind, gouging his face and shouting his last words. "Leave her alone!"

One swift blow to his head, and sunlight faded to black. Satyajit opened his eyes. He was engulfed in smoke, but the air felt cool and thin. Though the smoke was thick and crackling with flames, he felt nothing. He stood, recognizing that he was inside the church. The tin roof popped and rattled against the rising heat. A seam of light split the fire as the silhouette of a man stepped out of the flames toward him.

Inescapable eyes and the unmistakable voice of his dreams awakened him to a new reality. *"Thank you for bringing God's mercy to my father."* Warmth embraced his soul. The church dissolved around him as light poured like rain.

Satyajit lifted his head to welcoming glorious skies. He saw his thin sack of discarded flesh fall beneath him. A cool rush of air swirled around him and through him as new life pulled him away from the sorrow.

*  *  *

As Satyajit's limp frame collapsed at his feet, Natraj grunted and nodded. His minions gathered the crumpled and tattered body of their former friend and carried it into the house of worship. Obedient hands tossed him onto a mound of kindling, built from smashed chairs, a broken table, and a few Bibles.

A handful of his men wrestled the large wooden cross from the front of the sanctuary. Dragging it to the growing heap, they hoisted the cross, thrusting it down into the center of the pile. Natraj unleashed a victorious chuckle as he left the church, turning his sardonic eyes to Andrea.

In the shrinking shadow of the church, Andrea clawed the earth. "Please help me, God."

The sound of her cries ignited passion in her assailant. Natraj stretched a wicked smile across his face as he loosened his belt.

Andrea writhed, kicking the hands that held her legs. She dug in her heels to push away. As she scratched with her nails and wriggled her arms, the grip of hate grew tighter. *They are not going to let go. No fight will be enough. God help me and forgive them.* Struggling vanished into numbness, and she lay motionless.

With no fight, no passion, no whimpering, she felt Natraj loosen his grip. She opened her eyes. Startled as a child waking from a dream, she stared at Natraj. *Why? How could you?*

His eyes dispelled all that remained of her courage.

She buckled and rolled onto her side to vomit, expressing her misery all about her.

The crowd recoiled from the oozing flow.

Natraj gritted his teeth and spat. Repulsed as he was, anger still ruled over his passion. *I am going to have this girl no matter what.* Grabbing her by her belt loops, he twisted her hips, plopping her onto her knees. As he motioned with his hands, those of his troupe furiously grappled to claim their piece of Andrea, holding her anywhere they could reach. A horrendous moan and gasp heaved from her tiny frame as pain ripped through her abdomen and pelvis.

*Oh, God, what is happening?* Andrea's thoughts flailed. They're not even doing anything.

As Natraj ripped at her jeans, thrusting them down from her hips, Andrea felt a violent flood of warmth. Her flow, not due for another week, had come early. Contractions combined with fear unleashed a torrid flow of menses and urine. The timely blast disgraced and incensed her attacker.

Natraj had no more stomach for violating this virgin. *I will just beat her to death and burn her with the others.* His plan was to trap the parishioners inside the church and watch it incinerate. As he heard the familiar crunch of gravel beneath tires and saw the familiar cloud of dust, he knew the police were on their way.

Natraj cursed and screamed. "They are early!"

He was supposed to be done before the police arrived to "investigate."

Natraj shouted. "Get them inside."

*　*　*

Anila had tried to stop her, but Indu was a child, quick, agile, and stubborn. Anila had only one of those qualities, and her stubbornness could not compete with Indu's quickness. Shortly after Andrea left, Indu set out after her. Following from a safe distance, Indu would duck when Andrea paused to turn around. Indu followed her to the edge of the village. When Andrea slipped out of her sight, between the tiny houses, Indu dashed toward the south end of the village. She tip-toed behind Chandrika's house. Fear kept her from entering.

She squatted beneath her bedroom window, listening, hearing nothing. When she was satisfied that the house was empty, she crept behind the neighboring houses. She could only guess where they had taken Chandrika.

Indu passed house after house, each one dark and silent. *Where is everyone?* She crouched against the back of the house. Her hands folded, she whispered a prayer as she remembered the disquieting silence of her own village when those men came and took her father.

In the days after the attack, she had quietly observed the way her neighbors went on with their lives as though nothing had happened. She prayed as she remembered how the light returned to her village when Andrea and Marci came.

Indu continued praying. "God, please don't let that happen in this village. Please protect these people. You have the power. Please use it. Let these people know You are God." As though she was interrupting the thoughts of God, Indu continued. "Yes, I know You are God, whether You use Your power or not, but please do this for me. You know I love You."

The sweet waft of her words drifted through the halls of

Heaven, joining the prayers of the saints.

The Spirit within her and around her provided the strength to stand without fear. Indu passed to the next house and the next, peering through the rear windows, seeing nothing. She stood still at the sound of footsteps. They pounded like a fateful drum. As the mob marched past her hiding place, she slid along the east side of the home and into the shadows. Looking and listening, she chanced a peek toward the hostile gang. With sticks and clubs, they were grappling for space around the doorway.

Spying across the street, down the street, toward the church, she saw no sign of Andrea or Chandrika. Fear clutched her tender throat, but Indu swallowed her fear and clung to the words of her mother. *"No matter what happens today or tomorrow, always trust Him." Always trust Him.* The words played on a loop in her mind. With the giant faith of a child, Indu walked toward the crowd.

Standing behind them, she began to pray for each one of them, "God, let him know You today." She combed the mass of men with her eyes, pausing on each head to offer an individual prayer.

As the crowd turned, holding their focus on those who were leaving the house, Indu followed behind them, continuing her prayers. As the crowd neared the church, she caught glimpses of Andrea, but she still could not see Chandrika. Somehow immune to fear, she stood watching and praying. Two men, whom she did not recognize, stood beside her. One of them smiled and offered his hand. His gentle grip warmed her with strength and a soothing comfort. His eyes captured her heart.

The man nodded as if to say, "Keep praying."

Indu focused once again on the hostile crowd. She thought it strange that her prayers were for these evil men instead of being for Andrea and Chandrika, but something inside directed her prayers.

Her intent prayers were disrupted by the boil of dust pouring down the road. She saw the familiar ambulance from the hospital, followed by a police car.

\* \* \*

As the church doors flung open, Natraj shouted in Oriya, "The Lord calls all those who believe to enter and worship."

A few of the elderly women pulled away from their families and marched into the church. Natraj sneered at the dehydrated, almost lifeless body of Chandrika. He nodded, and his men dragged her up the slope to the church. With callous disregard and unfeeling hands, they tossed her through doorway. Chandrika flopped limply against the bloodied remains of Satyajit.

Andrea remained on her knees. Still numb, she lifted her head to the encroaching feet of those who would burn her alive. Through their legs, she eyed the tiny form of Indu praying. An inexplicable surge of calm rushed over her, and she marveled that no one seemed to notice the little angel. *I should be afraid for her, but I know she is ok. I should be afraid for myself, but I'm not.* Straining to look up at her attackers, she realized, *I am afraid for them.*

Each scowling face screamed at her with anger and fear. Their vacuous eyes opened into a chasm, void of any other feelings. Andrea lost herself in a flood of compassion. *They truly do not know what they are doing.* At the top of her lungs, she cried out, "God, please forgive them." As the sun blazed its course over the humble steeple, she prayed, "Let them know You. God, let them know You."

Natraj screamed, "Get them inside. The fire starts now!"

He clutched Andrea's arm, and dragged her to the church. He pulled her to her feet in the open doorway.

Andrea gripped her sliding jeans as she struggled to stand. She buckled at the horror inside. *Satyajit!* He bore no resemblance to the young man she remembered. She trembled at the sight of his twisted, tormented, brutalized flesh, his blood spilled completely.

Andrea turned away and heaved at the sight of Chandrika lying nearby. Chandrika! Her limp body lay naked, discarded like waste, breathing but unconscious. The unmistakable smell of kerosene breezed past her as four men with buckets entered the church and began soaking the pile of broken flesh and furniture. Andrea shuddered at their savage cries as they soaked the remains of Satyajit.

In the midst of such vile carnage, Andrea was enamored with the shameless love of three elderly women who entered the church unabated. Ignoring the splashing kerosene, one of the women knelt beside Chandrika. She squelched her tears and wiped the young nurse's face. Another courageous saint wrapped her in a beautiful cloth. A mix of kerosene and blood soaked through the delicate fabric. The third prayed next to Satyajit.

Andrea felt numb in the eye of her emotional hurricane. She gazed in wonder at the three aged saints respecting life in the midst of impending death.

Her wonder vanished as Natraj clutched her arm and whirled her around. Eye-to-eye, he blasted his hot, disgusting breath into her face. She caught a glimpse of the wannabe ambulance barreling toward the church. *Marci and Mitch!*

Natraj smacked her face. "Look at me!" He raised a club over her head and shouted, "This is for poisoning my friend."

Andrea lofted one last prayer as the club came crushing down. She felt herself falling as in a dream, falling and falling. Silence. No sunlight. No church. A warm darkness veiled her sight.

She landed hard on the slippery deck of that same boat in the storm. She was immediately drawn into the moment as though she had never left. The man in the stern was still smiling, arms outstretched. The boat tossed wildly on the angry sea. The man showed no regard for the rudder or the anchor. He closed his eyes and breathed deeply. Without saying a word, He spoke to her heart. "You know I can calm the storm, but you're not sure that I will."

He opened his eyes, their deep brownish-green scanning her mind. An unpretentious smile stretched across his face. Ignoring the storm, he stepped toward her. "If I called you to walk on water, you would try."

Andrea nodded with some hesitancy. Looking beyond the man, she could see Chandrika sleeping at the bow. Andrea rubbed her head. *How does she rest in such a storm?*

The man leaned into her view. He lifted his eyebrows. Without him saying a word, Andrea clearly heard him answer. *"Trust."*

The winds wheezed through the cracks in the boat. Waves slapped and shoved the modest craft, washing over the deck. The other men on the boat scurried about, frightened for their lives. The man in the stern wheeled around Andrea and headed back toward the rudder as it danced about wildly. He lifted his hand as though ready to seize control of the boat. Andrea followed his every move. With his hand hovering over the rudder, he paused as though he felt her eyes poised to watch him exert his power.

The storm raged with even greater ferocity, but he turned and stepped toward the edge of the boat once more. He stretched out his arms, palms toward the sea. He closed his eyes once more, inhaled deeply, defying the wind.

He smiled as he felt the warmth of Andrea's anticipation. He opened his mouth to speak to the wind and the waves. Andrea stepped toward him. Leaning to hear his words, she felt his unmistakable whisper roar through her heart and mind. *What if I call you to walk through fire?*

\* \* \*

Marci uncontrollably bounced around the back of the microbus. She choked on the cloud of dust in and around the ambulance. "Can you see anything?" she asked Naomi.

"Oh—my—god!" Mitch cried as all four of them witnessed a large plume of fire raging from the tiny church ahead.

As they pulled into the village, the incensed mob reveled in triumph. Smoke and flames surged from the church windows. The doors were shut tight, braced to thwart any escape.

\* \* \*

Mitch had no time to pause in disbelief. He immediately leapt from the ambulance and began shooting photos of everything, the gawkers, the angry throng, the miserable excuse for a church, stragglers slowly fleeing but still watching.

As the police car slid to a stop beside them, Marci stumbled out of the ambulance. Tears burst from her core, shaking her violently and washing the filth from her face. She pushed past the police car unaware of everything but Andrea. As Mitch clutched her arm to stop her, she choked on her dry scream. "I know she's in there. Dear God! Mitch! I know she's in there."

Mitch refused to let go. Pulling hard, he drew her into his arms. Slinging his camera over his shoulder, he wrapped her in a tight embrace. "You can't go up there."

*I know.* "Don't you dare tell me everything's going to be ok."

Mitch swallowed hard. *I can't say anything that would hurt her.* Surprised at his own thoughts, he realized, *I really do love this girl, and I don't want anything to harm her.*

His thought was disrupted by the brush of three officers darting past. "What's going on here?" the first officer demanded.

As the angry mob scattered, Mitch noticed one young man handing his club and bandana to another and walk toward the police. *He is staying.*

A familiar voice said, "That's Natraj." Vishal stood silent, staring at Natraj as though seeing himself.

"Vishal? What are you doing here?"

Vishal nodded toward the wounded motorcyclist. "This man was supposed to meet the police at the main road. Their plan was to say I escaped and led the attack. They would have burned me alive, and they may yet."

Vishal and Mitch turned toward a renewed commotion. A small crowd was growing again, near the church. Mitch reached for Marci's hand, and Vishal followed closely as they moved toward the crowd.

\* \* \*

Incensed youths cheered as Satyajit's macerated pulp burst into flames. As the perpetrators fled the church, they tossed Andrea's limp body toward the pyre. Slamming the doors, they sealed their victims inside.

The elderly women pulled Chandrika away from the flames. Rolling on top of her, they suppressed the fire.

Chandrika moaned. She half-opened her eyes. Then snapping them open, she turned her head to the nearest etched face. Dry, crackling Oriya wheezed from her throat. "My friend, the American girl, where is she?"

Two of the women immediately tore away from Chandrika. Rushing to the pyre, they stopped abruptly, halted by a wall of fire. As smoke covered the ceiling and began to ripple downward, their vision was challenged. Through the flames, they could see the young woman robed in fire. Strangely, it appeared she was standing.

The aging saints resumed their prayers as they stood amazed. Cinders drifted from the ceiling like falling leaves. They stepped back as the roof creaked and moaned.

"Do you see what I am seeing?"

The women embraced amid the scorching heat, eyes transfixed on the glowing image of Andrea. A furor of flames twisted around her, engulfing her. To elder squinting eyes, fiery robes appeared to be shielding her. Andrea was untouched.

Clinging to each other, their prayers shrank into whispers and silent muttering as they watched Andrea open her eyes. The smoke cleared from the center of the church as though driven by a silent wind. Andrea twisted to her right while leaning forward, bracing herself on nothing.

The blaze continued to rage, but the popping, crackling, and hissing faded. Chaotic thunder and violent winds unleashed within the church, crashing against the walls with hurricane force. The elderly women stood like statues in the eye of the storm.

The sound of heavy rain and crashing waves sent their minds reeling. They turned to look for Chandrika. She was standing beside them. As they smiled at her, the wall of fire buckled. A ball of flame shot out of the shrinking heap. Like a giant hand, the fingers of fire wrapped around Chandrika. As though entranced, she slowly and deliberately stepped toward the fire. The mothers of the village embraced each other and crouched to floor, trembling and closing their eyes. The sound of the mighty rushing wind continued to twist around them.

* * *

Indu opened her eyes. She had prayed for every face she had seen. She prayed for their families, especially their children. When she had prayed for them, she turned her prayers toward Chandrika and Andrea, Marci, Mitch, and Satyajit. With her prayers offered and eyes wide open, Indu walked boldly toward the church.

She gave no thought to the two men who had been beside her. She did not notice every eye in the village trained on her. She ignored the fierce crackling, snapping, and hissing that roared from the church. Her mind was intent on one thing.

The flames had softened to a mix of black, grey and orange. The tin roof rumbled and seized as the tortuous heat warped the metal. Heaves of smoke and sparks breached the roof. One spewing shower ignited a nearby tree and house. The immense heat opened a wide buffer, forcing onlookers to back away from the inferno.

Indu marched unabated. No one stood in her way.

* * *

The trio of Marci, Mitch, and Vishal followed the police officers from a safe distance. As they approached the church, the crowd seemed to part.

"What's going on?"

"I can't really see," said Mitch. "Someone is moving through the crowd toward the church, but he is too short."

Vishal stood breathless as he saw his beautiful Indu step out from the crowd. He squeezed between Marci and Mitch, nudging his way toward her. Mitch tried to stop him, but the lead officer, turning around, said, "No. It's okay. He is here to see his granddaughter."

The color washed from Mitch's face as he realized the cruel, vindictive plot of the police. Mitch kept his camera behind his back as he slid around the back of the crowd.

Sliding into the first house, Mitch peeled the camera off his back. Wheeling around, he began firing more pictures. He spied Vishal kneeling next to Indu.

Vishal was overwhelmed beyond speech. He could not collect one solitary thought. The flood of questions, regrets, lost moments, and wasted emotions blurred his mind. His parched throat and cracked lips made swallowing impossible. Placing his hand on Indu, he choked on emotion. "I am your grandfather."

Indu fixed on his face. Looking into his eyes, young Indu measured the depth of her grandfather's heart. She studied the etching of life, the invasion of gray, his spriggly eyebrows. When he sniffed and drew a sigh, Indu saw her father in him. *My mother prayed for you every night.*

Indu smiled without a word. She reached out to him. His giant fingers engulfed her tiny hand.

Mitch captured the moment.

When she touched him, he felt a strange cooling warmth. Warm inside but impervious to the mounting heat before him, Vishal followed as Indu led him to the smoldering doors of the church. Vishal wanted to embrace her and escape, but a strong urge within held him fast.

Indu smiled faintly and withdrew her hand. Stepping forward, she closed her eyes and pressed her palms against the door.

* * *

Andrea was soaked to the skin on the storm-tossed vessel. Despite the tempest, she felt calm. The man who had been sound asleep in the stern was still standing with his arms outstretched. She watched the rain pounding his shoulders, raindrops bouncing off his smile. The storm still raging, he turned toward her once more. She clutched the side of the boat as it lurched with a great wave. Her sense of calm was shaken, but his strong hand reached out to her.

"Andrea."

The sound of his voice calmed the tempest within her.

"I command the wind and the waves."

Andrea drew a deep breath as she waited for him to quiet the storm. Nothing happened. She studied his eyes. He spoke not a word, but in her mind, she heard his voice. "Sometimes I calm the storm, but today I invite the rain."

* * *

Amazement glazed the eyes of onlookers as Indu leaned against the door. She muttered inaudibly, eyes shut tight, arms stretched out, face against the curling paint.

Awe swept over the crowd. A cool rush shook those closest to the church.

The cloudless sky remained a startling blue, yet the sound of thunder quaked the village. Some swore they heard rain, their eyes dancing about in search of clouds. Others watched as Indu maintained her vigilant prayer.

Vishal trembled as he knelt beside her. *Oh, God, I don't*

*know what I'm doing,* he prayed and folded his hands.

Curious onlookers from all around had begun to gather at the sight of smoke from the otherwise unnoticed village. Marci stretched and squeezed her way through the thick mob. With her eyes fixed on Indu, Marci inched her way forward until she reached the church. She knelt behind Indu, pressing close to Vishal.

Placing her right hand on his shoulder, Marci began to whisper her own prayers. She poured her hurt and fear. *God, protect my Andrea and Chandrika.*

A voice within urged her. *"Pray for their attackers."*

*I can't, God! I just can't.* The image of Christ on the cross suddenly appeared in her mind. She felt his eyes as though he was praying for her, for those who crucified Him. She choked on the thought and offered a silent groan for those who so brutally attacked her friends.

A smattering of the village faithful gathered around the trio at the door. On their knees, prayer consumed their focus. Nothing else mattered. A father of six abandoned his fear as he bowed his head. A young mother, cradling her infant son, ignored the warnings from her family. One after another, villagers knelt to pray.

Natraj and the three police officers stood with arms folded. Natraj ran away in his mind. His triumph had soured. *Christians praying.* He could not imagine a greater failure.

Prayers continued as the crowd of observers stretched the village. Amazement and wonder captivated Gourpali.

*Who is this little girl, and what is she doing?*

As Indu and the growing faithful prayed, the roaring noise faded. The sparks died. The flames receded. The smoke began to hiss like steam. Black turned to grey and then white. The thunder ceased. The wind fell silent.

Mitch stood alone in the house across from the church. No longer shooting pictures from the shadow, he stood dumbfounded, watching as the unscathed child released her hands from the door. *How did Indu not get burned?*

Silence replaced the crackling of sparks and the roars of thunder. The quiet stilled the tears, the screams and shouts. No one moved. The tiny angel at door captured every eye.

Indu remained locked on her objective. She motioned to Vishal, urging him to open the doors. Marci and others stepped forward to remove the barricade.

*　*　*

Andrea felt the soothing coolness of the rain pelting her hot, parched skin. She puzzled at her dry throat in the midst of such a torrent. Although the waves continued crashing and tossing about, the boat seemed to calm, only gently rocking. Andrea let go and turned toward the bow. Chandrika was no longer there.

Scanning the vessel, Andrea spotted her walking slowly and deliberately toward her. She wanted to run to Chandrika but felt safer beside the man in the stern.

Andrea turned to him one last time. Something inside told her she would not be on the boat any longer. As the man opened his mouth to speak to the storm, her eyes opened to a cloudless blue sky through the remains of a tin roof.

Her hands brushed the dry, bare floor. Against the clear sky, she caught the austere shadow of an old wooden cross. Her thoughts awakened, rushing to Chandrika. *I'm in the church in Gourpali. They're going to set it on fire.*

Andrea leapt to her feet. Backing away from the cross, she bumped against the doors.

\* \* \*

Mitch left his hiding place and hustled toward the church, jostling his bulky, frumpish frame. A journalist, he was accustomed to swimming through crowds. He ran to the thinnest edge of the mob and hurdled his way to the doors. He shoved his camera into Marci's chest. "Hold this. Please." He pleaded eye-to-eye.

Mitch stepped to the door as the barricade came down. Vishal moved the latch and the doors flung open. Mitch thrust himself into the doorway where his arms met a falling Andrea. His world melted in his arms as he marveled at her smile, the two of them collapsed on the ground together.

Mitch gently gathered her in his arms. He drew a relieved sigh. *She smells like the woods, but there is no hint of smoke. Not one singed hair. No soot on her face.*

Andrea gazed at him, unaware of herself. Comfortably collapsed in his arms, she studied his eyes. *I know that you know.* She smiled as the wells of his soul sprung to life, her gentle fingers stroking each tear.

Marci shoved Mitch's camera right back at him. Reaching across his arms, she covered her half-naked friend in a crimson sāddhi. "Thank you!" Marci nodded to the gracious woman who slunk back into the crowd.

Neither Mitch nor Andrea had offered any attention to her nakedness. Despite her condition, Andrea felt no shame, no guilt, no anger, and no remorse. She held her focus on Mitch as Marci pulled up her jeans and fastened them for her.

\* \* \*

Anila stood bent and frail at the edge of the crowd. She was beyond weary, dry-mouthed, panting, pulse racing, and near collapse. She had left her wooded retreat to chase Indu as a snail would chase a rabbit. Threatening heartbeats forced her to stop many times. The rising tower of smoke added to her angst. *My church. My Chandrika, and young Indu.* Her worst fears unfolded before her failing eyes.

Too old to run but too stubborn to wait, she was dead set on finding Indu. When she rounded the corner and caught sight of her church, the smoke had faded, the doors opened. Her tiny village was flooded with people.

Anila persisted toward the church, her eyes too weak to identify Indu from any distance. When she finally reached the church, she saw a man she had never met cradling a young woman that looked like Andrea. She edged past them, nudging through the doorway. Her feeble eyes crinkled at the sight of the charred remains near the cross. *Dear God, No!* She stumbled toward the body. "Oh, my Chandrika! No!" With trembling hands, she patted the marred face. Sniffling and sputtering, her tears turned to wailing. A hoarse cry interrupted her grief.

"Anila." Chandrika wept at the sight of Anila beside the scorched shell of Satyajit. Her voice dry from dust and tears, she called out again. "Anila!"

"Chandrika?" The aging woman slowly stood and ambled toward her. Although age restrained her crumpling frame, nothing could confine her joy. Anila flailed her arms wildly. Her heart pulsed. *Thank You, God!* She pressed toward Chandrika as fast as her aged legs could carry her. Her joy was blunted as she realized Chandrika was kneeling over two of her dearest friends.

"Mother, your friends walked into the church on their own." Chandrika's words stumbled as she wept. "They didn't have to come, but they did." Her eyes met Anila's. "They did it for me! They saw me beaten and naked. This sāddhi belonged to them. They clothed me and "prayed for me."

Anila's arms spoke for her as she embraced Chandrika and Indu.

\* \* \*

The sun crested the torn roof as Vishal stepped into the church. He stood in silence, tears streaming sunlight broke through the warped metal and illuminated the cross and the charred remains. *Satyajit! It should have been me!*

The words rang in his mind as he stared at the cross. *It should have been me.*

Andrea rested in Mitch's arms as she watched Vishal. She studied his face as he entered the church. *He is not the same man I met at the hospital. Hate and fear are gone.* She felt his heart as he gazed at the cross and Satyajit. "He's not here anymore, Vishal."

Vishal did not waver. With his eyes fixed to the cross, he said, "I know. He is with my son." Tears of sorrow and joy mingled down his cheek. "He is with my son and my wife, with Pastor Joseph and his family. He is with his wife, the daughter-in-law I never met and my grandchildren I never knew."

Andrea stood and embraced Vishal.

He felt strength from her hug. "I know will I see them again. I am at peace." He looked into her eyes and continued, "I found the peace I saw in their eyes. The peace I see in your eyes now."

\* \* \*

Mitch sat with his hands folded, staring like an empty-handed child at Christmas. The world seemed to stop turning as he stared at Satyajit's blackened corpse. His stomach curdled. *Why? None of this makes any sense.*

Normally unfazed by the worst of humanity, Mitch could not lift his camera for even one picture. His eyes moved across the floor to the makeshift funeral pyre. The broken furniture was completely gone. There were only scarce ashes, but the cross remained.

Mitch gritted his teeth and stood facing the cross. *It's still here. How can that be? And how is it possible that Andrea and Chandrika survived? I watched the mob discard Chandrika's limp body against Satyajit, but she is unscathed.*

*I watched as they forced Andrea into the church. I cringed as the doors closed. The flames surely engulfed her. The house next to the church burned to rubble. Even the tree is gone, but the church is still here. The cross is still here.*

Tears welled as his eyes fixed on the rough wood. Years of emotions swelled and raged. Every frustration, every doubt, every angry thought for God stirred within. Everything else seemed to disappear, and all he could see was the cross.

*How can you stand there silent? How can you expect me to believe when you let evil run freely over innocent people? How can you just stand there? You have haunted me my whole life. You are silent, invisible, and untouchable, and you want me to believe.*

Mitch collapsed in a pool of his own tears. He covered his face and tried to forget, but the pain of past and present would not surrender even one moment of peace.

*Get a hold of yourself, Hawkins!* He drew a deep breath. *On your feet!* He grabbed his camera and aimed it at the charred remains of Satyajit. As he trembled, he felt a hand on his shoulder. He shrugged and gathered his poise. *Back to reality, Mitch.* He snapped pictures like a machine and buried his emotions once again. *I'm a journalist. This is what I do. I report what I see. I report what I know.*

He felt the hand once more and turned around, but no one was there. Looking through the open doors, he saw a mass of people.

*"Untouchable."*

"What?" Mitch turned back to the cross. *Still no one!* He pounded his fist against the rugged timber. "I can't believe. I won't."

The sturdy beam loosened and fell.

His world was suddenly dark.

\* \* \*

Mitch lay motionless, his head splitting and his vision blurred. The cold floor lilted beneath him. He felt his stomach lurch as the floor shook and water doused him.

He lifted his head and blinked. He saw Andrea and Chandrika standing in the wavering shadow of the mast. He watched the shadow. With the sail lowered, it looked like a cross touching the waves.

A man in a white kurta appeared between Andrea and Chandrika. Mitch saw no fear. His mind drifted into his past. He heard the faint voice of his mother singing.

*I take, O cross, thy shadow for my abiding place. I ask no other sunshine than the sunshine of his face. Content to let the world go by, to know no gain nor loss. My sinful self my only shame, my glory all the cross.*

Mitch clenched his teeth and groaned to void the noise. The wind howled around him but could not drown the song as it grew. He screamed, but her words still rang. He stood to run but felt no floor. He looked down. He was drifting away from himself.

*There I am on the deck of that ship! How can it be?* At once, the storm thrust him against the mast. The song stopped. Although the storm raged, he felt a strange calm and silence.

The man in white turned and lifted His arms. He whispered, "Be still," and the wind and waves ceased.

Everything was still. The waves disappeared. The deck was dry. The mast stood firm like a stalwart cross.

Mitch felt the song starting again. He struck the mast. The sturdy timber fell, striking him on the head.

# CHAPTER 62

All Saints Hospital
Monday, September 15, 2008
9:30 PM

Andrea kept vigil. She studied the lines on his face, watched the tide of his chest rise and fall. She held his cold, swollen hand and waited for the moment when he would open his eyes and everything would be all right.

Marci stepped through the door toting Mitch's backpack. "No change?"

"Nothing."

Marci plopped the bag next to Mitch's bed. "I'm not sure how much longer we should stay."

"The nurse said I could stay with him as long as I like."

"No, I mean I'm not sure how much longer we should stay in India. You were almost raped and murdered yesterday, Andrea."

"Yes, and God protected us. Do you think He would protect us more if we stayed home?"

Marci shook her head. *Sometimes I have better luck talking to the wall.* "I'll be in the nurse's lounge."

"I'm sorry, Marci. It's just…"

"No. It's ok. I understand, but I would like to go home. The train leaves tomorrow morning at 11. I would like to be on it."

As Marci left, Andrea noticed a partially unzipped pouch on Mitch's backpack. As she reached to close it, she noticed a fine leather journal. She looked around the room to make sure no one was watching as she untied the leather cords and flipped through the pages. *There it is. September 7, 2008.*

\*\*\*

## Mitch's Journal

I have no faith and I feel pity for those who do. Everyone wants to find meaning and purpose in life, but there is none, and so we invent hope in a hereafter and a higher power.

I grew up surrounded by faith and religious teaching. The nuns smacked my hands into obedience as they taught me about the love of Christ. My parents took me to mass faithfully. I was nursed on Bible stories. It was a good childhood really, but then I grew up.

Faith became what it truly is, a superstitious hope, a fantasy. The only god is time. Time measures our days and cruelly counts down the minutes until our last breath. Time, the great teacher, kills the pupil at the end of life's lessons.

So, all there is is all there is. We make the most of every day. We give life what it needs from us and we take what we can get. Life is in the experience, but for some the experience is tainted by religion and its plagues of guilt, grief, and intolerance.

I travel the world as a journalist, trying to understand this idea of faith, religion, voodoo, superstition, astrology, or whatever you choose to call it. It ruins life for the rest of us. I am baffled by wars fought in the name of religion, acts of terror, oppression, discrimination, and judgment inflicted on us all by people of faith.

Religion is the greatest evil.

And so I find myself travelling to India, to try to comprehend the why, the reason, if there is any reason, for the violence in Orissa.

Here I am in Amsterdam, awaiting my flight. I amuse myself with people-watching. Two untested American women cowered as I passed them in the bookstore, naïve college students no doubt. I ogled them just to watch them squirm. I hope they are going to Delhi.

\* \* \*

*He's writing about us.*

\* \* \*

I met the two girls from the U.S., Marci and Andrea. Neither has the first clue of what they are facing. Their plan, for lack of a better word, is to travel to the heart of Orissa with blind hope, out to save the world – on their own. Unbelievable!

I like these two girls. Something about their innocent, courageous passion is enticing. It would be nice to believe in something with as much heart as they do. I'm here to understand, to see and know. I want something to make sense when nothing does. These two young women seem fully assured in their beliefs. I wish I could believe, but it's a fairy tale. I can't believe in an all-knowing, all-loving god when I'm travelling to a world of suffering upon suffering, neither can I willfully suspend my disbelief.

Those who seem genuine in their beliefs intrigue me. Andrea is one of them. She is steadfast, a silent saint, always praying or pensive. She occasionally offers a look of consternation toward her friend, Marci.

Marci is the judge. She is my kind of Christian, knows all the answers and walks the straight line, mostly straight line. She has an eye bent on judgment before anyone can even think or move. She judged me by my shorts and flip-flops even before she noticed I was browsing porn. Her eyes popped, her face flushed, and she turned abruptly from the magazines in front of me. That's when I saw Christian written all over her. I can hardly wait to really get into it with her.

\* \* \*

Mitch opened his eyes to a fuzzy room. An ancient fixture dangled above him with a solitary glowing bulb. He followed its wobbling shadow on the ceiling. As the light swayed he felt his eyelids closing like immovable weights, and he drifted back to sleep.

Andrea failed to notice his open eyes as she continued reading his secret thoughts.

\* \* \*

No one grows up thinking, "I want to be an atheist." Something or someone tells him, "There is a God." He goes on believing, following, and, as he grows, testing to see if God is real.

The conflict arises when belief and suffering collide. Prayers go unanswered, leaving him to decide "God does not hear, God has a different plan, God does not care, or God does not exist."

"God does not hear" goes out the window first, because an all-powerful God can do anything. "God has a different plan" is a cop out and a different way of saying "God does not care."

Who would trust a god who does not care? Thus, I chose to no longer believe.

And so, I first gave up creation. It is easy enough to explain existence through naturalism. I dismissed the flood using the same reason. The virgin birth, the cross, and the empty tomb, they all fell apart.

For almost forty years, believing in myself has been enough, but this young woman I met in India is testing my resolve. Andrea Widener, what are you doing to me? When I challenged her faith, she said, "To say God has another plan is not a cop out."

That was my phrase, "a cop out." She said, "His ways are higher than ours. He sees what we cannot see. He knows what we cannot know."

Her words did not convince me. I have heard every tired cliché, but her passion was real, and she had followed it halfway around the world to reach out to people she did not know to show them God's love. I travelled here to affirm the absence of God's love. I have been chasing suffering for almost three decades trying to convince myself I am right and there is no God. I see this young woman, and now I am no longer certain.

My friends would say I have gone soft, that I faced a brush with death and started to fear my mortality, but I ask myself, "What if it's true? What if God is real?"

\*\*\*

Andrea closed the journal. *I can't read anymore right now. God, I don't know what to do or say to help Mitch. He is the worst kind of lost soul. He doesn't know he is lost, and he doesn't believe he is a soul. Please reach him. Please lead him to the cross as many times as it takes. Use me. Use anyone that can help. I trust You. Please save him from himself.*

Returning the journal to Mitch's bag, Andrea pulled out her own journal and tore out a handful of pages and began to write. She wrote until she could no longer stay awake.

"Andrea."

She turned to Marci. "Just let me stay with him."

Marci quickly returned with a blanket, which she rolled out on the floor. "You can sleep here next to his bed."

# CHAPTER 63

All Saints Hospital
Tuesday, September 16, 2008
7:00 AM

Marci entered the ward full of people and noise. *I don't see how anyone could sleep in here, but there she is. Neither of them has moved.* She watched Mitch slowly breathing as she walked toward his bed. She leaned over Andrea and pressed a kiss onto Mitch's forehead.

Kneeling, she nudged Andrea. "Hey, sleepy head. It's time to get up."

Andrea rubbed her eyes and sat up. "Any change?"

"No, but he is still breathing, and his vitals are good."

Andrea stood next to him. "Look at his face. Does he look calm to you?"

Marci said nothing but slipped her hand into Andrea's.

Andrea sighed. "No. He looks troubled. I prayed for him most of the night until I fell asleep. Marci, I don't know for sure why God called us here, but I feel like we are here now for Mitch. He is the one big piece of this puzzle that still doesn't know where he fits."

Marci tugged Andrea's hand and looked at her.

Andrea could not pull herself away. "I know. I know. We have to go. Marci, will you pray for him one last time before we go?"

Marci placed her free hand on Mitch's hand and bowed her head. "God, you know I got off to a bad start with Mitch, but you know how much I love him now. He was with us through all our struggles here in India. We needed him. Right now, he needs You. Andrea and I have done all we know to do to reach him, but now we have to go. He is in Your hands. Please God, watch over him and draw him closer to you. I pray in the Holy Name of Jesus. Amen."

\* \* \*

Andrea cried until they were aboard the train and well on their way to Bhubaneswar.

Marci asked, "Do you suppose we will ever see Mitch again?"

"I'm trusting God for that one. I hope so."

# CHAPTER 64

Thursday, September 18, 2008
Mitch's Flight from Delhi to London

*Comfort at last.* Mitch smiled as he sank into his first-class seat.

"Would you like some refreshment?"

"Pinot Noir, thank you." He slowly sipped his wine and then cradled the glass as he rested his head. *Finally, I can rest and put this trip behind me.*

"Sir, I'm sorry to disturb you, but the captain has asked us to prepare for takeoff. Would you like me to stow your bag?"

Mitch shook his head as he shoved the bag under the seat. *What's this?* He plucked some crumpled papers from his journal. Unfolding them, he wondered, *how did I fail to notice?*

* * *

Dear Mitch,

I am sorry I could not say good-bye. I hope this letter finds you well. Our trip to India didn't turn out exactly as I had hoped, but God was with us, and we met you. A bit stodgy at first, but over time we saw the person beneath the coarse, intellectual exterior, and you became a friend. More than that, you were a salvation for us. I don't know what we would have done without you.

I have prayed for you daily, not just for your healing, but for you to come to know Christ. I couldn't come close to you in an intellectual debate, but I'm sure by now you know how passionate I am about God. Maybe some of that passion spilled over, and then I think about what happened in Gourpali and wonder how anyone could doubt the presence of God when the church withstood the fire.

\*\*\*

*The church withstood the fire? How is that possible? How could I not remember that?* Mitch stuffed the letter back into his bag and pulled out his camera.

*The last thing I remember from that day, Marci and I were on our way to Gourpali to find Andrea.* Mitch turned on his camera and browsed the images. Quickly flipping past the burned-out car and shots of Sambalpur, he slowed as he viewed pictures of the motorcycle accident. *I'm getting closer.*

He paused on a photo of the church. The mob filled the street. Villagers huddled together near the church. Some were fleeing. Many wept and wailed with arms waving. Despite the dust and the crowd, he captured a clear glimpse of Andrea. *Did they rape her?*

In the bottom corner of the photo, he saw Indu by herself. She was standing as though holding hands with someone, but no one was with her. He felt a sudden all-over tingling. Ignoring the feeling, he scrolled to the next photo. He browsed the gradual progression of the scene as though watching a slow-motion video.

He watched as they opened the doors of the church and cast Satyajit's body onto the pyre. He watched them light the fire and close the doors, trapping his friends inside. *Why did I do nothing?*

He captured smoke wheezing from the window edges, the doors, and the seams in the roof. He caught a burst of flames heaving from the roof and the side of the church, catching the nearby jacaranda on fire, but as he continued to browse, he noticed a strange story unfolding.

Indu, frame by frame stepped closer to the church. As she approached, the crowd divided as though shoved out of her way. His pulse quickened. *How did she survive?*

In the next frame, Indu leaned against the church, pressing her hands against the doors. The next picture captured huge flames engulfing the tree next to the church and the crowd backing away, but Indu stood firm. There were no flames coming from the church and the black-gray smoke had turned white.

The tree and tiny house next to the church burned to ash while the church stood. The next photo was from inside the church. *There is a gap in my photos. What happened? I must have run to help.*

*"Then you came to the cross."*

Mitch trembled at the voice within. *I came to the cross?* He could not override his thoughts as his mind drifted back to the hymn of his youth. *The emblem of suffering and shame. Where my trophies at last I lay down. I will cling to the old rugged cross... The old rugged cross... The emblem of suffering and shame...*

He could still hear his mother singing those words. He imagined Andrea standing next to her, holding her hand and singing, *and I love that old cross, where the dearest and best, for a world of lost sinners, was slain. So I'll cherish the old rugged cross where my trophies, at last, I lay down. I will cling to the old rugged cross and exchange it someday for a crown.*

*Mum's favorite hymn. I still remember the words. To the old rugged cross, I will ever be true. Its shame and reproach gladly bear.*

He grabbed a pen and began to write.

\* \* \*

My Dear Andrea,

My whole struggle with God has been the problem of suffering. Why does he allow it? I mean if he is God, why not stop it or prevent it? But these last several days have got me thinking a bit differently. If I never suffered, if I never had a need for anything, why would I have a need for God? Did we invent God to explain suffering, or does God exist and use suffering to show us our need for Him? I can't pretend to have the answer, and I'm not ready to believe, but as I stared at that cross I felt angry. Nothing made sense to me, yet I felt the presence of God, and I was angry because I don't want to believe in God on His terms. I want God to be God on my terms. I was angry because he was not the God I invented, but I cannot deny what I saw. That cross should not have survived. You and Chandrika should not have survived. The tree and the house next door burned to the ground. The furniture and everything in the church burned except for you and Chandrika and the cross.

How is that possible? I can't answer, but I know what I saw. Perhaps someday I will accept it and believe.

If there were a God to thank, I would thank him for bringing us together. You are the only Christian I have ever met who honestly reflects the grace of Christ, aside from my mother, of course. If there were more like the two of you, there would be a lot more Christians, and the world would be a better place.

Unfortunately, most of the so-called Christians I have met are more like Marci was when we first met: presumptive, hostile, judgmental, holier-than-thou hypocrites. I don't base my decision to believe or not believe on the actions or attitudes of others, expect for the case of Christians. As a non-believer, I am told that Christ makes all things new. The believer is a new creation. The old ways are gone. New ways have come. The Christian is transformed by the renewing of his mind, but I fail to see the transformation. Where is anything new? Where is the change?

And then I met you. Are you the only Christian, you and my mother? Perhaps if I find more who have been truly changed, then I will accept that Christ can change me.

\* \* \*

He finished his letter and tucked it into his bag. He drew out his laptop and flipped it open. *Thank you, British Airways. Finally, a fast, reliable internet connection.*

*412 new email messages.* "Ugh." He scrolled through pages of junk until... *Joan Zweritt? Why would she send me an email?*

\* \* \*

Mitch, it's a small world. I want you to know I started praying for you the moment you disrupted my sleep. I know you don't count on prayer much, but I started praying years ago, in college, after I met my first real Christian, Maureen Widener.

I cannot explain it, but I started praying that God would send someone just like her into your life. I know how you think. From all those late-night discussions with Daniel, it is obvious that only real change can prove Christ to you. There are no fine arguments worthy enough to conquer the intellect of Mitch Hawkins. "Show me Jesus is real. Show me a transformed life full of grace and void of judgment, and I will believe." That's what I imagine you saying.

When Daniel told me of your dreadful circumstance, I had no powerful string to pull, no one to call on except God alone, so I prayed for you. I prayed, "Dear God, watch over Mitch and send him a comforting angel like Maureen whom you sent to me."

Little did I know God was answering my prayers before I prayed. Not terribly long after your call. I received a chilling ring from my friend Maureen, now Maureen Sturgis. I am giggling as I write because you have met your match. Maureen tells me her daughter, Andrea is with you in India. If she is at all like her mother, you, Mitch Hawkins, have met a real Christian. Do take notice and don't try to explain away the miracle of God's transformation in this child.

When I found out Andrea Widener was with you, my worries faded, because I knew God was with you, watching over you and answering the lifelong prayers of your mother. You march into wicked predicaments searching for the failings of religion, but the success of the hound of heaven is to seek and save those who are lost. I'm giggling again because He has sniffed out your foul stench (written in Christian love, of course), and he is ever on your trail.

Why do you suppose you have survived so many encounters with hostility and remain alive? God is watching over you, protecting you because He has a plan for you. I find it strange that you are in His hands, but in a mysterious sort of way, He is in yours at the same time. You hold the choice whether to embrace Him or discard Him, but know this: He is on your trail, following you, guarding you, even guiding you toward truth. I pray you embrace Him.

# CHAPTER 65

Guest Lecture – Taylor University
Dr. Abhiraj Jeremiah
Thursday March 5, 2009

Andrea sat between her mother and Marci, holding their hands. She'd marked her calendar the instant she'd heard Dr. Jeremiah was going to speak at Taylor. She'd read most of his books and followed his blog. Andrea considered him a pillar of the faith. He could explain what her heart felt about God—what she believed but couldn't express.

Marci squeezed Andrea's hand and whispered. "You alright?"

Andrea offered a weak smile, nodded, and looked down to hide the mist in her eyes. "I wish I'd known what to say to Mitch. I wish he was here. If anyone could crack his shell, it would be Dr. Jeremiah."

After a brief introduction, Dr. Jeremiah stood. His deeply bronzed skin and short dark hair blended into the black floor-to-ceiling curtain behind him. His smile popped in the spot-light. He grasped the podium and stood tall—as tall as he could at five feet and four inches, his chin barely visible above the podium.

Chuckles wafted across the auditorium as Dr. Stott, the dean of students, walked onto the stage carrying a small plat-form. Dr. Jeremiah grinned and rubbed his chin as Dr. Stott set the platform behind the podium.

Dr. Jeremiah surveyed his audience, his smile stretching

wide, then he stepped onto the platform and gripped the podium. "I think I just grew a foot taller. Thank you, Dr. Stott. You and your family here at Taylor are most accommodating and *uplifting*."

Chuckles turned to laughter.

"Thank you for the opportunity to speak. I've been asked to respond to the question of suffering. I'm sure you've all heard someone ask, 'How can an all-loving, all-knowing God allow suffering? Perhaps you've asked that question yourself.

"I grew up in a world of suffering, a world of callous disregard. My family, my neighbors, my entire community were Hindu—except for my mother. She died when I was very young. It wasn't until years later that I learned she had become a Christian. It was unclear whether she had been murdered for her conversion or whether she ran away.

"In either case, I had no mother, and I felt abandoned." He lowered his head and drew a deep breath. Then he lifted his gaze and stretched his open arms toward his audience. "We had all the trappings of religion. Too many gods and goddesses to count. Too many festivals. But none of these gods or goddesses seemed to care." He shook his fist then folded his hands as though praying. "I desperately sought some kind of transcendence, but all I could see was the bitter reality of poverty, pestilence, and empty traditions.

"Emptiness filled me. A great nothing consumed my desire to believe in something, but I found no god who listened or cared. Eventually, I felt no reason to live. Life had no purpose, so I decided to end it.

"My grandmother had died. Among her things, she had left a full bottle of sedatives. I ingested the whole bottle and welcomed a forever sleep.

"But, instead of dying, I awakened in a hospital—a Christian hospital. Apparently, the government hospital had refused to take me. They said it was too late and they could do nothing. As a last resort, my father took me to the Christian hospital."

He closed his eyes for a long moment. Another deep breath. He gripped the podium once again as though bracing himself. The crowd remained silent.

"My first memory was the kind eyes and gentle smile of my nurse. Her name was Naomi." He smiled and flung his arms wide open. "She gave me *hope* and told me God had refused to let me die—that He had a purpose for my life." He folded his arms and continued. "He words felt good, but I didn't know her god, and I refused to naively accept her words as truth. But deep in my heart, I wanted to believe. I wanted to have purpose—to have meaning—to be filled.

"I left that hospital with a sense of determination and set my mind on finding the truth. Nurse Naomi gave me a Bible. It was the first Bible I had ever seen. I read it day after day. Finally, after months of wrestling with the Living God, I surrendered. If there was truth, I felt I'd found it in him."

Andrea tried to listen, but heartache distracted her. India held her thoughts. The carnage of Pahireju and her personal horror in Gourpali. Mitch. *God, I hope you can reach him. Indu. I hope she is ok. God, please protect her and Chandrika and Anila. Vishal.*

She buried her face in her hands. Her silent prayers drowned out Dr. Jeremiah's stories of persecution and suffering until he said a name that grabbed her attention.

"Jeevan Joseph was a pastor in the tribal areas of northern India. When a Hindu leader was killed by Maoists, Hindu extremists blamed Christians and vowed to purge Orissa of all Christians. Pastor Joseph was one of their victims. His home was burned. His family were killed, and he was burned alive in his humble church building.

"When confronted by the stories of those who live their faith among people who hate them for it, I am confounded, inspired, saddened, and thankful all at once. The murder of Jeevan Joseph startles those of us at ease in our faith and gives us pause to reflect.

"I want you to imagine the courage it takes for believers —for followers of Christ to live among those who do far worse than hurl insults. How treasured is the Bible when it must be buried in the backyard for protection—not only protection of the book but of the owner? How sacred is the faith of those willing to die for what they believe—for whom they believe?"

His gaze bore into his listeners as though asking if they would be willing to die for their faith.

"For those of us who live in comfort, news of persecution is foreign, frightening, and difficult to fathom. The experiences of suffering believers bring the words of the apostle Paul to life. Nothing will separate us from the love of Christ—neither 'trouble or hardship or persecution or famine or nakedness or danger or sword.' He spoke of real struggles—not far off stories."

His eyes swelled and tears dribbled down his cheeks. Knuckles white as he gripped the podium. "These things happened and happen still today." He swallowed his tears and cleared his throat. "They happen today because our faith is real, our faith is strong, and the One in whom we believe died and rose again for us. And He is worth dying for. And He will raise us to eternal life.

"Even when 'we are afflicted in every way,' we are 'not crushed.' We are 'perplexed, but not driven to despair; persecuted, but not forsaken; struck down, but not destroyed; always carrying in the body the death of Jesus, so that the life of

Jesus may also be made visible in our bodies.'

"The apostle Peter also encouraged persecuted believers to stand firm. 'Do not be surprised at the painful trial you are suffering, as though something strange were happening to you. But rejoice that you participate in the sufferings of Christ.'

"These words do not erase the injustice of murder. But they do temper the impact. Jesus said, 'Blessed are you when people insult you, persecute you and falsely say all kinds of evil against you because of me. Rejoice and be glad, because great is your reward in heaven, for in the same way they persecuted the prophets who were before you.'

"Persecution is earth-shaking and terrible, but it is not unexpected for those who follow Christ. Maybe it's more strange when it doesn't happen. For those of us who live with our faith unchallenged, comfortable, and without trial or risk, perhaps it is time to examine the depth of our faith—to prepare ourselves for what may come and ask ourselves if we are ready."

He stared at the silent audience. Tissues and sniffling dotted the crowd. Some heads bowed. Some listeners wiping their tears. Some waiting for his next word.

"Have we closed ourselves off from the world and from any risk of suffering for Christ? Are we so at ease that we avoid venturing among those who might hate us and even hurt us?" His words became like distant echoes to Andrea. She couldn't stop thinking of Mitch—wishing she'd said or done the right thing to help him know Jesus as she knows him.

The room fell silent once again. Andrea lifted her head and watched as Dr. Jeremiah studied the crowd. She gulped as he fixed his eyes on her. Everything around felt dark. She could only see his face—his eyes looking into her heart. She couldn't hold her tears. Her lips quivered. Marci's arm slid around her back and rested on her shoulder.

Dr. Jeremiah held her gaze and said, "Some of you are shaken by my words. Perhaps you know someone who has suffered for Christ, or you yourself have suffered for His name, or perhaps you hurt for someone who does not know Christ or has rejected Him."

His face blurred in her tears.

"I must tell you there is hope. Hope trumps despair. There is light. Light pierces the darkness, and there is joy which erupts at the end of the long night.

"Tonight, I am compelled to do something very different from my usual discourse. There is a light in this building which cannot be contained, and I want to introduce you to that light."

Andrea clenched Marci's hand. "I can't stop thinking about Mitch. I wish he could hear this." Her mother handed her a tissue, and she wiped her tears.

The room fell silent once more. Dr. Jeremiah surveyed the room, glanced off stage, then bowed his head as though praying silently.

Footsteps interrupted the silence. A figure emerged from the shadows behind the curtain.

Warmth rushed through Andrea's body. She leaned forward, her pulse drumming in her ears. Fresh tears joined her uncontrolled smile.

A spotlight startled the man walking toward the podium. He smiled, squinted, and missed a step as he held up a hand to shield his eyes from the light. Dr. Jeremiah grinned and swept his right arm toward him.

"Even in the darkest places of this world, the light of Christ shines. I introduce my new friend who encountered the light in the darkness of suffering in India.

"Please welcome Mitch Hawkins."

# EPILOGUE

Dear Andrea,

I will never forget our trip to India. I've been around the world more times than I can count. I've seen so many different people and been in so many different places but none of my experiences have been as painfully relevant as our journey together. I relished the thought of devouring your tiny presumptuous faith. You and Marci were easy marks to me. I thought, "Here are two completely naïve Americans, two Christians with no comprehension of reality."

You proved me wrong. My eyes were opened in that tiny village. I saw myself standing in the midst of a storm ready to consume that entire village and me with it. When Indu pressed her hands against the doors and began to pray the storm broke loose, but instead of consuming the village, it doused the flames.

I could not explain what happened there. I blamed it on my concussion. I believed only in what I could see and know. I was jealous of your peace even in the midst of a storm, but I would not allow myself to believe until I encountered the power of the cross.

My faith is not a nostalgic collapse into childhood fairy tales. My faith is tested in fire, literally. My faith is more than belief in what I see and know. It is believing in the One I cannot see, the One who knows me inside and out and loves me anyway.

My mother is a dear woman of faith. I know she has worn out her knees praying for me, but her faith and example were not enough. I had travelled the world trying explain away God, but there was no where I could go that

Andrea, you live that life. I thank God for bringing you into my life. Because of you, I believe.

Your friend,

Mitch

# AFTERWORD

I find bits of myself in each of the characters in this story. I am the wide-eyed Andrea who wants to save the world and sees good in everyone. I'm Marci who can't be fooled by smooth words and is skeptical of anyone she doesn't know and many of those she does. I am Mitch who wants crisp and tidy answers and deep down wants all the chaos to somehow make sense.

I see myself in Satyajit, wanting to do the right thing, wanting to be a part of something important, something real. But I'm not always sure what that is. I am Vishal, fervent in what I believe to be true but not so dogmatic as to hang on when I'm proven wrong.

I am Indu, an orphan who is not an orphan but a child of the mysterious yet personal God who is father to the fatherless.

I hope you can see something of yourself in this story.

# ABOUT THE AUTHOR

John Matthew Walker spent his earliest years in southern Africa, the youngest son of a missionary doctor. He grew up with a heart for the down-trodden, destitute, and desperate. In his journey, he has been to many places around the world and seen all kinds of hurt.

But no hurt pricks his heart like the suffering of those who are persecuted for believing in Jesus. He wrote this story after a trip to India where he met people who had endured or witnessed violence against themselves and others for believing in Jesus and talking about Him.

He writes stories that delve deep into darkness to awaken hope and inspire compassionate action.

Follow the author at johnmatthewwalker.com

# BOOKS BY THIS AUTHOR

## *Moonlight Awakens*
### *a sex-trafficking story*

At only seventeen, Emma is used, abused, and discarded. She runs a thousand miles away from shame and judgment and falls into the arms of a stranger. One careless mistake, and she plummets into the hellish world of sex-trafficking. Her pimp takes everything from her, starting with her name. Deep in that darkness, Emma must find herself and find a way out. Her story is a tantalizing suspense that awakens hope.

## *Tiny Blush of Sunlight*
### *a slave story*

Nkembe is a young slave in South Carolina's lowcountry in the 1830s. After witnessing a murder, he runs for his life. Hounds chase through the woods and into the marsh. Trapped between a bitter past and a desperate future, his only hope is to find a place to hide and someone who can help him escape the reach of his master.

Made in the USA
Monee, IL
25 September 2021